Adirondack Sundown

BOOK ONE: THE LOST IN THE ADIRONDACKS SERIES

By Heidi Sprouse

ISBN-13: 978-1512393682

ISBN-10: 1512393681

Cover photography: Patrick Sprouse

Other Works by Heidi Sprouse

The Cordial Creek Romances

All the Little Things: Book One

Lightning Can Strike Twice: Book Two

Aging Gracefully: Book Three

Sunny Side Up: Book Four

Free on smashwords.com to see the birth of a writer:

Lakeside Magic

Deep in the Heart of Dixie

To all those who are missing a loved one,
May you have a homecoming of your own.

Dedicated to my husband, Jim, and son, Patrick—I thank God they are the reason I come home every day.

How to describe the Adirondacks? Pristine, primal, awe-inspiring. Words do not begin to do them justice. The Adirondack National Park, or Forest Preserve, of upstate New York is the largest national and state park in the United States with the exception of Alaska. The pride of New York and a national treasure, it is protected, preserved, and loved by many. While most of it is unsettled wilderness, it is the only national park where people live on the fringe and in isolated areas while maintaining its spirit and beauty.

It covers approximately six million acres in area. The task of finding something as inconsequential as one human being, particularly one that has been hidden within its vast boundary known as the Blue Line, is daunting if not impossible.

Prologue

"*THIS EVENING AT MIDNIGHT*, there will be a prayer vigil held in Colonial Park on Main Street in Johnstown for Sarah Waters, the thirty two-year-old teacher who disappeared a little over 3 months ago. Authorities are still investigating her whereabouts…" *Click.*

Graham Scott turned off the television. No more reports. He didn't need the news, not when he knew every detail, inside and out. An environmental conservation officer for the past twelve years, he played a key role in the on-going search for the young woman. Finding her was a priority on a professional level; on a personal level, it was all-consuming.

Sarah was his best friend. She was more than that if they both stopped tiptoeing around the truth—she was his everything. She was the person he had planned on spending his life with until everything changed. He was only 34 and felt like his life ended when the nightmare of her disappearance began. That day played out in his mind when he dreamed and in his waking moments. Whether his eyes were closed or wide open, the reel would keep playing until there was resolution or Graham took his last breath—whichever came first.

It happened in early May. Spring had the upper hand, nearly giving way to summer, wiping away the remains of winter. The leaves were popping on the trees, wildflowers exploded in the countryside, crocuses that had broken through the soil in the gardens in town long before were being replaced by the next round of perennials, and the air had lost its bite. The assignment was an easy one, a patrol of the Rockwood State Forest, a quiet network of trails in the Adirondacks of upstate New York. A piece of cake, in and out, then on to the next area.

Graham pulled into the parking area in his green truck, recognizable by the distinctive symbol of his office, and spotted a familiar, red Volkswagen Beetle with a beautiful blonde propped against the hood. A surprise, picnic lunch waited in the basket beside her; Sarah was dessert.

The blood thrummed pleasantly in his veins, giving him a head rush at the sight of her. Maybe not so brief a visit after all. "Hi, Gorgeous. You are the prettiest thing I've laid eyes on all day."

Sarah pushed away from the car and stepped into Graham, the scent of apples drifting around him from her hair. She grabbed hold of the lapels of his shirt, gave them a good tug, and planted a sweet kiss on his lips. "You're looking none too shabby yourself. I thought you could use some company." One kiss was only a teaser; she had to give him another.

Graham's fingers threaded through the smooth, shining fall of gold that fell to her shoulders. He breathed deeply, caught something floral and definitely feminine, mouth-watering. She was warm, reassuringly solid, and made it hard to concentrate on anything as trivial as work, but he tried.

"I can always use your company. Shall we?" He took hold of her picnic basket while she set her hand in his and they took the winding trail into the heart of the forest.

"I woke up early and thought this day should not be wasted. It's got summer written all over it." Sarah walked ahead of him, stopping him in his tracks at the swish of those hips, such a tease in form-fitting jeans with the sun in her hair. She turned around, the sky in her eyes, and started to laugh. "If only you could see your face! Come on, we can't stand here all day!"

She came back, grabbed his hand, and pulled him forward. The sun was high overhead when they dug into the wonders of her picnic basket. Sarah spread a blanket for them to sit on and pulled out a thermos of coffee because guys like Graham couldn't survive without a regular infusion of coffee.

"I do not know what you do to coffee but that settles it. I'm your slave." He drained his cup and nestled her in the crook of his arm, pushing picnic remains aside. "God, woman. I do not want to go back to work. I'm seriously considering calling it a day and coming home with you." She leaned her head against him and he could feel her heart fluttering, the weight of her as appealing as all the rest of her.

Sarah reached up and brushed a strand of hair out of his eyes, lip thrust out in disappointment. "Sorry, Charlie, but I'm heading to dinner with Mom, Dad, and Lila. A private evening will have to wait. Why don't you join us when you get done?" She pushed up on her elbow, her smile as inviting as her words.

Graham shook his head and gave a little groan. "Stop torturing me! Now you tell me I'm missing your mom's cooking *and* Lila? I've got too many stops left and I've really got to head out if I'm going to get done before dark. Save me some dessert, all right?" He stood and offered her a hand up.

It was Sarah's turn to run her fingers through his hair. She stood on tiptoe and gave him a kiss on the cheek accompanied by a wink. "I'll save you more than dessert, all right?"

They made quick order of packing up the basket and completing the circuit of the trail. Hand in hand, full from lunch, feeling a little lazy. Wishing the day could stretch a little longer.

The sun was making its downward slope when they emerged and set the basket in Sarah's car while she shrugged into a sweater to ward of the coolness under the shade of the trees. They leaned up against the beetle's frame and Graham kissed her long and slow, smelled the season in her hair, felt her touch, vibrant and alive.

Forced to come up for air, he pressed his forehead against hers, breathing hard as if after a hard run. "I'll call you when I get in tonight, okay? Tell everyone I'm sorry I couldn't be there and let Lila know I owe her a piggyback ride."

Sarah rested her hands against his chest, making an effort to catch her breath. "All right, but if something changes, you know you're welcome. I'm not leaving yet. I want to take a few pictures of the sundown for Lila's photo album." She walked him to his truck and hung on the door frame. "You be careful, you hear?"

She shook a finger at him as only a teacher could then handed out one more kiss. He nearly turned the truck around at the sight of her hair catching fire in the light of sundown, her daughter's pet word for sunset. Sarah stood and waved to him as he watched in her in the rear view mirror. It was the last time he'd seen her.

Snapped back to the present, Graham turned on the electric candle that sat in the large picture window overlooking Pleasant Lake. Her photograph sat beside it, bathed in a soft glow like a benediction. Looking beyond, his gaze rested on the mountains, dark shadows looming over the still water. In his heart, he believed they held the secret to finding Sarah. He kept a light burning, as he had every night since her disappearance. He would keep it lit until the sun came up and he held her again, ending the night his life had become. But right now, he had a vigil to attend.

1

GRAHAM WALKED THE TRAIL, scanning to the left and the right, sweeping the area for anything off, or out of place, that said, “Not quite right.” He rounded the bend to see a dark figure up ahead and a flash of blonde. “Hey! Hold up!” He gave out a shout.

There was a scurry of movement into the underbrush and a shriek that sounded like a woman. Could it be? “Sarah?! Sarah!”

Graham put on a burst of speed until a root sent him sprawling. Infuriated with himself for his uncharacteristic clumsiness, he scrambled to his feet and nearly pitched to the ground with pain streaking through a wrenched ankle. Again, a scream pierced the forest, carrying his name.

“Sarah!” His hoarse cry echoed off the walls of his bedroom. So real, it had been so real. She’d been within his sight…within his grasp. Graham leaned forward, elbows on his knees, hands pressed against his eyes as if he could blot the images from his mind.

Night after night, he fought for a reprieve that would not come and if it did, his head was crowded with imaginings. Nothing in his experience had prepared him for this. It had been hard for Sarah to lose her husband to the war, a sudden snuffing out of a life. Harder still for Graham and his mother to lose his father to cancer as the pain whittled him down to nothing. But this missing Sarah, this not knowing, was the worst.

Her disappearance grabbed hold of him, sank its teeth in, gnawed deeper with each passing day. When someone stole Sarah, the predator stole Graham's sleep, robbed him of his appetite, and took away his peace of mind.

The shreds of his nightmare forced him out of bed before the dawn. A new search could only begin with the coming of the light. A daily run ate up some time until the sun rose. The air held a chill, his breath a frosty cloud, hinting at winter. His feet slapped the pavement, names flashing through his mind with each step. Ephratah. Rockwood. Lasselsville. Oppenheim. Caroga Lake. Bleecker, Pine Lake. Towns that surrounded him, each a possible starting point for the day's search.

It was the area Graham knew best, like the back of his hand. He'd grown up on Murray Hill Road, picked strawberries at the neighboring farmer's field in the summers, hiked at Nine Corner Lake in the fall with his mother, gone fishing on Caroga Lake with his father, watched the fireworks at Sherman's, went skiing on the slopes of Royal Mountain. In the months since Sarah vanished, he had fanned out from Rockwood State Forest and expanded to different sections of the Adirondacks, but he was still drawn to the area. He believed somewhere close to home held the beginning and the end of what happened to Sarah.

Push harder. Pick up the pace. Heart pounding. Lungs bursting. No matter how fast or how long he ran, there was no stopping the relentless memories of that night when all hell broke loose.

He walked in the door at eight o'clock. His keys jangled on the table as he tossed his coat on the couch. Grabbing a beer and flicking on lights, the first tendrils of anxiety settled in with the words that accompanied the blinking red light of the answering machine. "Graham, it's Sally. Sarah hasn't been home yet for dinner. We thought maybe you'd seen her. Give us a call."

The voice on the machine sounded brittle, the tone of a mother trying, and failing, to hide her worry. A cold lump sank into the pit of Graham's stomach, the beer forgotten in his hand. Door left open, lights still on, his truck peeled out of his driveway as if of its own will and flew down the road to Rockwood.

Twenty minutes later, his headlights found Sarah's empty car in the parking area, making his stomach clench so hard he almost lost his lunch from the picnic laid out by her hands. "Sarah?!"

His shout rang out as he hit the ground, tried her doors, found them locked. His flashlight panned inside her car, catching sight of her purse tucked under her teacher's bag, nearly bringing him to his knees.

"Sarah! Baby, can you hear me? Sarah?" The small patch ahead, covered by the glow of his flashlight, revealed nothing.

Damn the darkness! Graham canvased the area and ran into the forest, frantically calling her name until his voice went hoarse, with no response. Was she hurt? Unconscious? His feet carried him down one trail, but it turned into a maze and he lacked the resources to find her on his own. Within the hour, all area law enforcement and environmental conservation officers were undertaking a full-scale search.

Head pounding. Heart hammering. Repeatedly circling the network of trails and all of its variations. No stopping until a fellow officer in green blocked Graham's path. A gray haired veteran with his face lined by time, he was seasoned by many searches of his own.

His steel gaze met Graham's while his palms pressed down on the younger man's shoulders and steadied him. "Son, she's not here. Go home."

Eyes burning, stomach hollow, Graham walked out of the woods—without Sarah. Time to break the news to her parents...and her little girl.

In the days that followed, investigating officers interviewed all homes within a reasonable radius and news bulletins asked people to call with any helpful information. No one had seen anything suspicious at the remote trailhead. It had been late in the day, a time when people were settling in at home, not heading out for a nature walk.

There were tire tracks in the lot that could have belonged to anyone. No strange fingerprints or footprints were found by her car. There was no sign of a struggle, no evidence of foul play. For weeks, they scoured the area but Sarah Waters had vanished without a trace, as if the wilderness had taken her and swallowed her whole.

Every time Graham's feet pounded the pavement, the wondering, worrying, and questions bombarded him. What happened in the window of time they were apart? Did she walk back into the woods? Did someone pull in, asking for directions, only to abduct her?

That a stranger might have been huddled in the trees, stalking her, rammed Graham's heart into his throat and covered him in a cold sweat. Why hadn't he waited for her to get in her car? Hindsight was cruel. He should have stayed while she took pictures, never should have left her. But it was a peaceful area with very little crime. Nothing bad ever happened there.

The light began to change, darkness fading to gray. The mountains and trees became more sharply etched against the sky. Time to shower. Let the hot water beat on his head. Slam back some coffee, black and scalding, a desperately needed shot of caffeine. Choke down a protein bar.

The first burst of color burned on the horizon as he climbed into his truck to follow through on the next part of his daily regimen. All intents focused on finding Sarah and bringing her home.

THE CRACK OF A 357 MAGNUM rang out, breaking the silence at the Pine Tree Rifle Club, a small, practice range tucked away on a quiet road heading out of Johnstown. It was Sunday morning. The rest of the world was sleeping, being lazy, eating donuts, or reading the paper while Graham's pistol fired repeatedly at the paper outline of a man. Dead center in the chest with every shot.

Sunday had become family day for Graham, not that Sarah and Lila were his family yet. In the year that they had been seeing each other, they had taken their time weaving each other into the fabric of their lives, slowly forming a solid mesh.

Both had been hurt. Sarah's husband, Lee, had been away in Iraq for nearly a year when he was killed without ever seeing his baby girl. Graham had been burned by a relationship gone bad when his fiancé, Mandy, changed her mind about spending her life with him at the drop of a hat. A chance encounter on a hike in Rockwood was the beginning of many meetings between a family with an empty space and a man who needed to be whole.

Sundays were theirs. Lazy, lay about with the paper days. Read the comics in a fit of giggles and give chase to Lila days. Go out for breakfast, go for a drive days. Stay in, his place or hers, didn't matter which days. God, how Graham loved those Sundays.

His hand shook and he realized his cheeks were wet. Over three months had gone by and it wasn't getting any easier. It was getting harder. The only thing that kept him going was the search, asleep or awake. He shot off another round, watched it go haywire. He put on the safety, set the gun down, and bowed his head. How much longer? Alive or…dead, he would bring her home.

"Graham," a voice called out, faint through the protective earmuffs and a hand came down on Graham's shoulder. Jim Pedersen, his best friend and a Johnstown police officer, stood by his side.

He was off duty, dressed likewise in jeans, flannel, and work boots. He came to practice at the range on a regular basis, knew Graham had become a fixture every morning. Jim was quiet and didn't get in the way, a strong shoulder when Graham came close to crumbling. "Buddy, have you ever had to shoot anyone with that pistol? That last shot would've missed the broad side of a barn!"

"Don't worry. I'll be able to make my mark when it matters most." Graham hadn't been prepared a few months ago, had trusted life would be good. He picked up the gun, took aim, fired. Bull's eye.

Jim digested his answer. "Be that as it may, take a breather and come on back to the house with me. Jeanie will cook us breakfast. You know she won't do it for me, but she's got this soft spot for you. Take pity on a man who's been married too long to be spoiled anymore and has to fend for himself. What do you say?"

Graham studied the man who looked like he could be his brother. They were tall, lean, and solid from their work and time spent outdoors. Both had dark hair, though Graham's had been lightened by the sun and was hard to manage as it brushed against his collar. Jim's was straight, in a no-nonsense, military cut. Graham had just a bit more height, giving him the ability to look down on his friend when he needed that advantage in an argument.

He considered arguing now, but didn't have the fight in him. Green eyes that used to be filled with light, but had grown dark, were reflected in the warm, coffee colored gaze of his friend. "I've got to hit the woods. There's so much ground to cover and the days are growing shorter. She could be there. I've got to. . . ." He bit off his words before he lost it.

Jim reached out, gripped his arm. "Graham, you've got to stop doing this to yourself. You won't be any good to anyone if you burn out. You have to be practical, realize no matter how hard you look, you may not find her. She could be anywhere, she could be…"

"Don't. Don't say it. Please." Graham closed his eyes, overcome by a sudden chill. "I know I'm not being sensible, but my gut tells me she's here, somewhere close. You don't know how hard this is. I'm not the husband. I'm not even the fiancé, but I thought…dammit, I knew it was going to happen and I cannot give up on her!"

He pulled away, kept it together. Somehow, he hadn't fallen apart yet. The breaking point wasn't far.

Jim stood by, waiting for his friend to unravel. Graham knew from the face he met each morning in the mirror; it hurt to see others hurting. This kind of loss was much harder than any other he had ever known. There was no closure, only grieving. Patient beyond measure, the police officer set an arm on his shoulders. Graham's body went loose with a ragged sigh.

"I know you won't quit and I'll even go out there with you today to help, but you have got to take a break. Come on home with me, Graham, please. Humor your best friend." There was a slight hesitation and surrender. It was easier to give in and Graham was so tired of everything being a fight.

THEY HIT THE WOODS WELL BEFORE NOON. It was a late start for Graham, making him anxious as time slipped through his fingers. They came with full stomachs, a thermos of coffee, and sandwiches that Jeanie insisted upon making.

She forced them into Graham's hands, would've sent him with a sack to feed an army after taking a good look at him. He didn't have the patience or inclination for something as trivial as food. He'd accepted her fierce hug, a kiss on the cheek, and the warmth in her eyes, but Jim's wife reminded him too much of Sarah and he had to go.

Out on the trail, his hearty breakfast turned into a churning lump, it had been so long since he'd had a big meal. The discomfort added an edge to the knot in his stomach, his constant companion.

Graham chose Rockwood. He felt closest to her here in the last place they'd been together. He'd searched it countless times since her disappearance. If he looked carefully enough, if he took long enough, if he came when the time was right, maybe he would finally find a clue that would lead him to her.

The trees had ignited with the varying reds, oranges, and yellows of autumn. The mountains were a backdrop, rising above, keeping watch in their primal beauty that stole his breath away. They knew the secret, had seen what took place as well as so much of mankind's past, but they remained silent and steadfast.

He had always loved this place until it became tainted by Sarah's absence. Graham had grown up here, exploring, hunting, fishing, and hiking with complete respect for the land. He had known from an early age that he wanted to make a career as a steward for the national park, protecting his way of life. The woods had brought him peace, his livelihood, and the woman he loved. Walking side by side with Jim, his mind carried him back to that first meeting with Sarah and Lila.

A few cars sat in the trail parking area on a beautiful day in May. Graham checked the log to sign in and was satisfied that no one had gone in by themselves. It was foolish to hike the woods alone, no matter how confident an outdoorsman. He could've gone on his way, but something made him decide to take a walk—perhaps the perfect day or fate. Graham walked about an hour, soaking up the sun, sucking in the spring air, feeling pretty good to be alive.

"Hey mister! Help! Mommy hurt her ankle and she can't get up!" A little slip of a girl dashed around the bend, dirt smudged on her clothes, twigs in her hair, her eyes wide with fright. She plowed straight ahead, knocking into Graham's legs.

Graham knelt down at her level and offered his hand to shake. "Whoa, whoa, whoa. Easy there. I'll help you and your mommy, but my mother taught me to always introduce myself first. I'm Graham Scott, the environmental conservation officer that patrols this area and who might you be? Are you a woodland fairy?"

The little girl giggled in spite of her troubles. "I'm Lila Waters. Mommy's right this way, hurry!" She took hold of his much larger hand and tugged until he followed her back the way she had come.

They didn't have to go far to see a woman sitting on a log with her foot propped in her lap, a sheepish grin on her face. He noticed how the sun lit her hair at first, then the deep blue ocean in her gaze that could pull him under. She made Graham come up for air to catch his fleeting thoughts in a way that hadn't happened since Mandy left him. The woman smiled when she saw him, but her eyes were cautious like the deer he sometimes startled on his way through the forest.

"I see Lila didn't have to go far, thank God. Come here, young lady," the woman ordered. The little girl dug her toe in the dirt, her cheeks flushing as she came closer.

Her mother pressed a finger under her chin and forced her daughter to look her in the eye. "Lila Elizabeth, you should never take off like that even if it's to help me. You could've been lost or there might have been something dangerous out there."

The tears started to fall. "I'm sorry. I was just so worried about you, Mommy. My feet just started running." Lila's bottom lip trembled and her face scrunched up, a full storm of emotion in the making. She tugged on Graham's heart and he didn't even know her yet!

Her mother gathered her daughter into her arms and kissed the top of her head. "It's all right." She looked up at the conservation officer. "I'm Sarah Waters and this is my daughter, Lila. I'm so glad you found her. I don't know what I would've done if something happened to her. She's all I've got."

Graham gave her an easy smile, took it slow, and knelt down beside her. "Well, in all the time I've been working these parts, there's never been a serious animal attack or crime so you needn't worry about that. Now, how about you let me take a look at your ankle and then we'll see what's what. By the way, the name's Graham Scott."

He was soothing, his touch gentle because he sensed that was what she needed. Graham didn't think it was anything serious. As a precaution, he wrapped Sarah's foot in an ace bandage and let her lean on him on the way out to her car. He put an arm around her waist, felt her stiffen with his touch, then a gradual loosening like a flower opening as they continued.

Lila skipped ahead, flitting from one of nature's wonders to the next while Graham and her mother took their first steps in building a bridge between one another. "Look at the sundown, Mommy! Look! Isn't it pretty?" Lila shouted as they left the forest.

Sarah laughed. "That's a sunset, honey, and it is really beautiful." Her limp had stopped quite a ways back. She thanked Graham and exchanged phone numbers. It would be the first of many sunsets they would share.

"*HEY BUDDY. COME ON BACK* to the here and now and tell me which way you want me to go." Jim stood beside him in the parking area of the Rockwood State Forest, a well-worn map spread out on Graham's truck with the various trails highlighted in different colors to make them easy to identify.

Meticulous notes were jotted in the margin—the path they'd taken that fateful day of Sarah's disappearance, the timeline, any possible scenarios. Jim couldn't help but shake his head. "You've spent way too much time obsessed with this map, but I don't blame you. If it was my Jeanie, I'd probably camp out here until I found her."

Jim started in surprise when Graham gestured to his notes; he *had* spent a few nights in the parking lot, trying to recreate that day, to lie in wait for her abductor, to do the impossible—turn back time.

A slight shudder ran through Graham's body, shaking himself loose of bad memories. "I'll head in here, at the main entrance, circle around, take the side trails one at a time. Why don't you cross over to that entrance people hardly ever use, you know, the road less traveled?" He traced a finger over the network of trails he would cover even though they were already imprinted on his mind.

Jim nodded and took his own thermos of coffee. "All right. Let's meet back here between three and four. Make sure you save me some of those sandwiches. They're my favorite and Jeanie doesn't make them for me unless I'm incapable of moving." With a wink, he set off on his course for the day.

Graham passed the sign-in log, resisting the urge to flip to the page where Sarah signed her name. It was still there, toward the front of the book. No other names came after hers on that dreadful date. He pushed himself to not break his stride and took to the woods.

A short way in, he branched off to the right on a lengthy trail that would lead him in deep before circling around to the beginning. There was a change in the light as it filtered through the trees, throwing off his sense of time. His footsteps became muffled on the forest floor, the sweet scent of the pines filling his lungs. It was this gathering him in that had made him fall in love with the woods. Nature cast a spell on him, making him forget about the outside world, but the outside world wouldn't let him forget.

Graham's feet led him to the spot where he first saw Lila and Sarah. Funny thing about life, where it carried a person. If he'd taken another path, he never would've met them. What if they'd taken a different journey the day she disappeared or she never got in the car, went in his truck instead?

He sank down onto the log where Sarah had favored her ankle that afternoon. He let his head drop into his hands and pictured that final walk. Graham shot up, retraced their steps, replayed that afternoon over and over, tried to picture what happened next. Every time, he hit a wall because his mind wouldn't allow him to go there.

Drawn into the web of possible trails, Graham could've continued on through the night. He'd left the charted paths on other visits, thinking it would be more likely for someone to break off into unfamiliar territory. His theory hadn't panned out.

Besides, it wasn't humanly possible to cover every inch of the six million acres of the Adirondacks. Lord knows, he had tried. With discouragement weighing him down until he thought it would flatten him, Graham headed back out of the woods at sunset to find Jim leaning against the truck, glowering. He glanced down at his watch. It was six o'clock.

Jim raised a hand, eyes stormy; the delay had cost him. "I don't want to hear about any excuses. I just want you to stop and think about how I'm feeling right now. I'm hungry. I knew I should've taken the sandwiches but more importantly, you had me worried sick. Two hours past our time, Graham. Two hours! You've had my stomach in knots. I couldn't call you with no service out here. I thought about going in after you, but realized we could wander around day and night without ever meeting up. You've had me imagining every scenario and believe me, a cop has quite an imagination. Will you please try and step outside of your head for a while?"

Jim stood with his hands on his hips then looked down at his feet, cutting himself off before he regretted whatever spilled out of his mouth.

Graham cleared his throat and tried to close the gap that had opened between them. "I'm sorry for being irresponsible. I, of all people, should understand how it feels when someone doesn't come out of these woods. I won't let it happen again. There was nothing new my way. How about yours?"

Jim gave him a smile and there was an easing of the tension between them that said Graham was forgiven. "Nothing unless you count some teenagers drinking beer. I scared the hell out of them when I showed them my badge. They probably won't set foot out here for the rest of their lives. They took off so fast, they left the beer." He reached behind him and pulled it out of the back of the pick-up. "It's crap beer, but I'm thirsty. Want one?"

Graham accepted the peace offering. He dropped the tailgate and they hoisted themselves up, popped the cans open. The trees were etched in black against a deep, pink sky that could not be matched on a paint palette. They didn't talk, just let the calm settle between them while they drank.

Graham finished his first beer; it was cold going down and took the edge off. He picked up another, let it hit the pit of his stomach. He already felt a bit of a buzz. His last drink had been a long time ago and an empty stomach didn't help matters any. It growled in protest, reminding him that breakfast had been a hours ago.

Jim rolled his eyes at him. "I heard that. You didn't even touch those sandwiches. Break them out, let's go. I deserve some compensation for my pain and suffering." He held out a hand, waiting expectantly.

Graham rustled around in the pack and brought out a handful of sandwiches. He handed two to Jim and started in on one for himself. He chewed slowly. It was a chore that had to be done. By the time he finished one, Jim was polishing off the second and eyeing the remaining sandwich. "You're going to spoil your supper and then Jeanie will have it in for you."

Jim took the sandwich, split it in half, and gave one to his best friend. "Not possible, not with Jeanie's cooking. I could eat a five course meal in a great restaurant and still find room for Jeanie's food. It's in the husband handbook—you have to eat whatever your wife makes, under penalty of starvation. Besides, she's the best cook I've ever known and…crap! It's Sunday! That means Sunday dinner is waiting for me and I didn't tell her I'd be late. I am in deep you know what if I don't get home and you are coming with me to save my butt, got it, buddy?"

He hopped down and headed around to the passenger side, shutting the door on any possible arguments.

Graham closed the tailgate and climbed in behind the wheel. He scanned the area one last time. She wasn't here. He knew that, had known for months even though something kept him coming back. It was a waste of effort on these trails. He would have to move on.

The sound of fingers drumming on the armrest made him push the search to the back of his mind and start the engine. Graham pulled out and turned the truck toward town. Time to shut the door on Rockwood and focus elsewhere. It was like trying to find a needle in a haystack.

2

JEANIE PEDERSEN SAT AT HER KITCHEN TABLE with her arms crossed, simmering. Small in stature yet curvy, with brunette hair in a pixie cut and snapping, dark eyes, she was an Italian spitfire. Everything had been ready two hours ago and was being kept warm on the stove. She was tempted to eat, turn it off, and make her husband have cereal.

The sound of the opening and closing of the door had her on her feet. "James Patrick Pedersen, you had better be unable to talk or have a serious injury or I," She broke off when Graham stepped into the room, Jim close behind him.

Graham gave her his slow, heart-melting smile that wasn't around often these days. It didn't take away the haunted look in his eyes. "It's all my fault, Jeanie. I lost track of time in there and Jim chewed me out for it. Don't take it out on a loyal lawman just doing his job."

Jeanie pushed a long strand of hair out of his eyes, nothing but welcome in her manner. All of her frustration was quickly forgotten. That Graham was here now, making an effort to join his friends, even for a little while, was a big deal. Make that twice in one day. He'd closed himself off in the past couple of months and she wasn't going to let him get away this time.

"It's all right, Graham. I'll forgive you, but don't let it happen again. The only way you'll make it up to me is by joining us for supper. Go wash up while I set a place for you."

Jim came up behind her and wrapped his arms around her waist, burying his face in her hair. "Thanks, baby. He scared the hell out of me. He was supposed to come out between three and four. It was six when Graham finally made it back. I'd almost called out the search dogs."

It was hard being a police officer's wife. She never felt completely secure that he was safe, that he was walking through her door again, until he was home. Even though they lived in a relatively peaceful town, things happened. Sarah and the changed man that Graham had become were constant reminders. Jeanie's only defense was to pretend to be tough on her husband because if she was soft, she'd never let him go.

Jeanie turned around and hugged her husband with all she had. "I was worried, especially since you went to the place where Sarah. . .You almost ended up sleeping on the porch."

"That would've been terrible. It's getting cold out there, baby." Jim knew it was her way of dealing and played along. He knew how lucky he was to have her; he'd chosen to become a cop after they married. It wasn't like Jeanie knew what she was signing up for when she accepted his proposal, but she supported his decision. As a police officer's wife, she had never done otherwise since the day they said their vows. If a sharp tongue was all he had to worry about, he could take it.

The sound of footsteps made them break apart. Graham propped a hip against the counter and crossed his arms. "Are you sure you two want a dinner guest? I can let myself out." There was humor in his eyes that couldn't conceal the pain. It was hard, feeling their closeness.

Jeanie wagged a finger at him, using the same gruff voice she usually reserved for her husband when he was in trouble. "Oh no, you're not getting out of this one. If this roast is dried out and my mashed potatoes are lumpy because of you, you are going to suffer along with us." She directed him to a chair then went about serving their meal.

Jim poured drinks and they both sat down. He leaned over and whispered to his friend, "No matter how it tastes, you tell her it's good and you clean your plate or you're in for it." He grabbed a hot biscuit, slightly darker than usual, but not burnt, and slathered the butter on. "I've got a stash of chocolate if we're still hungry."

"I heard that and you can forget about it or I'll make you do the dishes." Jeanie filled each of their plates and sat down at her place. They all bowed heads and took each other's hands. "Thank you, Lord, for the food on this table and for bringing Graham and my husband, even if he is a trial to me, home safe. Please bring Sarah back to our table as well. Amen."

AT HER SIMPLE WORDS, Graham's throat began to choke up. He pushed away from the table. "Excuse me, I have to use the bathroom."

Once sealed away from his friends, Graham leaned against the sink and fought back the tide of pain always so close to the surface. Couldn't he be like a normal person just this once, share a meal with friends?

He splashed water on his face and set his shoulders. He would do this for the sake of two people that had done so much for him. Graham returned to the table, forced a smile. "It smells wonderful, Jeanie. I can't remember the last time I had a meal like this."

Jeanie passed the platter of roast beef, her voice gentle. "We're glad you could join us, Graham. We wish you would come around more often. Dig in before it gets cold."

She busied herself with eating, but Graham saw her fighting not to cry. Jeanie wanted to fix everything, something impossible. The best the woman could do was try.

The meal was quiet, everyone lost in their own thoughts, although they each made an effort at conversation. When he was done, Graham sat back and patted his stomach. "That was really good, Jeanie. Jim is a lucky man."

He stood up and started clearing the table. With a jut of her chin, Jeanie directed Jim to the living room before she stood next to Graham. He had filled the sink with soapy water and had his hands buried in the suds.

Jeanie nudged his hip with her own. "You don't need to do that. Guests don't clear." She picked up a dish towel and started drying. Her hands made quick work of putting things in their place.

"They did in my house. My mother taught me you should always help clean up when someone else made the meal, at home or when away. I remember how I hated the stack of dishes after a holiday dinner. How could I say no when Mom had slaved all day on that mountain of good food? Sarah said…" He bit off the words, kept washing.

Jeanie laid a hand on his arm until his hands became still in the warm water. "Sarah said what?" She asked quietly. They all avoided saying anything about her around Graham, as if she didn't exist. Maybe it was better to talk about her, to remember the good things about her.

Graham's voice held just a hint of laughter. "Sarah said it would be easier to just throw the dishes out. I remember one time I was looking in the fridge and there was a mystery plate. You couldn't tell by sight or smell what was under the aluminum foil. Sarah took one look at it and tossed the whole thing in the garbage. I told her she should start using paper plates."

Jeanie giggled. "I know what you mean. At one of our barbecues, you should have heard her complaining about washing the plastic spoons and forks. I told her it was a matter of principal, we had to save the environment one piece of tableware at a time. She squirted me with the water gun at the sink."

They were quiet while they finished the job, caught up in their memories. Graham turned around and dried his hands. He met Jeanie's eye, smiled in a way that brought the shadows to her eyes. "Thank you," he said softly.

Jeanie leaned forward to brush his cheek with a butterfly kiss. "You're welcome. Go sit down with Jim while I bring out dessert."

She turned away to avoid a refusal or excuses and started pouring coffee. By the time she carried out a tray filled with cake and steaming mugs, the boys had turned on a ball game.

Graham polished off the cake, even though he was so full he thought he'd be sick, because there was no other choice when Jeanie was cooking. It must have been her Italian heritage that made her prepare so much and expect everyone to eat until they could burst.

He carried his dishes out to the kitchen and walked back to the living room, stopped by the sight in front of him. Jeanie sat cross-legged on the floor by Jim's feet while he played absently with her hair. It was a simple thing, a sweet moment.

Why did it feel like he couldn't breathe? "Well, I'd best be getting home. Morning comes fast. Thanks again, guys."

Jeanie and Jim stood as one and walked him to the door. Jim slapped him on the back and pressed his hand on the nape of his best friend's neck. "We're glad you came. Don't be a stranger around here."

Jeanie wrapped him in a hug as strong as a mama bear's. "Take care of yourself, Graham." She stepped back and leaned against her husband. They were a united front. Spend enough time with someone and they became a part of one another.

Graham hugged both his friends. "I'll try but I can't promise, not until I bring her back."

GRAHAM PULLED INTO THE DRIVEWAY of an empty house that seemed even emptier after an evening with the Pedersens. No one was waiting for him, not even a dog. He'd thought about getting one, maybe a golden retriever or a black Labrador, early on when the pain of missing Sarah was so bad it almost sent him over the edge. In the end, he'd decided against it. It wouldn't have been fair to the dog. Graham was never home and wasn't fit company.

He'd built his log cabin on Pleasant Lake, just outside of Caroga Lake, because it was a small, quiet lake that gave him his own little piece of the Adirondacks. He'd thought the name was a good omen, that it held promise for the future. Now, he wondered if it was a curse. Mandy had lived with him for nearly a year in this place before she found herself in someone else. He had planned on bringing Sarah and Lila here next until life had other plans.

Graham walked out onto the dock and stared out over the still water. The moon was full, its reflection so clear it looked like he could reach down and pluck it out of the water. Maybe if he dived into the middle of it, he could be the man in the moon and find the girl in the world, his Sarah. A breeze picked up, setting him to shivering. The image distorted and shattered.

Graham sat down on the dock and drew his knees up under his chin. He had to plan for the next day, but he was so tired and there was a nagging at the back of his mind that he was forgetting something, something important. "Lila," her name drifted through his mind. Tomorrow was a big day for her. The search would have to start a little later.

"I DON'T WANT TO GO!" Five-year-old Lila Waters sat her bottom down on the porch step, crossed her arms, and poked her lip out as far as it would go. Sally Anderson, her grandmother, stood over her and tried to decide what approach to take. In any other child, this would be normal on the first day of kindergarten, a challenge in households across town for such a major milestone. For Lila, it was one more mountain to climb.

Since her mother's disappearance, she didn't want to do any of the normal things five year olds liked to do anymore. She didn't play house. She didn't talk to her dolls or have a tea party with her stuffed animals like she used to every day. She didn't dress up in her mother's clothes and put on her make-up. Sally's heart sank. Her granddaughter didn't want to do anything. Who could blame her?

She sighed and sat down by Lila. Sally had passed on the sunshine in her hair to her daughter and granddaughter, but it was threaded with silver, more so since Sarah was gone. There were lines around her eyes and on her cheeks that had been etched deeper as well. The face that greeted her in the mirror each morning looked much too old.

Everything was a struggle these days. "What do you mean you don't want to go, Talulah? It's time to walk up Pleasant Avenue to the school, just like we used to when we would meet Mommy at the end of the day."

"I have to stay home and watch the Gingerbread Cottage! What if Mommy comes home today?" Lila's eyes were glued to the little, yellow house next door. "I have to be here to wait for Mommy."

Surrounded by the last of summer's glory in an explosion of blossoms around the picket fence, the home was aptly named because it looked like it belonged in a fairytale. Sarah's father, Sarah, and Lila had worked together to make the identifying sign that hung over the door.

Sally's arm wrapped around the small, sturdy set of shoulders. Her gaze fell on her daughter's home, but in her mind's eye she saw the note Lila had made with her help, posted on the front door. It read, "*Dear Mommy, I am at Nana and Pop Pop's waiting for you. I didn't forget about you. Please come and get me as soon as you come home. I love you. Love, Lila.*"

Feeling the trembling in the little girl beside her, the crack in Sally's heart grew wider. "Honey, you know that Pop Pop and I will be waiting for your mommy. We'll come get you right away if she comes home."

"But Nana, I have to be the look-out! It's my job!" Lila pulled away from her grandmother, ready to run next door if she got the chance. No one else knew that the Gingerbread House was magic and could bring her mother home. Only Lila believed it. Lila was always thinking about her mother, watching and waiting for her. It was how she had started her day.

"*Lila, are you ready? It's time for breakfast*!" That morning, when Lila was supposed to be getting dressed, she stood in front of the big mirror on the back of her bedroom door at Nana and Pop Pop's. She searched really hard for Mommy in the little girl that looked back at her. People always said that she and Mommy looked alike. They both had sunshiney hair and eyes as blue as her favorite marbles in her marble bag. But there was something wrong…Mommy always smiled and laughed a lot. The little girl in the mirror looked really sad.

Lila imagined that the little girl in the mirror was actually her mommy and she'd been put under a spell like Snow White and the Wicked Witch in the movie she had watched with Nana. She stared very hard at the little girl and whispered, "Mirror, mirror on the wall, let Mommy out and make her tall!" It didn't work. She really wanted to believe it anyway so she blew a kiss to the mirror girl and told her, "I love you, Mommy."

LILA STARED DOWN AT HER NEW SHOES. They were shiny black and looked really pretty. She even had white socks with lacy tops. Her dress was really pretty too. It had short, white puffy sleeves and the rest was like a red and black checkerboard. Mommy had bought it for her. Nana did her hair in two long braids and put little, red bows at the ends.

Everything looked right, but everything felt wrong without Mommy. They were supposed to start the first day of school together. Mommy would go to her kindergarten class and Lila could wave to her from her room across the hall. "I want Crackers!" Lila's hands tightened into tiny fists and she nearly stomped her feet.

Nana reached down and took her hand. "Lila, you already had your breakfast. You'll have a snack at school in a little while. Just you wait and see."

She always knew what to say and do. Nana was the best babysitter ever. She had watched Lila since she was a baby. There was one problem. Mommy always came home at the end of the day in the time before.

Lila's eyes started to fill with tears and her lip began to tremble. "I don't want to go without Crackers!" She stared hard at the ground. She didn't want to go at all. Why didn't anyone understand?

Nana stood up slowly as if very tired all of a sudden. "Lila, I can pack you some crackers in your lunch. I'll be right back out." She stood to go inside. Anything to make Lila happy. A truck pulled into the driveway, stopping her with her hand on the door.

"Crackers! You came, you came!" Lila shouted, running off the porch and down the walk as Graham climbed out of his truck. "Crackers" was their special name, like graham crackers. She didn't call him that all the time, but it was her favorite name for him.

He picked her up and swung her around in a circle. Graham always made her feel like she was flying. He smelled like pine needles and wore his green uniform that Mommy said made him look so handsome. He had a great, big smile, but his eyes, green like the summertime leaves, were so sad. Lila knew why they were sad. It was because he missed Mommy too.

"Lila, my lovely! Of course I came. Don't you look like a picture! I am here so I can walk the prettiest little girl in Johnstown to school." He looked up and gave Nana a smile too, although it was a sad smile, like Nana and Pop Pop's smiles. "Good morning, Sally. How are you and Steve doing?"

Sally walked down to give him a hug and a kiss on the cheek. "We're managing, all things considered. Come on in for a cup of coffee, Graham. We've got time. I started early because I thought we'd have to work on her a while." She turned and went into the house with Graham and Lila close behind.

Graham carried Lila inside and gave her a wink. "You're not going to give me any problems about going to school, are you, Lila? I can't go by myself and you have to be there to make sure they're taking good care of Mommy's kindergarten across the hall. Besides, Miss Ashley can't start the day without you, right?"

Lila scrunched her face up and tried to wink back. "You're right. I didn't think about that. I have to go get something."

She waited for Graham to set her down and ran upstairs in search of a picture she made for him. She felt better. Her tummy ache that had kept her from eating a good breakfast was going away. Having Graham there gave Lila a little, happy bubble inside and she wanted to make him happy too.

SALLY SMILED AS SHE LISTENED to the thumping of feet upstairs. "You've made her day, Graham. Thank you so much for coming. I thought we were really going to have a fight. How would you like your coffee?"

"Black, please." Graham used to take it with cream and sugar, had especially loved Sarah's sweet blend, but couldn't stomach it now. He sat back and took in the sunny kitchen, Lila's drawings on the refrigerator, along with a photograph of Sarah, Lila, and Graham from a backyard barbecue when everything was right in the world. He had to look away.

Steve Anderson came in from the bedroom, still in his bathrobe and slippers. He'd also been altered by Sarah's disappearance. There was more salt than pepper in his brown hair and his gray eyes didn't seem to shine as much. An early riser in the past, he often slept in now and took naps every day. His wood shop out in the garage used to be the place where he spent all of his spare time, a place he shared with his girls. He hadn't gone in again since the night that their world turned upside down.

Setting his personal struggles aside, he extended his hand and found a genuine smile for the young officer because it was needed. "Good morning, stranger. It's good to see you again. How are you?"

Graham, reminded of his father, stood up and took Steve's hand in a firm grip, then stepped in to give Sarah's father a hug. The older man put him to shame, managing to pick up the pieces of their lives and carry on with some semblance of normalcy for Lila's sake. It made Graham vow to himself to try harder as he pulled out a decent smile of his own.

"What's the Joe Nichols' song say? 'I'm doing all right, for the shape I'm in.' I'm sorry I haven't been around sooner. It hit me last night that this was Lila's big day or I would've come before, given her a pep talk." He took a sip of coffee, scalded his tongue, and gave himself some small satisfaction at the discomfort that was only a fraction of what everyone in this house was going through.

Steve sipped at his own coffee and nibbled one of his wife's homemade blueberry muffins. They had been one of Graham's favorites, but he couldn't touch one today. The conservation officer was not indulging in any extras of late.

Always lean, his reflection in the mirror was honed down now, the lines of his face sharper, his eyes shadowed, their light nearly extinguished. He shifted under the older man's scrutiny and studied the inside of his coffee cup.

Sarah's father chewed for a moment, deliberated on asking, then asked… because he had to ask. "What news on the search effort?"

Graham shook his head and took a deep gulp of the coffee. His insides twisted. "Nothing yet, Steve, but I'm not giving up. I'll find her."

The search for Sarah was the only thing he could do, the only reason to could get out of bed each day. After that fateful night, Graham had gone to his superiors and demanded they make it his full-time assignment. He had come close to begging, would not take no for an answer. They acquiesced. He knew the area better than any of their other officers, was excellent at search and rescue, and the powers that be knew—he would do it even if it meant quitting his job.

Graham realized they were humoring him. They didn't truly believe he'd bring Sarah back, at least not alive. He managed to contribute in other ways while on his mission, catching poachers, helping lost hikers, and spotting forest fires, but they were all on the back burner. One goal topped everything else: find Sarah.

Sally laid an arm across Graham's shoulders and winced. There were no soft places anymore. "If anyone can find her, it's you, Graham. We have faith in you. We don't say it often enough but thank you for all that you are doing."

Graham stared into his coffee mug, his eyes stinging. It wasn't enough. Nothing would ever be enough until he brought Sarah back through their door. The scampering of little feet was a distraction as Lila scurried back into the room, waving a picture she had painted with her watercolor paints.

"*LOOK, CRACKERS, LOOK!* I made this for you! I want you to hang it on your frig'rator, okay?" It was one of her best pictures ever, one with Mommy, Graham, and of course, herself and they were under a rainbow and there was a big sun in the sky. She made another one a lot like it hanging over her bed. Lila thought it would make Graham happy but when she looked up at him, his eyes were wet like he was ready to cry.

Graham scooped her up and hugged her, hard. He always gave the best hugs. She thought they must be like Daddy hugs and hoped he would be her daddy someday. "Thank you, Lila, my lovely. It's a beautiful painting. I'll hang it up as soon as I get home." His voice sounded funny, hoarse like when he had a cold.

Lila hugged him back and put her hand on his cheek. "Okay. I knew you would like it. Hey, Crackers, how come you haven't come over in so long? It's been ages and ages since we went on our hike in the summer and I haven't been to your house since—," she stopped herself. She didn't talk about what happened to Mommy because then it wouldn't be real.

Graham leaned his forehead against hers. "I'm sorry, sweetie. I'm going to see you more often. It's just that I've been working, really hard." He closed his eyes and she saw dark spots under his eyes, like bruises.

Lila looked up at him, her little face very serious. "Working at finding Mommy, right?" She saw one tear slip down his cheek as he nodded. She wiped it away and hugged him back with everything she had, a squeeze-the-stuffing-out-of-you hug like Mommy's. She hoped that would make him feel better.

Nana cleared her throat behind them. "Well, Talulah, it's time to go. Let's head on over to kindergarten!" She picked up Lila's backpack and lunchbox, gave Pop Pop a kiss, and went to the door. Lila climbed down from Graham's lap and went to her grandfather next.

"Bye, Pop Pop. You watch for Mommy while we're gone, 'kay? I love you." She gave him a big hug and a kiss. His arms closed around her and he surprised her by picking her up.

Pop Pop carried her to the door and set her down. He smiled but had that same funny sound when he talked, like Graham. "I will, baby girl. You have a great day and I love you more. See you later, alligator." When Lila looked back, he was still there, waving goodbye.

"In a while, crocodile!" Lila took Graham's hand and they joined Nana.

It was a short walk to the school and a really nice day. It wasn't too cold. Nana put Lila's new sweater in her Tigger backpack that went with her Tigger lunchbox full of her favorite things. Tigger was the one she liked the best. He reminded her of Graham, before the bad thing happened to Mommy. The birds were singing and flying from tree to tree. Graham pointed out a squirrel sitting on one of the lawns, holding an acorn and watching them. He made Lila laugh. Just a few more steps—there were 400, she knew because she and Mommy had counted them once—and they walked inside Mommy's school.

Now Lila's feet started to slow down and the tummy ache was back. Graham squeezed her hand. She looked up at him, saw how he stood straight and tall. Lila swallowed hard, but nodded at him and started walking again. There were lots of other families and boys and girls walking in the hall, just like Lila. Some of the little boys and girls were crying. Lila decided she was too big to cry.

Miss Ashley stood at the door across the hall from Mommy's room. When they weren't in school, Lila could call her Melissa. When they were at school, she had to call her Miss Ashley. Miss Ashley had really curly brown hair that was short and bounced when she was excited. She also had green eyes with brown in them that reminded Lila of the mallard duck she'd seen in the pond in the park.

Miss Ashley knelt down to give Lila a big hug. "Good morning, Lila! I'm so glad you're here. Come on in and go find your cubby, your table, and take a look around."

Lila nodded slowly then turned to look behind her. "Can Nana and Graham come in too? They want to see my classroom." She took their hands and pulled on them to come along.

Miss Ashley laughed. It was a nice laugh, a lot like Mommy's. "Of course, Lila! Everyone's taking the tour today. Go ahead!" She waved them inside before turning to the next family on the way.

Lila did what she was told. It was easy to find her cubby because it said "Lila" in big letters and she was the only Lila. She hung up her sweater, her backpack, and put her lunchbox inside. Next, she found her spot at her table. She was lucky. She had a red chair and red was Mommy's favorite color.

She walked around the room and looked at everything. It was almost the same as Mommy's classroom across the hall. Lila found a chair in the play kitchen corner and sat down. If she turned the right way, she could look at the other kindergarten classroom. The substitute teacher was at the door.

When the teacher moved, her blonde hair swished back and forth, just like Mommy's. Lila pretended it was her mother, that she would turn around and come and get her, and everything would be okay again. The teacher went inside and closed the door. Lila stared at it for a long time, but she knew—Mommy wasn't coming out of that door today.

Nana knelt down beside her and gave her a hug. "It's time for us to go, Lila. I'll be here at the end of the day. I'll even try to get Pop Pop moving. I love you, sweetheart." Nana squeezed her hard and tickled her a little even though her eyes looked wet and her voice was funny.

Graham was next, picking her up one more time and whispering in her ear. "I'll come too, I promise. Have a good day, lovely Lila." Lila gave him one more hug and he set her down.

Miss Ashley called all the boys and girls to come pick a spot on the rug. Lila picked the ladybug spot because Mommy said they were good luck. She sat down and turned to wave. Nana and Graham waved back and left. She watched the door. Her tummy ache was really bad now and she wanted to cry but if she did, it might make Graham and Nana cry too. Lila bit down on her lip and stared at the ladybug. Maybe if she tried really hard, her wish would come true.

3

COMING HERE WAS HARD. Walking into that school was like ripping a bandage off a healing wound, made fresh and raw again. Graham had dropped in often—a surprise meeting for lunch or at the end of the day. He had been a visitor in her classroom, as well as others, to talk about his job and environmental conservation. This was his first time without Sarah.

The staff knew him. They used to stop and talk. Today, no one made eye contact or said a word. They kept on moving, not even acknowledging him. Beneath the newly opened heartache, it festered and burned. How could they forget, go on with their lives as if nothing ever happened? The mother of all headaches bloomed at the base of his skull, making him lengthen his stride and aim for the exit, set on getting out before he did or said something he'd regret.

"Mr. Scott, wait!" A deep voice called out and Andy Vicenza, the principal, joined Graham in the hall. He was Italian through and through, with a full head of dark hair and eyes like cappuccino. Everyone recognized his big laugh and bigger heart. The principal gave his all when it came to his school.

His grip was firm as he pumped Graham's hand and he looked him in the eye. Whether the conversation was good or bad, this administrator would meet it head on. A competent principal, he had a great deal of experience doing just that with parents and students on many occasions. "Have there been any new developments? I've kept my eye on the paper. I didn't catch anything."

Graham wanted an easy way out. There wasn't one when it came to Sarah. It was getting harder to answer the questions. "I'm afraid not, but it's not over yet. I'll be sure to keep in touch with any updates."

Mr. Vicenza patted his back. "Thank you. I have to give you a great deal of credit for your dedication. It was difficult starting the morning today without Sarah's smile and cheerful spirit. Every night, my family and I say a prayer for her safe return. We won't give up and we know you won't either."

"Never. Have a good day," Graham told him in a voice suddenly gone hoarse again and slipped outside.

Coffee. He needed more coffee, something to override feeling so low down he wouldn't be able to get up again. Truth be told, he needed something strong enough to take him to oblivion. *Not an option. Stay sharp. Keep going.*. He joined Sally where she waited on the sidewalk and they walked back to the house.

The trip to school had taken a toll on Sarah's mother as well. She was uncharacteristically quiet and seemed deflated. When they reached the front steps, Sally turned to Graham and finally spoke. "Thank you, Graham. Would you like to come in for a while, have something to eat?"

"Thanks, Sally, but I have to pass. I'm getting a late start and I've got a lot of ground to cover today. I'll see you this afternoon." Wasting precious time put him on edge.

He brushed her cheek with a quick kiss, gave her a hug, and climbed into the truck. Sara Evans' song, "No Place That Far," played on the radio, pushed him to start the engine, and get going. It was getting harder to keep the faith.

Where to stop for coffee? Johnstown was a great place. He loved the small town feel, spiced up with a dash of an interesting blend of Colonial and Revolutionary landmarks. But right now, his familiarity with the people and their familiarity with the case rubbed him the wrong way. The Railside was tempting but too many regulars went there. Graham would feel their stares on his back, listen to their hushed whispers, and be forced to deal with people when he couldn't deal with much anymore.

The more impersonal atmosphere of Dunkin Donuts with its steady flow from all directions was a possibility.

Catching sight of Jim's cop car in the lot swayed his decision. Graham pulled in and beat a path through the crowd revolving through the door to grab a spot in line.

"Hey Scottie, over here!" Jim gave a shout and gestured to the empty seat across from him. He shoved aside the newspaper to make room. "Did the world stop turning? This is very unusual for you—coming in this late *and* stopping here for coffee. You don't ever go to Dunkin Donuts. What gives?"

Graham dropped down into the chair, took his first sip, and winced at the bitter taste without sweetener. The only solution—drink the strong brew down so fast blisters were sure to be popping up on his tongue. "I had to get something quick before my body stopped functioning. What are you doing here? Just because you're a cop, it doesn't mean you have to go to the donut shop. It's not in the police handbook or anything."

Jim sat back and shrugged. "Jeanie forgot to buy anything sweet. You need your coffee to get started, I need my sugar high. You still didn't answer my question. Why are you here now? Most of the time you are long gone at the crack of dawn." He eyed the box of donuts on the table intended for the station, debated, and hooked one more double chocolate.

Graham shook his head at an offer of a donut, tipping his head back to slam back the last swallow before meeting his friend's eye. "It was Lila's first day of school. I figured she'd need someone to go with her." He stood up abruptly, shutting the door on any conversation on the matter. "So, that's the deal.

I've got to get going. Have a good one and try to stay out of trouble."

"You, too. I'll talk to you later," Jim called out, offering him a pinch of reassurance. Someone would be there when he crashed and burned.

Graham turned on to the road, mentally plotting his course. Each day began with a debate on how to conduct the search. He went by his considerable knowledge of the area and probable locations, his instincts, and luck of the draw.

In the beginning, the primary focus was the area of the Adirondacks closest to where she was seen last. Canvasing homes and businesses to share Sarah's picture and ask questions was another part of the job. Always methodical and meticulous, he had patience beyond measure, but impatience was mounting for himself.

Today, due to time constraints and the need to meet Lila, Graham chose a peripheral search. That meant hitting the trailheads, residences, and any public place along the way. As he had in the past, Graham posted Sarah's picture at each trailhead, in every business he passed, left flyers, and handed them out whenever he stopped for questioning. A glance at his map urged him to head through Wells, Speculator, Indian Lake, wrapping up in Blue Mountain Lake. At this point, being blindfolded and throwing a dart at a map might be best.

The day was clear and crisp, the roads quiet as normal people went about their routines in normal jobs. Graham traveled through Wells, a quaint, little town that was gone in a blink, and noticed a camper high up on a hill with a sign, "The Rock." That sounded really good right now, to go somewhere to get away from the world and leave it all behind.

With a sigh, he shut that thought in the back of his mind and tortured himself with the hindsight game of "what if" for a while until he pulled into Speculator. The town had some tourist traffic and a bit more action, several businesses, a state park, and trailheads to provide plenty of distractions. Graham pulled into a small gas station with an auto shop to fill up and get another installment of coffee.

The shop manager came out of the garage and wiped his hands on a greasy rag before offering a hand to shake. "What can I do for you today, officer?"

Graham looked down at the man's pocket, embroidered with *Doug* and made eye contact. It was important to encourage a sense of connection. "Hi, Doug. I'm searching for Sarah Waters, a young woman from Johnstown that disappeared back in May. Have you seen her?" He held up her picture and waited. *Let this one give me a lead.*

The mechanic was small and wiry from all his hard work transforming hunks of metal into running machines again. He was good at what he did with an attention to detail. He pulled his glasses out of his pocket to give his full concentration to the photograph in the young man's hand. He took his time and studied the image closely. Graham resisted the urge to tap his foot.

When Doug looked up, his gray eyes were troubled. "I'm sorry, officer. I'm sure I'd remember a pretty, little thing like that. I'd be happy to post her picture and pass them out to my customers if that will help."

Graham nodded, swallowed his disappointment, and handed him a pile of flyers. Each bore Sarah's photograph and contact numbers for the authorities. "Thank you. I knew it was a longshot, but I had to try. If you think of anything or see anything out of the ordinary, don't hesitate to call." He climbed back into the truck, drank coffee that had grown cold, and continued the journey.

The drive was uneventful heading through Indian Lake all the way to Blue Mountain Lake, the pockets of civilization becoming sparse. A work van with the name *Down in the Glen's Building and Roofing—Your Adirondack Source*, made him stop at a large, log home. There was always the possibility that a builder would see or know something. Only one way to find out.

"Excuse me, can I talk to you for a few minutes?" Graham called up to a man working on the roof, pounding away.

A large man with gray hair and a booming voice shouted down, "Sure thing, officer! Be right down!"

Minutes later, he was down the ladder, huffing and puffing with exertion. He wiped his forehead with a bandanna and met Graham's eyes with a bolt of blue that was piercing. "What's the story? I've got work to do, got to finish this before the weather gets too cold."

Graham tried to stomp down his frustration. Some people went out of their way to assist him. To others, he was an imposition. "I'll only take a brief moment of your time. I'm sure you've worked in many places around these parts. Have you ever seen this girl, Sarah Waters?" He handed the man the picture and searched for patience.

"You're right saying I've been all over. I've been to Hadley and Luzerne, to Corinth, Queensbury, out to Lake George and beyond. I've roofed all the houses you see around here. Fell off a few times too! Got right back up and finished the job. Have to keep busy is what I always say!"

Graham's head started to pound again as the man hit him with a flash flood of information. "That's great sir, but can you tell me if you've seen Sarah? She disappeared over three months ago and we can use any help you are able to give us."

The man glanced at the picture and shook his head. "I'm sorry but I can't say as I have seen her. Now if you don't mind, I've got work to do." The roofer turned without further comment and climbed back up his ladder.

Rage, never far from the surface, sparked and threatened to flare up like a bonfire. On the brink of snapping, Graham stepped into his truck, slammed the door, and revved the engine. He also had work to do, something much more vital than home improvements. He had just turned his head to back out when there was a tapping on the glass.

The roofer was standing next to his truck, motioning for him to roll down his window. "Hey, listen, you want to give me some of those flyers? I'll pass 'em out on my jobs, put 'em in my shop. I've got a daughter. I'd appreciate someone looking out for her the way you are, but I got to get my work done." Graham gave his thanks and continued on his way.

The last exchange left a bad taste in his mouth and soured his mood in Blue Mountain Lake. He had to head back in the early afternoon. Another useless day—over. What if he was going about it all wrong, not even in the ballpark? He shook off his doubts. His gut told him she was somewhere in these mountains. That meant follow his gut.

LILA SAT IN THE SCHOOL CAFETERIA and waited for someone to come get her. It was loud and big and really crowded. It gave her a tummy ache. At lunch, she didn't even eat anything because her tummy felt so bad. She liked it when she came to school once for Green Eggs and Ham Day.

Mommy was there that day and she read their favorite Dr. Seuss book.

Thinking about "Green Eggs and Ham" made her tummy hurt more so she stopped and stared hard at the ladybug crawling across the floor. Mommy had ladybug earrings. Lila squeezed her eyes shut really tight and made a wish like when she blew out her birthday candles. "Please ladybug, bring my Mommy home." She didn't know if ladybug wishes worked. She hoped so.

"Lila!" a deep voice called out. She would know that voice anywhere!

She opened her eyes wide and there was Graham, standing in the doorway with his arms out. Nana and Pop Pop were right next to him. Lila felt all warm inside and forgot about not running in school. She went as fast as she could and jumped into Graham's arms. He swung her around in a circle, like always, and then he hugged her really hard.

"You're here! You're finally here!" Lila shouted. She gave Graham a big smacker on the cheek. Nana and Pop Pop were next when they stepped up to give her a hug. She smiled at everyone. It was the first time she felt like smiling all day. "I thought you'd never get here!"

Graham laughed. It was a deep, rumbly sound from somewhere way down in his belly. Lila thought it sounded kind of like a bear. "I thought the end of the day would never get here. All I could think about was you. How about we all go to Friendly's to celebrate your first day of school and being such a big girl?"

"I love Friendly's! I'm going to have a hot fudge sundae with peanut butter sauce on it just like Mommy." Lila held on tight while Graham carried her down the hall and outside. She knew she was a big girl and could walk, but she liked being way up high in Graham's strong arms. Nobody else had a "conversation" officer—Lila couldn't say conservation—in a special uniform. Besides, everything was better when Graham was around.

GRAHAM SLID INTO THE SEAT by the window, staring at the flow of traffic going by without really seeing it. He felt bouncing next to him and winked at Lila. Being with her was a sweet torment, a constant reminder of her mother. His thoughts were pulled from that dead end track by the arrival of the waitress. Show time. *Act human.*

"Sally, Steve! It's good to see you. It's been a while. And wait a minute…this cannot be Lila! Look at this big girl!" Betty Smith, an old friend of the Andersons stood by their table.

She always made a splash in bright colors and unconventional styles. Today it was a black and pink polka dot shirt with huge, pink, hoop earrings that dangled when she walked. Her fingernails and make-up matched what the waitress was wearing and she was soft on Lila.

"It really is me, Betty! I started kindergarten today. I'm high five now." Lila started to color on the coloring page on her placemat. Her tongue poked out in concentration while she hummed a tune. She was endearing, as always, and made Graham's heart ache for every moment her mother missed.

"Well, congratulations, Lila. What can I get you all?" Betty took out her note pad and wrote down the sundaes everybody wanted. She stopped when she got to Graham and looked at him—hard. "As for you, young man, you had better order more than coffee this time and you need to clean your plate. A body can't keep on doing a job if you don't take care of it."

Graham raised his hands in the air in surrender, waving his napkin like a white flag. "All right, Betty. I'll take a large Reese's Peanut butter Cup sundae…and don't forget that coffee, please." He ducked when Betty pretended to hit him with the menus and bustled back to the kitchen.

"So, how was school today, Talulah?" Nana asked as she stirred her coffee. Her eyes softened watching her granddaughter, her tone tender. Somehow, when it came to Lila, everyone melted. Loving her came with the package.

"It took forever. We sat in our seats and we sat on the rug and we sat in our seats. We had to do the calendar and we sang our ABC's and we colored. We did everything Mommy used to do with me. Do I have to go back? I already know everything. I can stay at home and wait for Mommy to come home." Lila looked at everyone, but they all looked at their hands, fiddled with their napkins, or rearranged the silverware.

"Sweetie, I'm sure there is something for you to learn and you know that Mommy would feel really bad if you didn't go to school, especially when you are watching her classroom for her. You have to make sure her sub does everything right." Steve reached across and hooked her pinky with his to do a pinky hug. Before she could say anything more, their desserts arrived with lit candles and balloons. Perfect timing for a distraction.

"Wow! It's not my birthday!" Lila shouted. She took one look at the candles and blew while those gathered at the table made the same wish. Everyone laughed and Graham hooked her cherry with his spoon.

Catching Betty giving him the evil eye several times, coming by more often than was necessary, he managed to polish off the sundae. Being one of the ever-impressionable young, Lila mimicked him with her considerably smaller dessert only to groan. "I ate too much."

Graham nodded at her and slid down in his seat. "Me too, Lila. What do you say on Sunday, I come get you and we'll go on a hike, okay? We have to walk off this ice cream tummy ache." Lila snuggled in close and lit up with her smile. She sent its badly needed warmth all the way to his heart.

IT WAS LIKE FAMILY DAY AGAIN. Lila woke up really early that Sunday. She couldn't sleep anymore. She was too excited. Graham was coming to get her and take her on a real hike through the woods. That meant she couldn't be hungry or she'd get tired! She stood on a chair so she could reach the cereal box and the milk. She only spilled a little of her frosted flakes into her big bowl with the red stripe, Mommy's favorite.

"Talulah, it is six o'clock in the morning! What are you doing?" Nana sounded a little cranky. She wore her bathrobe and her hair was standing up. She usually slept late on Sundays.

"I'm getting ready for Graham. I need my hiking boots and my lunchbox 'cause I'm gonna share lunch with him on the trail. We're gonna find Mommy today, I know it."

Nana almost dropped her bowl of cereal that Lila handed to her when she climbed down from the chair. Nana made sure Lila was nice and toasty with a warm blanket around her then went in search of coffee—and a lot of it.

Nana waited until Lila was all done eating before she sat down next to her on the couch and put the little girl on her lap. "Lila, we don't know if you'll find Mommy today. No one is sure about where she is. You're going to make Graham feel very bad if you tell him that's why you want to go with him today."

Nana's blue eyes were shining like when she was ready to cry in a sad part of a movie. Lila didn't want Nana to cry any more. She had heard her too many times in the middle of the night when everyone was supposed to be sleeping.

"I don't want to make Graham feel bad or you either, Nana. I won't say anything but I'm going to keep my eyes wide open just in case, okay?" Nana kissed the top of her head and then she hugged Lila so hard, she was sure her stuffing was going to come out.

GRAHAM CAME WHEN HE PROMISED, nine o'clock on the dot. He recognized the importance of keeping commitments, especially for this little girl in particular. A quick cup of coffee with the Andersons before installing Lila in her booster seat and they drove to their favorite hiking spot, the trail on Kane Mountain.

It was the perfect kind of day—not too cold, not a cloud to be found, and the distinct smell of fall leaves filled the air as they made a cheerful rustling under their feet. The sun was shining bright enough to burn off the early morning chill, had the blood thrumming in his veins, and Lila singing some song about Mr. Sun. Cute.

"Crackers, I bet I can beat you to the top of the mountain!" Lila called and started running ahead of him up the trail.

She knew the path well because her family had taken this journey several times. Her mother and grandparents made it a tradition each year when the leaves turned. Small trail markers in bright yellow with a picture of a hiker made it easy for Lila to know she was on the right track plus so many people came here, all she had to do was look for a brown roadway of muddy foot prints.

"Whoa Lila! It's not a race. Remember what I've always told you—you have to stay close to me, where I can see you. Besides, we have to take our time and see if we can catch autumn on the mountain." Graham stretched his long legs so he could catch up to her quickly and took her hand. She looked at his face; whatever she saw there was enough to make her slow down. They were quiet for a little while, looking for the season.

"There's autumn over there! Look at the tree that's got yellow and orange on some of its leaves!" Lila pointed to a little tree tipped with gold, bathed in the rays of the sun. "That oak tree looks like magic, doesn't it?" She stood under the boughs and reached her arms up to the sky, the spill of light trailing over her as well.

Graham smiled at her. He'd caught his breath from the run, but it was taken away again by the innocent beauty of the moment. It was a struggle to gather his thoughts. "How do you know that it's an oak tree?"

He always did that, asked her questions like she was a detective. She loved Scooby Doo and the Mystery Gang, always solving mysteries. Graham said there were mysteries all around in the woods if she looked really hard and Lila could figure them out by wearing her smarty pants.

"See the squirrel underneath holding that acorn? That's how I know it's an oak tree 'cause acorns come from oak trees and that's what the leaves are like. A maple tree has leaves like the tree in front of Nana and Pop Pop's house, more like a star, and those other trees are pine trees. How come they don't change colors and turn naked like all of the other trees?" Standing with her hands on her hips and her face scrunched up in concentration, the little girl made quite a sight.

Graham started to laugh so hard he had to stop walking. "I don't know, Lila, but I love how you call them naked trees! I'm glad the others aren't naked yet and still have all of their pretty colors. I always feel a little sad when the leaves fall down." More than melancholy, this year the season filled him with dread as the shedding of leaves marked the passage of time.

Lila took his hand and squeezed with all of her heart. "It makes me feel sad too. At least the leaves always come back."

Graham nodded in understanding; the conversation had shifted to more than leaves. They moved on. The path seemed to go on forever until they finally reached the top. In the beginning, someone had to carry Lila. Not anymore. She was a big girl now. With a tug on Graham's hand, she brought him straight to the fire tower.

Graham stopped, tipped his head back, and stared up at the top. "Are you sure you don't want to rest first, Lila? It's a big climb."

He sat down and took out his water bottle, gulped the whole thing down without taking a breath, and handed Lila her Tigger bottle. Lila tried to copy him, spilling half when she tried.

"I'm not too tired. Come on, Graham, please!" She tugged again and they were off, climbing, climbing, climbing until they got to the top and it seemed like they could see forever.

There were more mountains dressed in colors from the leaves that made them look like a quilt, dotted with blue by the lakes scattered below as well. "Can I use the 'noculars, Graham? I want to see if I can find that something red again. You remember our mystery from when we came in the summertime?"

They had hiked in the summer and climbed the fire tower. Graham let her look through his binoculars and the little girl was captivated by a splash of red in the sea of green leaves. Graham had seen something too and was intrigued. When they tried to find that slip of scarlet again, the wind picked up and obscured their view. He made sure the lenses were adjusted and handed her the pair he brought on every hike. Lila poked her tongue out, but couldn't even see over the railing on the tower.

Graham picked her up and held on to her really tight. "It was this way. I remember because we could see that lake right below us, the one that looks like a hand. Look up a little higher and I bet you'll solve our mystery today."

He scanned the area himself, searching for anything out of the ordinary. There was a nagging sensation of missing something important. There was nothing strange, only the ocean of foliage flowing away in waves to the soft rolling mountains. "What do you see, Ladybug?"

Lila looked straight ahead, then side to side before handing the binoculars back to him. "I can't find anything today. Everything is red, orange, and yellow. We'll have to try when everything is brown or the trees are naked. Then we can see lots more. Why do they call this a fire tower, Graham?" Lila talked fast, her words running into to one another with her busy mind .

Graham stared out at the landscape spread out below them, the wind making his hair dance. He loved these mountains and the woods. "Long ago, environmental conservation officers like me actually stayed in the woods in little cabins like the one by this tower. Part of their job was to climb up the fire tower every day and search for fires. If they saw any, they would call for help so there wouldn't be a big, forest fire. Now, airplanes fly over to check so they don't need someone to stay up here."

"But we stayed up here, 'member? It was my very first camping trip. Let's go to the cabin." Lila yanked on his hand.

Graham groaned like a bear. Still, he went down the steps with her, only stopping once for a rest. They reached the bottom and walked over to the little cabin. It had a porch, an open doorway without a door, and two rooms. When they camped, Graham had brought sleeping bags, a lantern, and all kinds of good things to eat while they sat by a cheerful campfire at night. Lila liked it so much, they went on camping trips every weekend after that until the weather was too cold to go anymore. They were planning their first trip for the summer when disaster struck.

They sat down next to each other on the edge of the porch. Graham handed her a granola bar and she swung her legs back and forth while they chewed. He took another long swallow of his drink and put an arm around her. "We had a lot of fun here, Lila, but I miss your mommy. It's not the same without her. I hoped…I thought we would find her today, together. I'm sorry we didn't."

Lila climbed into his lap and wrapped her arms around his neck. Her eyes held such sadness, the shadows of someone who had seen too much at such a young age. "I thought so too,

Crackers, but it's okay. You'll find her. You can find anything."

POOR KID, SHE'S BEAT. Graham glanced at the seat next to him. Lila was out before they hit the main road. It was just as well. He wasn't much on conversation for the moment. Anxiety was creeping up on him, getting harder to ignore.

He'd neglected the search for a day, something that hadn't been done since the beginning, but Lila needed him and days like this. Sarah's loss wore on her the most. If it meant giving his Sundays to Sarah's little girl, so be it. Graham reached across and ran his hand over her hair. She didn't move. The hike had been hard work for someone so little, yet she never asked him to carry her, not once. He felt his heart squeeze at the thought. She had changed so much and Sarah was missing it.

After a twenty minute drive back to Johnstown, he pulled into the Andersons' driveway as the sun dipped down to the horizon. Lila didn't even wake up when he unbuckled her and carried her to the door. It was a shame. She was missing an amazing sundown, with reds, pinks, and a hint of purple. Graham turned to watch, soak in the sight, and find a scrap of short-lived peace.

"Graham, come on in. Why don't you set Lila down on the couch until she wakes up?" Sally stood with the door open and a welcoming smile.

He nodded his thanks and walked inside to be surrounded by warmth and the smell of home cooking. He bent down and set Lila on the couch, careful not to wake her, covering her with a blanket. He paused to watch the little girl's sweet face and pressed a feather of a kiss to her forehead. Sally motioned for him to come into the kitchen. He straightened, settled his emotions, and followed her.

"Sit down, Graham. You must be tired. Have a cup of coffee while you're at it." Sally handed him a mug of steaming brew and puttered with her dishes on the stove. Steve came in the back door, gave his wife a kiss on the cheek, and filled his own cup.

"Well, if the hearty hikers aren't back. You *are* staying for dinner and you're just in time for a good one." He took a sip of his coffee and inhaled deeply. "Just smell that chicken pot pie. It's the kind of meal that just sticks to your ribs and if you don't mind my saying so, you could use it."

Graham gave the older man a weary smile. "I've been hearing that a lot lately. I must be worse off than I thought. I was planning on stopping off at the range, but I guess I could stay, for Lila's sake."

Steve reached across and grabbed his arm to give it a hearty squeeze, grabbing his attention as well. "You need to do it for your sake, Graham. We know how hard you're trying and how much you're hurting. We all are. You know Sarah wouldn't want to see you this way. Try and find pleasure in the little things while you're at it."

Graham bowed his head and blinked hard as his vision started to swim. He gave a nod and spoke when he could. "You're right, Steve. I'll try to be more like you and Sally, I really will. Thank you for all you've done for me."

Lila walked in, rubbing her eyes, rosy cheeked and still sleepy. "I'm really hungry. I think I could eat a bear. When are we gonna eat dinner?" She managed to make everyone laugh. Sally settled Lila in her seat and started to serve. Everyone enjoyed their meal and a night of company. It almost felt like Sundays with Sarah.

LILA WAS TRYING NOT TO GO TO BED. She went to the bathroom. She asked for milk and cookies. She had to go tell Pop Pop something else she forgotted about their hike. She asked Nana to read her a story. She got up to say good night to Pop Pop—again. Bedtime used to be her favorite time of the day. Lila didn't like it anymore.

Night-night used to be the time when Mommy climbed into bed and read to her until Lila fell asleep. It would be all warm and snuggly with Mommy there and she wasn't as scared of the dark. Lila burrowed down under the covers, holding her teddy bear in one arm and Mommy's picture in her other hand.

Her bedside lamp was turned down low like a night light. Nana bought it for her because it was so scary at night now that Mommy was gone. She had turned it on every night since she came to stay with Nana and Papa along with a little candle they used at Christmas that was in her window. She would keep them on every night until Mommy came home and could see the light in Lila's window.

She closed her eyes and said the same prayer she said every night. "Dear God, please bring Mommy back to me. I'll be good, I promise. I ate all my vegetables and I listened to Nana and Pop Pop. I'll do anything if you bring her home. Just let me know, dear God. Thank you and amen."

4

SHE WAS COUGHING AGAIN. A terrible rattling sound, deep in her lungs, getting worse each day. Caroga was whittling away before his eyes. Whatever was wrong was taking the shine from her fair hair, stealing the light from her pale, blue gaze. He brought her water, propped her up with more pillows, and tenderly took her hand. She fell into a fitful sleep. His eyes fell on the blood on her handkerchief and he fled.

Kane Johnson met the day on the mountain that was his namesake as was his habit, searching desperately for peace. Regardless of the weather or the season, he made his way from deep in the forest to reach the top. The climb wasn't vigorous, but got the blood pumping and made his lungs burn on the journey.

The mountain's steady solidness soothed him, settled the mind. Along with the surrounding woodlands, it was all he'd ever known. Kane Mountain had given him his livelihood, his pleasure, his home. He would honor the gentle peak at sunrise, without fail, born again in a baptism of sun's fire, seeking solace from his sister's pain.

In that sweet pause, waiting for morning to come, Kane pondered his life, seeking answers. Forty-five years. A blink, considering that the Adirondacks had been born when the Earth was young. Kane had only spent forty-five years delving into its secrets. There was so much more to learn, so much more he didn't know, like how to heal Caroga.

His eyes scanned the rolling mountains that surrounded him, but in his mind he saw a tall man standing over him on the same peak, the wind ruffling sandy hair like Kane's. Eyes of an intense blue honed in on his little boy.

"A body never stops learning, boy. These schools in America think they give young people all they need in a few, measly years, fill their heads with facts, and spit them out with no idea about what really matters in life. I don't have much faith in schools or where they send someone after graduation. My son will get the best education by going back to the basics through experiences and living. The land is the best teacher and her lessons won't end until you take your last breath."

Kane longed for his father's knowledge now, to draw on that well of strength and find answers for his sister, but Daddy had never found it easy to let the words flow. He was reticent, only handing out tidbits of his past. *I wish you were here now, Daddy, to tell me what to do for her, to help me carry this burden.*

Mama had tried to fill in the gaps, showing Kane a photo album she'd kept secreted away. She'd pull it out whenever Daddy was out in the woods, which was most of the time. All Kane had to do was close his eyes to remember her.

Mama gathering him up onto her lap, the smell of the wildflowers that grew in a carpet on the forest floor in her hair, cinnamon and baking bread in her clothes. She was his first home and every time she tucked him in her arms was a homecoming. She let him turn the pages, giving him a little tickle, humming or whispering the tale of the time before.

Kane often looked through the book to hold them close, to try and understand. It was all he had left of his parents, a smattering of photographs. Ben Johnson as a baby, flags waving around him, celebrating the end of WWII. His father playing a stickball game in an Albany alley, pretending to the great Babe Ruth. A snapshot with Kane's grandparents outside a little white house in a row of white houses. Ben as a young man, his hair long with his girl by his side, Mary, Kane's mama, their hands raised in peace signs.

The last photograph. Daddy in a soldier's uniform, drafted, and Mama in a simple sundress on the steps of city hall. Their wedding day. He looked so young, not much more than a boy. His eyes were wide, afraid. Mama looked like a flower that had begun to wilt.

Kane closed his eyes, felt Mama's arms around him, heard the creaking of the rocker as the scent of her perfume, made from her own flowers, floated in the air. " *That war was like blowing out a candle in your daddy. It still haunts him, what he saw, what he had to do. That's what you see in his eyes. He'll carry it with him always, why he had to leave it behind.*"

The war in Viet Nam changed Ben Johnson, soured him on the taste of American Pie. Like the adult child that could no longer live with his parents, he could not live under Uncle Sam's roof anymore. Not when the government sent their boys to slaughter, to see and do the unthinkable.

He came home, gathered up his young wife, the essentials, and took his jeep off to the woods. To a place that beckoned from childhood, a place that could soothe the raw patches in his soul, where healing could begin. Except for rare excursions on the winding roads of the Adirondacks into the small towns interspersed amongst the stretch of wilderness, it was all Kane and his sister, Caroga, had ever known.

Above all things, Ben Johnson was a survivor. He'd learned the hard way, making him a hard man. In the name of his country, he had been forced to do terrible things, unspeakable things that went against his conscience and God. His country had taken his peace. It was up to him to take it back. He tucked his home deep within the forest and camouflaged it. A person would not see it until he was on top of it and even then might walk by.

Kane was born in the small cabin in the woods, the mountain that gave him his name standing watch. Caroga came when he was ten, a slip of sunshine. He was over the moon about his baby sister, couldn't get enough of her. Mama said she'd never learn to walk what with Kane carrying her around all of the time.

Sitting on the mountain top now, he likened it to his father, steady and strong, weathering all storms. That was the man that Kane knew. Daddy was a store of invaluable lessons and passed them on to his son. Kane loved to work with his hands and would spend hours carving figures out of wood. Caroga was his shadow, tagging along after him everywhere. She'd settle at his feet and watch, mesmerized as the animals took shape in the wood and became hers.

The soft sighing of the wind in the pines, that was his mother. A gentle, quiet woman. Kane loved the sound of her sweet voice. There was no picture book holding Mama's past. In their flight to the woods, hers had been left behind, but she painted pictures with words. From the time Kane was a baby, she read to him, and later to his sister, from a small collection of books. She and Daddy revered the Bible. What books she did not have, she told him by memory, nursery rhymes, her favorites, some out of her own imaginings. Mama taught both of them how to read and write, passing on a piece of herself.

IF ONLY A CAMERAMAN HAD THE POWER to take a photograph, make their contentment last forever. In their little cabin in the woods, the bonds that held his family together were as strong as the mountains, their love as deep and gentle as the clear, blue waters. Every minute was a gift until it all came down.

Mama died, inexplicably, suddenly. One morning she collapsed in the kitchen and never got up again. She was the heart of their family and left a gaping hole. Caroga tried to fill the gap, but fate was most cruel, taking Daddy within a few, short months as he followed his heart. The hole became dark and bottomless. When Kane lost his parents, he lost himself. If not for Caroga, he would have lost his mind.

One year. On their own. They survived it, if one could call it that. Time was no longer a friend, empty, with too much of it. Kane kept his hands busy with projects, tried to crowd his mind with the words on the pages of his mother's favorite books, made his body weary with the labor of chopping wood, carrying and skinning animals from the hunt, scrubbing his home and clothing.

His sister sewed, making them both clothing, more blankets for the cold months. She dabbled with cooking, trying new dishes to tempt her brother's taste buds when he was too depressed to eat. She would read aloud or sing to him, sometimes dancing over the forest floor, as light as the wind in his arms, making Kane forget the terrible sadness for a little while.

Until the day she took ill. Kane thought it only a cold, a cough that left her winded and shaken. Strange. There was no fever, no runny nose, no bright eyes or hectic color in her cheeks. In fact, the pink bloom faded from her skin and her gaze lost its sparkle as the cough persisted. Day after day, the fits became longer, harder, more terrifying. His baby sister grew weak and thin. Nothing helped. One day, Caroga couldn't even get out of bed anymore and Kane knew. She was dying.

KANE WOKE UP, LISTENING TO THE DEATH RATTLE…AGAIN. Unable to stand the noise or the consuming sorrow, he comforted his sister with an herbal tea to soothe cracked lips and a throat worn raw until she drifted off. The gratitude in her eyes tore at him and forced him out.

He pulled on his tattered jeans, Daddy's army jacket, and headed out into the woods. Took to the mountain, reached the top, and the heavens opened up. Head tipped to the sky, fists raised, Kane shouted like a wounded creature, "How could you leave us alone? She needs help and I don't know what to do!"

A rush of anger at his abandonment, an overpowering grief, pushed him back down the mountain and out of the woods. Kane had to get away, find a small reprieve.

There was no destination in mind. His feet found the way of their own accord and Kane came to a halt next to the old jeep, tucked under a cover of branches. It fired up with a little coaxing and rumbled out of the woods, navigating the winding roads that wove through the Adirondacks.

Round and round, the tires hummed on the pavement. The hours of the day wound down and the aching inside only intensified. For the first time in his life, he thought about ending it, but that was out of the question. Kane couldn't leave Caroga alone.

Guilt ate at him for leaving her this long. She needed someone to watch over her, to ease her suffering. He needed to hunt and gather for their survival. It was not possible to be two places at once and Kane didn't know what to do.

The sign for the Rockwood State Forest loomed ahead, old, stone posts from a former gateway acting as guardians. If only they held the solution to his dilemma…and then, God was good enough to bring him a woman. She was a torch, hair gleaming in the dying light of the day, surrounded by sunset's fire. The answer to his prayer.

THAT HAD BEEN ON THE BRINK OF SUMMER. Kane waited patiently for the sun to show its face, hoping to soothe the rough places. Caroga was still with him, but for how much longer? Light burst over the horizon, a flaming torch dispelling the darkness. He cast up a prayer of gratitude then took out a bit of wood and his pocket knife.

Hands quick and sure, they carved the pictures from his mind. He tucked the lifelike miniatures into his pocket and made his way down the mountain. The sunrise was a daily reminder of his one blessing. The woman. The reason his sister still lived.

A small line of smoke drifted at ground level, resembling nothing more than some fog. Daddy had found an ingenious way to make a chimney that would not reveal their presence. A few items of clothing and some towels were hung on the small clothesline that stretched between the house and a tree in back. Birds were gathered outside his door and scattered at his approach. She must have been up early today, preparing for Kane's return, caring for Caroga.

He stepped inside the cabin to be met with the smell of coffee and food simmering on the wood-fed cook stove. Kane didn't know what the girl did, but her coffee was better than any other he had ever tasted. His woman stood by the window, staring out at the dawn. She reminded him of his mother and something she used to say, "*Still waters run deep.*" Quiet, her eyes were like the lake waters on a calm day when they mirrored the sky.

At the sound of his footsteps, she turned to him and bowed her head. "Good morning." Her soft voice was almost a whisper.

"It is because of you," Kane told her with the gentleness he would use to tame an animal of the forest.

He sat down at the small table and chairs, sturdy as his father's hands. A steaming, stoneware mug was set in front of him along with homemade, cinnamon bread. Kane savored the meal while she sat across from him sipping a cup of tea and nibbling on her breakfast.

"This is wonderful, thank you." He smiled at her and set a carving by her plate as he did every morning.

Her fingers reached out to stroke the image etched into the wood, a pair of geese, wings outstretched. Kane had chosen them because they were one of his favorite birds. They represented new beginnings with their return in the spring, and they mated for life. He needed a symbol of hope more than anything else.

There was a tremble in her voice and she would not look him in the eye. "They're beautiful."

Kane reached out to take her hand. She started to pull away but he held firm, a simple reminder of his strength, until she became still. "I'm glad you like them." He rubbed the back of her hand for a moment with his thumb, letting go when he sensed her reluctance. "How is she?" He asked, his voice dropping down low.

In answer, the coughing started again. Kane was out of his seat in an instant, the woman trailing him as they entered Caroga's tiny bedroom. His sister was bathed in sunshine, but the light did nothing to brighten the scene. Her breathing was becoming more labored each day.

Kane sat down beside her and gathered her into his arms, wincing at how brittle she'd become. The woman acted as a nurse, took the handkerchief, replaced it with another, and held water to his sister's lips. Eventually, the fit lost its grip and Caroga fell back, exhausted.

Kane eased her down, stroking her hair from her face, struggling to hold back his tears. She did not need his weakness. "Look, little sister. I made you an eagle today after I saw one soaring high above the mountain. You would have wanted one for yourself."

She took the carving and held it up to the light, closing her fingers tightly around it. Her eyes closed and a tear trickled down. "I wish I could take flight like this beautiful bird."

Kane pulled a chair beside her bed and continued to sit with his baby sister while the light shone through bits of colored glass in her window, casting brilliant shadows of blue and green on her face and her pillow. He didn't even notice when they were alone.

He found the woman clearing the table, wiping at her cheeks from time to time. Kane didn't know if the tears were for his sister or for her own plight. The thought of life without Caroga was too overwhelming, one he shied away from. Instead, he pictured finding a partner in this woman.

Kane handed her a flannel shirt and opened the door. "My father always taught me—ladies first," he said with a small bow.

She walked outside and inhaled deeply of the fresh air of autumn, taking pause to wait for his guidance. "Where will we go? Your sister really shouldn't be left alone." Her caring for another human being who did not belong to her amazed him. Kane wanted her to care for him in that way.

A hint of wind lifted her hair, catching the sunlight. Kane longed to touch it, feel its silky smoothness, bury his nose in that soft spot between her jaw and her neck, breathe her in. He had laid awake in bed many nights, picturing her beside him while he ran his hands over her body. He wanted her with a need close to aching, but resisted. She was timid like the woodland creatures and required his patience.

Finding his inner balance, he set the wanting aside and cleared his throat. "I thought a short walk and some fresh air would do you good. You've been cooped up for too long."

They spent an hour in the heart of the forest. Kane pointed out animals and their tracks along the way, their droppings, and marks they made. He showed her plants that were safe to eat as well as those that were poisonous, told her how tools could be made out of many things found in nature. His tongue kept running, sure to become unhinged. The woman said little, yet her eyes were wide and she drew it all in, like a sponge.

They stopped to eat lunch before turning back, a homemade bread and tree nuts, when two deer walked close to them, grazed, and moved on. Wonder lit the face of the woman beside him. "Aren't they amazing? There's always something new to see if you'll only take the time to see it."

The light flickered out and a wall of sadness came down, strong enough to take Kane's breath with it. He took her hand again with nothing but gentleness. "I know you're not used to this place, but I need you. My sister needs you. You'll find peace here if you let it in. It's the reason my father came. Make sure you leave the door open."

They turned back and made haste across the forest, anxiety nipping at his heels. Walking inside the cabin, they were met by silence. Fear clutched at Kane's heart, making it start to pound, and he hurried to her room. She was still, so white and small that he thought it must be over.

A sound of distress broke free as he dropped to his knees beside the bed and took Caroga's hand. It was so cold and yet…there was a flicker of movement as the blanket rose and fell with the slightest of breaths and her eyes opened. They glowed softly, staring at him, and Kane moved beside her to take her in his arms and press a kiss to her forehead.

Glancing back, he watched a single tear slide down his helpmate's cheek. Kane wiped it away with a tentative touch and spoke in a hushed voice. "She is all right and you will be as well. Give it time."

The woman nodded and stood. "I'm really tired. I'm going to go to bed now. Good night." She turned and walked out.

Shortly after, she made the climb to her bedroom in the loft. He felt his sister go loose in his arms as she fell back to sleep. Up above, he could hear footsteps and a rustling of motion from time to time, his ears highly attuned to the slightest sound. He eased Caroga back on her pillow, pulled up the covers and kissed her good night.

Kane went to his room and changed for the night then sat in his rocker to mull over his day. It had felt good spending time with the woman, even with the specter of sickness hanging over him. If only he could take away her unease and unhappiness, a current that ran strong beneath the calm surface she presented each day while nursing Caroga.

With a sigh, he banked the fire, turned off the kerosene lamps, and went to his small bedroom off of the living room and kitchen area. Sleep did not take long, not with all the work a body needed to do in the wilderness. He drifted off, holding a picture of his visitor in his mind.

In the middle of the night, Kane stirred in his sleep. He didn't know why he awoke—perhaps the wind rattling at his window or the sound of an owl, loud and clear in the tree next to the cabin. Hearing no sounds from above, he tiptoed out to check on Caroga, found nothing amiss, and went upstairs to make sure her nurse was still there.

In sleep, she looked younger, like a child. The fear and sadness were missing. He wished he could make her look that way when she was awake. He reached out and laid a hand gently on her hair. With a start, she pulled away, but never opened her eyes and her breathing remained even. Even in her sleep, she was scared of him.

With a heavy heart, Kane turned off the lamp she had left burning on her bedside table. He would have to be patient and bide his time. Eventually she would turn toward him, not away. "Good night, Sarah. Sweet dreams," he whispered and went back to bed.

5

GRAHAM CONFRONTED THE DAY on the peak of Whiteface, overlooking Lake Placid. Hoping to find some peace. He ran in the middle of the night, shot at the indoor range because it was still dark, and headed out because his mind, his body *couldn't* be still. He parked at the top as the sky began to lighten from black to gray, climbed out of his truck, and leaned against the front bumper. Graham hadn't paid attention to the sunrise in God only knew how long. Today he would wait for it, make the time before he went out of his mind.

In the wee morning hours when most of the world was still sleeping or just rolling out of bed, Graham felt completely alone with the wind as his only company. If only there was someone to share this burden. Most people thought he was crazy and it was time to let Sarah go. Graham couldn't let go, not until it was finished.

God, how he missed his father. Graham could come to him no matter what the problem, big or small. The man always had sound advice, a strong shoulder to lean on, an open ear. They used to talk for hours about anything and everything. He wished desperately that his father could help to see him through the greatest fight of his life. Instead, the only thing Graham could do was live by his father's example and be the kind of man Dylan Scott would want him to be.

Patriot. The word defined Graham's father. Dylan Scott beat the draft board to the punch and signed himself up for the army. Four years of his life, given freely to the service in Viet Nam, and he came back home to build a family. Graham's father did not dwell on the horrors of war; he tried to teach others how to avoid them in the classroom, through his example.

Hero. That was how Graham would always think of Dylan Scott, especially at the end. His father fought the cancer that invaded his body with everything he had, but the monster was vicious and took him down fast. Wearing him away to skin and bones with nothing left but pain. Graham and his mother were devastated. Each found their own way to cope. Pamela moved to Florida. As for Graham, he threw himself into his work, Sarah and Lila, until Sarah was taken from him. Now the search was all that he had.

Graham came back from the past, the tears running down his face once again. He looked up at the sky and shouted, "Dad, if you can hear me, I could really use a hand down here. I'm not doing so hot on my own."

The sun answered his plea, breaching the horizon, a ball of fire with brilliant reds, oranges and every shade in between, streaking across the sky. If Graham stretched out his hand far enough, he could touch it. It was a perfect sunrise, one that Lila would love. He stood still as a statue and let it wash over him, a balm for a soul worn raw. At the same time, it cut him to the quick. A double-edged sword, the dawn was a reminder of yet another day without Sarah.

No sense in lingering. There was work to do. Graham climbed in his truck, turned around, and headed back to the base of the mountain. He drove into Lake Placid, home of the winter Olympics the year the US Hockey team beat Russia. The town was quiet today on an off-season weekday Reluctant to resume the discouraging task of questioning people again, he went into the local diner to find coffee and some optimism.

The place was quiet. Graham chose a stool at the counter, set down a stack of flyers with Sarah's picture staring up at him on the cover, and eyed the menu. He supposed he should eat something. He was feeling a little light-headed, couldn't remember the last time he ate. He settled on coffee and a bagel when a waitress approached.

She looked to be in her twenties with highlighted blonde streaks in brunette hair piled up on her head, way too much makeup on an attractive face, and over-sized hoops dangling in her ears. She was snapping gum when she stopped next to Graham.

She glanced at the picture on the counter then up at him. "Pretty girl. You know her?" She placed a mug in front of him while waiting for his response and filled it with coffee at his nod.

"Yes. She's a good friend of mine." He'd almost said *was*. What was wrong with him? If he wavered, everyone else would give up. He took a sip of his coffee and looked into the girl's eyes which were faded compared to Sarah's brilliant blue. Her name tag said *Sandy*. "Have you seen her or seen anything strange around here? It's been over three months and we're searching for any leads."

Sandy shook her head and popped a bubble. "Nah, nothing like that. Sorry. Can I get you something to eat?" She propped a hip against the counter and acted bored out of her mind.

Graham wanted to tell her to get a personality. Somehow, he behaved. "Just a bagel, please. Could you top off the coffee too? Thanks." She nodded and walked away to help another customer while he stared up at the television airing the local news.

It was supposed to get cold with the potential for a first frost. To Graham, that meant time was running out. Once the Adirondacks were locked in winter's ice and snow, it would be near impossible to find Sarah or any sign of her. He tipped his cup absently until he realized the coffee was gone. Perhaps he should just go, continue his wild goose chase.

Five minutes later, Sandy returned and set down the bagel with packets of butter. She stayed this time, watching Graham and making him uncomfortable with her attention.

She caught his eye and gave him a smile that only filled him with a sinking feeling while he methodically chewed. "You know, a few months is an awfully long time to go without a *friend*. I get out at two if you need someone to ya know, talk to, or something."

Graham was off the stool so fast he nearly bumped into another customer walking behind him. He grabbed the bagel, set money on the counter, and pressed a handful of flyers into the waitress' hands. "I'm sorry, but I've got a job to do. If you could put the flyers out somewhere, post some, I'd really appreciate it."

His cheeks were burning and his heart started to trip on his way out to the truck as he shoved the rest of the bagel in the trash. What gave the woman the idea he was available? Graham didn't know if he could ever be with anyone else after Sarah. She had spoiled him on all other women.

The rest of his day was spent going to every business and as many homes as possible with his flyers. He left them at the post office, the police department, the fire station, and made a point of hitting all of the bars because they had the most traffic. No one had seen anything, no one knew of something out of place, no one encountered a strange individual. Another dead end.

Dinner time found him at McDonald's because he could use the drive thru and didn't have to interact with a waitress with a personal agenda. The result: a pain in his gut that suggested his body would be rebelling later on. He ate half and tossed the other half out the window, disgusted with himself.

Passing through Johnstown, he turned off at the rifle range and went inside for some more practice because it was too early to go home and go to bed. If Graham went to bed, he would simply lie awake and stare at the ceiling. Better to stare at a target.

A few other guys were practicing that night. They nodded to Graham and minded their own business until they had a chance to watch him shoot. With a low whistle, the others gathered around to watch a master at work. Graham never missed. He quit when his ammunition was gone and was met by applause.

"That was amazing," one man told him while another patted him on the back in a show of camaraderie. Others were speaking in hushed tones and nodding to Sarah's picture on the wall. They had figured him out. Time to go.

Back on the road, his stomach griped hard enough to put him down on the couch. McDonald's and stress were not a good combination. Graham wouldn't be surprised if fast food had nothing to do with it. He probably had an ulcer what with the endless coffee and the constant worry chewing at him all the time.

It was only seven o'clock. He turned on the television, but could find nothing in the span of one hundred channels. The remote landed on the country music video station, turned down low for background noise. Graham set his head on a pillow and stretched out, closing his eyes and trying not to think. What a joke. His brain never let up.

The phone rang, providing a timely distraction. "Hello?" He waited for a response. No caller i.d. There was a pause on the other end. Give it about thirty more seconds and he was hanging up. Probably a telemarketer or something and his patience was threadbare.

"Graham, honey, how are you? You sound beat." Pamela Scott spoke with forced cheer on the other end of the line. His mother tried to call at least once a week. At the beginning, when she thought Graham might lose his mind, she had come up to stay with him until he respectfully asked her to go home. No sense in two people going down with the ship.

Graham felt another twinge. Had to be an ulcer. He tried to put some life in his response. "I'm all right, Mom. It's been a long day. How about you?" His voice cracked on the last. Damn it! He would not break, not now.

Her voice was soft and reached out; he could almost feel her touch. "I'm fine. You're not. You're torturing yourself. Ease up, Graham. If you need me, I'm here. I love you, sweetheart." Conversation was pointless. There was nothing to talk about.

"'Night, Mom. I'll call…when I can. Love you too." He hung up. Restless, Graham went out into the night and ran *again*, pushing his body as far as it would go until his lungs were screaming and there was a bite in his side. His feet dragged on the walk back.

That killed some time. A scalding shower killed some more. When Graham stepped out, he was so exhausted it was hard to put one foot in front of the other. He would try bed. He shut out all of the lights save Sarah's candle in the window. It sent out its glow, a small beacon in the night.

Graham stared at the light for a moment and whispered, "Good night, Sarah. I love you." She was his nightly hope and prayer. He slipped into bed, pressed a kiss to Lila's painting on the wall, and waited for sleep to take him. Maybe there would be a respite, however brief, before it all began again in the morning.

SARAH WATERS WAS STRONG. She had learned to be strong when the messenger from the army appeared on her doorstep in full dress uniform, knew what his arrival meant before he said a word. Sarah dropped to the floor only to pick herself up when she heard her baby crying.

She learned to be stronger in four years of being a single parent, doing her best to raise Lila and give her everything two parents would normally provide.

She became strongest, steel strong, the day Kane Johnson found her at the Rockwood State Forest and made her his.

She lay very still, listening to the woods waking up. The bird chatter was followed by the darkness slowly lifting until it was almost like looking through a fog. If it was a clear day, the walls of her tiny room would be washed in pink before the full glory of morning arrived. There was the sound of a door opening and closing, heavy footsteps crunching in the leaves, receding into the distance. He would be on his way up the mountain and for an all too brief span of time, she could breathe again.

Kane brought her along with him in the beginning because he did not trust leaving her alone. Otherwise, he locked her in. He no longer slid the wooden bar across the outside of the door, his hold on her strong enough to keep her. A moth beating its wings against the glass, Sarah was trapped within the small confines of his cabin. She wouldn't be going anywhere, not yet. Like a snake in the grass, one day…she'd catch him unawares and then…

Upon waking, Sarah tried to figure out the puzzle that was Kane Johnson. He spoke sparingly about himself, gave only bits and pieces of his parents, was silent more often than not. The wilderness and his little sister were the only thing that opened him up. They were his passions and he tried to share them with her.

Sarah had heard of hermits before, but found it difficult to comprehend what would drive someone to cut themselves off completely from others. Most challenging to understand was Kane's compulsion to steal someone to nurse his sister. Why not bring her to a hospital or a doctor? Maybe…earlier on, it might have helped. Now, Sarah feared nothing could help.

She strained her ears, listening for the ailing woman. Caroga's breathing was a wheeze that worsened as time went by. How she was still clinging on, Sarah did not know. At least there was no coughing first thing that morning. Maybe the day would be restful for both of them. Watching someone die inch by inch, stranger or no, was gut-wrenching, exhausting work.

Reaching under the bed, Sarah pulled out a walking stick with a wolf carved on top. Kane had made it for her, one of his daily gifts, his way of courting her she supposed. It looked real with intricate detail, head tilted to howl at the moon. She felt as if she could howl every morning that she found herself in her loft again, loud enough for the world to hear her and find her.

She slid a pocket knife from under her pillow and made another notch in the wood, keeping track on her makeshift calendar. It would be September, time for her Lila to start school, for Sarah to share another year with those magical creatures—kindergarteners— and Lila would be among them. Her eyes stung and her throat burned with a longing strong enough to crush her.

Sarah climbed out of bed and knelt at the window, pressing her forehead to clasped hands. She whispered fiercely in prayer. "Please God, take care of my Lila, send her my love while I am away and bring me back to her. Give my parents strength and faith. Walk closely by Graham's side because I know *he* will need You, perhaps most of all."

Her throat closed and tears made tracks down her cheeks. Sarah closed her eyes to concentrate on the pictures in her mind that she took out at the dawn, as well as the close, of each day. In the beginning, she had looked at the images stored within the digital camera that had been tucked in her pocket. She'd even managed to take pictures of the cabin and Kane when he went outdoors; they might come in handy someday. Seeing the faces of the people she loved gave her the strength to get up each morning, but the battery died after the first month.

The memories flashed in her mind's eye and Sarah focused on each one with intensity because she would not forget anything about them. Most had Lila at its heart because her baby girl was her everything. She came to rest on a snapshot of Graham and Lila. Sarah's eyes snapped open with tears running down her face. Time to stop or she would not be able to pick herself up. She said one more prayer. "God, please help me to stay strong until we are together again."

Sarah waited at the window until she was rewarded by another breathtaking sunrise, something Lila would love. It also meant the start of her daily preparations for Kane's return. She pulled on her jeans and a wool sweater that had belonged to his mother. On quiet feet, she padded down the steps. The kettle was still warm on the cook stove. She set two herbal teabags of Kane's making in a cup to steep and poured water into a washbasin to wash up with a bar of homemade soap.

That accomplished, she took her first sip of tea and walked to the window. She picked up the brush that had also been left by Kane's mother. It was soothing, running it through her hair again and again, unwinding the knots that were her insides, at least for a little while.

Sarah wished there was time for a full bath in the tiny outbuilding not far from the outhouse, but that would have to wait for the weekend. Kane's father had been quite ingenious.

There was an outdoor shower that worked well when the weather was warm. The bathhouse was beside it, a snug building with a large copper tub. Kane would carry in stones that had been warmed in the fireplace to line the walls and heat the tiny room. The job of filling the tub with water from the stove came next. It was hard work and a lengthy process, making it a once a week luxury. Otherwise, she did her best with a basin of water and soap.

The outhouse was well ventilated with a seat and lid carved out of wood. A basket of soft leaves sat on a shelf, replenished daily. A bottle of perfume, made from flower petals gathered by her captor's mother, acted as an air freshener. Kane took care of the bucket beneath the seat that caught the waste. Sarah was quite certain that Kane's father had made many innovations to accommodate his wife because there was consideration for a woman in many aspects of their home. She finished using the outhouse, washed in the basin on the shelf, and returned to the cabin.

Sarah paused to soak up the sun and glanced back at the small buildings. It was fascinating. Even though she knew they were there, they had been built in such a way as to blend so well with the surroundings that it was hard to pick them out. The cabin was built in the same manner with consummate skill. During some of their outings, she had practically tripped over it upon their return.

In her early attempts at escape, their camouflage had been terrifying. She had made her way into the woods, turned to find her bearings, and it was as if the cabin had vanished. Unable to go back and forging ahead, everything around her looked the same, trees in all directions without any marked paths for guidance. She had no idea which way to go, but needn't have worried anyway. Kane was there within minutes, his hold on her gentle but insistent, leading her back to her prison.

Sighing deeply, Sarah went back inside and took out the Johnson family cookbook, a collection of handwritten recipes, and the ingredients for cinnamon bread. She enjoyed cooking, even though it took some getting used to doing the job like a pioneer woman. She had to stoke the fire in the cook stove and experiment with getting the right temperature and baking time.

Kane had been patient as was his way. He demonstrated the process first and accepted her disastrous, early attempts with good humor. In the same manner, he led her through all of her duties and left her to them. It took three months and a lot of burnt offerings until Sarah considered herself a decent cook. No one would die from it anyway.

She set the bread in the oven, poured herself another cup of tea, and sat down in a rocker made from young saplings. The chair set to rocking, the scent of cinnamon filled the room, and she sipped at the tea, striving for a calmness to settle over her.

Too much idle time set her mind to working like a dog worrying at a bone, always searching for a way out. It was torture, acting as if she accepted this life, feeling as if she was doing nothing to end her captivity. In the beginning, she had fought it, tooth and nail, from the moment Kane found her. Even though she was awake, Sarah only needed to close her eyes to relive that nightmare all over again.

6

GRAHAM'S TRUCK DISAPPEARED OVER THE HILL. The wind picked up, carrying a chill with the dying of the day. Sarah rubbed her arms, wishing she'd worn a coat instead of a sweater, and aimed to snap one more picture as a vehicle drove into the parking area behind her. She started to turn at the sound of footsteps when a blanket was pulled over her head and she was slung over someone's shoulder as if she was no more than a sack of potatoes. It was someone tall, someone strong and undeniably masculine.

Heart slamming against her ribs until she thought it would explode, Sarah started to smother in the rough, scratchy material. She kicked and screamed with all of her strength until a hand clamped over her mouth. She bit down hard and there was cursing when he almost dropped her. A gruff, deep voice warned her to keep quiet or she might be hurt.

A rope wrapped around the blanket to immobilize her and she was set on the floor of a vehicle. The engine cranked and they drove for hours, round and round with twists and turns, taking away all sense of direction. Jarred by bumps in the road, sheer panic building, Sarah thought she was going to throw up.

The man parked somewhere off the road, that much she knew because of the change in the sound of the tires as they left the hum of asphalt and rolled quietly over dirt. He scooped her up with ease and carried her, the strong scent of pine surrounding Sarah, the sounds of the forest closing in on her. She started writhing and kicking again until the rope loosened and she punched at a wall of hard muscle with her fists.

He dropped her and Sarah scrambled out of the blanket. She ran, her breath coming in a sob, but her sweater snagged on a low-hanging branch. Relentless, her captor grabbed her feet, dragged her back to him, and yanked the cover back over her head before he picked her up once more.

They arrived at his cabin where he brought her to the loft, set her on the bed, and removed the blanket. Sarah looked up at a mountain of a man. He was tall, broad of back, with a mane of sandy hair threaded with a smattering of blonde and white strands. His callused hand cupped her chin even as her stomach clenched and the bile rose up in her throat, forcing her to meet his eyes. They were golden, like the gleam of honey in a jar. Steady. Unshakeable.

"My name is Kane Johnson. This is my home and this will be your place. I'm not going to hurt you, but you *will* stay from now on, God willing. My sister is sick and needs more help than I can give her."

Lying on the bed in the darkness that first night, Sarah stared up at the ceiling until the wee morning hours. She tried slinking to the door, but he barred her path. In the days that followed, she bided her time, watching, waiting for her moment. When Kane finally left, he locked the cabin from the outside by dropping a wooden bar across the door and closing the storm shutters on the windows. Sarah still tried to slip out when he returned, shooting out the door the second it opened at every opportunity. He hauled her back in every time.

She was left to care for Caroga, a sweet, wan woman, beautiful even in illness. Each day refined Kane's sister more and more, bringing the bones in her face closer to the surface, showing without a doubt the end was near. Sarah did what she could, but it was no use. Caroga needed medical attention in a hospital with advanced treatment options…and even then, Sarah didn't know if anything could be done.

From time to time, Kane took her with him in the woods for short journeys. She tried to run, but he was always one step ahead. One day on an outing to gather edible plants, Sarah caught a glimpse of an army-green jeep. It was a good distance from the cabin, tucked away in a camouflaged, lean-to. A flicker of hope flared, but quickly died. Only Kane knew the whereabouts of the key and he led her back to the cabin on a completely different route. No chance of finding that means of escape again.

When attempts at escape proved futile, Sarah begged and cried, told him she had a little girl who needed her, especially now that Lila's father was dead. She pleaded with him every day, all day. She feigned illness and would not get out of bed, but guilt tore at her about the woman downstairs. Sarah didn't eat or drink. She even tried absolute silence. It didn't matter. Kane was quiet, he was kind, but he was relentless. He wanted Sarah for his sister…and perhaps more…and he was going to keep her.

SARAH CAME BACK TO THE PRESENT, stopped rocking, and picked up a book off the shelf next to her. Jane Eyre, one of her favorites. She tried to get lost in the pages and ease her mounting frustration, but she could not concentrate. Her thoughts turned to Graham, as they so often did, the need for him so strong it ached. She could not help but compare him with the man who had made her his prisoner. Both men had a great love and respect for the land. Both were caring and peaceful, but Sarah felt that their similarities ended there.

Kane had been taught a mistrust of others, raised in isolation, and kept the forest to himself. Graham was a people person. Others were drawn to him and his magnetic personality. He felt compelled to share his knowledge and love of the wilderness. He also found the best in others and had faith in the underlying good in most people.

It gave Sarah a cold lump in her stomach when she thought about what her disappearance must have done to Graham, how it might have changed him, her family. While she lived in relative comfort, her disappearance had to be eating away at them. It would have been easier if Kane was cruel and violent, making her suffer in the same way that she knew everyone at home suffered.

Her only solution was to play the charade with Kane. Sarah had to have faith that her opportunity would come and she would take it. Her gaze wandered outside, unseeing, when a horrible sound started in the next room, forcing her away from thoughts of herself. She took the cup of tea, kept warm on the stove along with a basin of water and a towel, carrying everything in to Caroga.

The ill woman was sitting up, pillows propped behind her because she could no longer lie flat or the coughing would consume her. Hunched over her bent knees, the noise was hideous. Sarah thought her lungs would come up soon. Caroga's hair fell down over her face, a curtain to hide behind but Sarah knew…Kane's sister was in torture.

She never complained, struggled to put on a brave face for her brother, and each day sapped more of her strength. How much longer? "Shh. You'll be all right. Hang in there, Caroga, just hold on." Sarah rubbed her back and waited until the fit finally let go. A body could only take so much.

Kane's sister sank into her pillows and closed her eyes, her tongue darting out to lick at chapped lips. Droplets of blood marred her handkerchief, something that happened now with alarming regularity. "My…I'm…plumb tuckered….That was…a tough one."

An understatement to say the least. Sarah pushed Caroga's hair from her face and rested a palm on her cheek, a simple comfort. She held the tea and helped her drink it down before washing her face with the cool water from the basin. Their morning ritual was completed after Sarah brushed her patient's hair and braided it in a long rope.

Caroga caught her hand and gave a gentle squeeze. "Thank you." She whispered. If she spoke softly, it was less likely to aggravate her condition and she might have peace for a little longer. "Kane loves my hair in a braid. Our mama often wore hers that way."

Sarah patted her hand and nodded as the woman's eyes drooped. Already worn out, Caroga fell back into a restless slumber. There was the sound of footsteps, making the hairs rise up on the back of Sarah's neck, and Kane stepped inside. She steeled herself and lifted her head to meet his gaze. "Good morning," she told him quietly. Oh to have the satisfaction of spitting on his feet.

"It is because of you." Kane's golden eyes glowed and he smiled at Sarah with part of his face tanned and creased by the sun. The rest was hidden by a beard. A pleasant face, like his personality. His sandy hair, streaked blonde by the exposure to the light and threaded with strands of white, was pulled back in a tail at the base of his neck to tame unruly waves. He was sturdy of build and strong from his life in the outdoors. Kane exuded an inner calm that could only be taught by nature and all Sarah wanted to do was scream. No one would hear her.

He settled in a chair at the table carved by his father. Sarah set a mug of coffee and plate of bread in front of him. The brew's strong scent gave her a pang for Graham. How he had loved her coffee and lit up for it every time. Such a little thing. She sat across from Kane and cradled her own cup of coffee in her hands, imagining it was Graham that sat with her.

"I made this for you today." Kane's ritual, every morning. He set his latest carving by her plate.

Her fingers trembled as she ran them over the smooth image of a pair of geese. Graham loved when the Canadian geese flew overhead, announcing the change of season. Anytime he heard them, morning or night, he would take pause, and listen to them with a smile stretching from ear to ear. If Lila was with them, he would pick her up and point out their "v" formation. Once there had only been two. "*See them Lila? They're a couple, like a mommy and daddy. They'll stay together for life.*"

"They're beautiful." Sarah would put them in her room with the rest of the collection. Rather than link them with Kane, she found a connection with her life in every bit of wood. Sometimes, when she awoke in the night and could not sleep, she held each piece and told herself what they represented until she could sleep again. These geese—they were for her and Graham. One day, they would become Mr. and Mrs. Scott. Her eyes began to burn and she bit down on her lip, fighting back tears. Her captor *would not* make her cry again.

The brief letup in the next room ended and Caroga's bark broke the silence once more. Kane, attentive to his sister's needs as always, was at her side, caring for her, comforting her. Watching their strong bond, Sarah couldn't understand how someone with such tenderness could do something as cruel as stealing a woman.

Kane came out shortly after and methodically began to clear the table, setting the small kitchen area to rights again as he must have done on so many occasions. Sarah couldn't help but wonder if he had performed this chore since he was a toddler at his mother's hip. In Kane's small world, this was what a body did.

Not spontaneous in nature, abducting someone was completely out of character. For at least the thousandth time, Sarah cursed fate that she did not get in her car and leave that day before Kane stumbled upon her. She stood at the window, hands knotted together, and fought to not come unglued. *Today. Dear God, please open a door today.*

As if he heard her thoughts, Kane dried his hands, and went to the door. He handed her a flannel shirt and took a little bow. "My father always taught me—ladies first."

It was an order sheathed in courtesy. Refusal wasn't an option; she'd tried it and felt his firm, vicelike grip on her arm, reining her in. Sarah did everything possible to keep him from touching her. He followed her out the door, keeping her within reach, and closed it. Kane dropped the wooden bar and scanned his home, assuring himself all was in order.

Arguments about leaving his sister didn't work. Sarah waited quietly. The wind running through her hair and the crisp autumn air helped her to find a slip of peace. It was smothering—always in the tiny cabin taking care of someone so ill, with the shadow of Kane's relentless presence at her side. He set off and she followed because standing still or walking away were not a choice now. All the while, her mind was working on a solution. One day, he would leave a crack open and she *would* slip through.

Throughout their journey, Kane became her nature instructor. Graham had already taught her the same information, but Sarah kept that knowledge to herself. While the woodsman alternated between periods of rambling on and silence, she concentrated intensely on the direction they were walking and any distinguishing features that might help her to get out of this place. She paid close attention to sources of food and water. If, no, *when* she had the chance, Sarah *would* find her way out.

They took a break for lunch and had a visit from two deer, another heartbreaking reminder of Lila and Graham. Early Sunday mornings at Graham's practically guaranteed a visit from the deer. He left feed for them year round, providing them with a sure thing even in the winter when the pickings were scarce. Each time they arrived on his front lawn, Lila would stand with the conservation officer and watch them at the window before they tiptoed outside to get closer. One day, a doe cautiously approached Sarah's little girl and ate out of her hand.

Kane studied Sarah, unable to miss the heavy weight of sadness that nearly pressed her to the ground. He said something about finding peace in the wild like his father did. He then made the sign of the cross over the deer and whispered a prayer or blessing. How could a gentle, God-fearing man commit the act of keeping Sarah against her will?

As Sarah accompanied Kane through the forest, she mused about her years of growing up and was certain of one thing: nothing had prepared her for her current situation. She grew up in historic Johnstown and the Adirondack Park was her playground. Sarah said nightly prayers, grace at the dinner table, and learned to have faith. Most importantly of all, she was taught to treat others the way she should be treated. She loved the world of make-believe, singing, the magic of books, and going to the movies. Drawing and writing were favorite pastimes, making it easy to imagine new worlds and adventures. Never had Sarah dreamed her life would take such a bizarre twist.

Her first love was her high school sweetheart, Lee Waters. Lee was an athlete. Sarah thought he was strong enough to take on any challenge. He had black hair that was hard to tame, an easy smile, and a laugh that made everyone want to join him. His eyes were a smoky gray that pulled Sarah in every time he looked at her. She'd been crazy about him and the war stole him from her. His loss had nearly broken her, but Sarah was a survivor. Maybe life had prepared her in some ways for Kane after all.

Kane led her home, taking a different route yet again in a zigzagging pattern that left Sarah at a loss. The quiet in the cabin was deafening when they stepped inside and she feared the worst. Following Kane into the bedroom, her lungs squeezed tightly in her chest until she found it hard to breathe. Was the wait finally over? There was grief and at the same time, calculation. Now…Sarah could slip out while he was distracted.

She inched toward the doorway when Caroga's eyes opened. Relief warred with sorrow and the stinging in Sarah's eyes gave way to tears. Kane's hand, rough from hard work, gently wiped away a drop from her face.

Her insides flip-flopped and she mentally cringed at his touch. "She will be all right and you as well. Give it time," he whispered. Unable to stand another minute beside him without screaming, Sarah feigned fatigue and headed upstairs to bed.

All the while, the sharks were circling in her mind while her feet were mired in quicksand. What was Lila doing? How were Mom and Dad coping? And Graham…had he given up on her? Sarah was drawn to the rocker and turned to watch the sundown. She made herself wait from beginning to end because Lila loved them so much and her little one could be watching it too.

Sarah didn't turn away as the color bled from the sky, the trees became dark silhouettes against a pale canvas, and it faded into black. Her heart sank. Another sunset without her baby girl, the nightly snuggles, and the sweet task of tucking her into bed. Another night without a dish of ice cream with Mom and Dad before goodnight hugs. Another day closing without Graham saying goodnight and stealing a kiss before heading home. She turned to stare at the ceiling and thought her heart would fall to pieces.

Dreading Kane's presence, she slipped on a long, woolen nightgown that had belonged to Kane's mother. A small dresser stood in the corner with more of the woman's clothes and her favorite belongings on top. There was a picture of Kane, his father and his mother, taken by a photographer at Sherman's when they took their little boy to see the fireworks. Another photo depicted Caroga as a bright-eyed baby with a streak of fireworks in the sky. There were a few of his mother's favorite books, carvings inscribed from her husband and son, and a small collection of jewelry.

Sarah picked up the brush next to the first photograph and began to brush out her hair, trying to understand how a woman could have given up the world to come here. Her eyes fell on the picture and she studied the image closely. The man's eyes were filled with a deep sorrow but an equally deep love when he looked on his family. If Kane's mother felt the same way, and it looked like she did, it could explain a willingness to do anything for her husband. Sarah realized she had felt that way about Lee. With a start, she knew Graham had that hold on her now.

Sarah crawled into bed and pulled the quilt tight around her. The nights were getting cold and her room was drafty. With fingers that trembled, she struck a match and lit her lamp, turning it down low. Kane had given it to her when she said she was afraid of the dark. A grown woman, afraid of the dark. She hadn't been before she was taken. She'd laughed when Lila said she was scared at night. Sarah wasn't laughing anymore.

She stared at the dim glow and waited for sleep. Her mind played a mean trick on her, playing the game of "lasts" as her last times with those she loved replayed and she couldn't turn them off. There was her last time with Lee, at the airport to see him off, whispering the news that he would be a daddy. Her last afternoon with Lila and her parents. And of course, there was her last walk with Graham in Rockwood Forest, the beginning of the end.

How his eyes shone like the sunlight on the leaves in springtime when he saw Sarah waiting for him. With each passing day that Graham was in her life, Sarah had a hard time picturing the rest of it without him in it. One moment during that afternoon stood out in her mind.

Sarah let her hand rest on his head so she could relish its warmth. "Graham…I've been meaning to ask you. How did your mother come up with your name? You're the first one I've ever met."

Graham snorted with disgust and looked up at her with long suffering in his eyes. "You do not know the grief this name has caused me. Lila is not the first to call me Crackers and it's easier not to fight it. My name is a source of great embarrassment. While my mother was pregnant, she was reading a romance novel about a Scottish highlander that swept her off her feet. It means 'home.' Pretty lame reason for a name, don't you think?"

It was the perfect name for a man who was steady, strong and true. Sarah felt like she was coming home every time she saw Graham. What she wouldn't give for a homecoming now. She kept a light burning by her bedside.

Every night she sent her love to her family, along with a hope and a prayer that Graham would find her to bring her home.

7

THERE WERE CERTAIN THINGS GRAHAM had to do to get out of bed every morning. First, he looked up at the picture Sarah's daughter painted for him and found hope…for Lila. Next, he picked up the photograph on his nightstand of the three of them, together, and found faith…for Sarah. Last, Graham built a picture in his mind, visualizing that he found her. He took her hand, stroked her hair, inhaled her scent, listened to the sound of her voice, and concentrated with unwavering focus. He *would* find her.

He swung his legs over the side of the bed and leaned his elbows on his knees, rubbing at his face because he couldn't stand himself. A moment of self-pity and he was up, pacing. It was a wonder there wasn't a tread worn in the floor.

Graham mentally scrolled through the list of destinations, chose one that pulled at him that morning, and stuck another colorful pushpin into the map of the Adirondacks on his bedroom wall. A quick, red "X" on the calendar to mark the start of another day, perhaps the day that he would find her, and he shrugged into his running clothes.

The length of the run varied, depending on the weather, the state of his mind, and his stamina. He had an hour in him today. Made it home, hit the shower, downed the coffee. Fifteen minutes, tops, and he was back on the road. Graham headed east to Prospect Mountain in Lake George. He thought it fitting; the name was symbolic of new beginnings. Over an hour later, he crested the top and waited for daylight to come.

He didn't have to hang on too long. Once the sun was over the horizon, he scanned the area in all directions with his binoculars. Lake George was sprawled below, quiet at such an hour. The town did not appeal to him. He didn't want to deal with people today, show her picture, see the same sympathetic stares. Finding nothing amiss, he drove back down the mountain, drove up route 9N, and parked on a side road. Graham's actions were programmed. Get out of the truck. Check his pack. Head into the woods.

It was easy to lose a sense of himself in the forest, to let it wash over him. Time stopped. The rest of the world disappeared. His footsteps carried him further in to where nature had not been tainted by humans. Graham willed it to be his medicine, but nothing eased his pain. Rather, the ache deepened until he thought he could not go on.

How easy it would be to keep on walking and never go back. Let the woods take him. The urge was strong. Only one thing stopped him: Sarah. Hours passed with nothing. No leads. No hope. What if she wasn't in the Adirondack Park at all? Unthinkable.

It wasn't easy to shake off the woods after hours spent in their depths. With each step, Graham mentally prepared himself for rejoining civilization until he walked out to find his truck waiting. He checked the time. Darkness would be falling soon. Another day, just spinning his wheels. He wrenched the door of his truck open, slammed it, and turned toward home.

Driving for well over an hour did nothing to improve his state of mind. He was seriously considering a bar when his cell rang. He hit the speaker. "This is Graham." He bit the words off.

"Whoa buddy, what did I do to you? You really should wait to see who's calling, pull out a little sunshine. It could have been Lila. What are you up to?" It was Jim, a constant light shining in a murky night.

"I'm heading home from Lake George. I just passed the sign for Broadalbin. What's going on?" His eyes scanned the forest on the side of the road. Nothing. After all this time, he still came up empty handed.

"Listen, Jeanie and I are going to Applebee's because she doesn't want to cook. What do you say about joining us?" There was a pleading tone in his best friend's voice that had Graham smiling in spite of himself.

"All right, what did you do? Saying Jeanie doesn't want to cook means you are in trouble. The woman lives to cook." There had been many a fight in the course of their twelve year marriage that ended in an eating establishment. It was rare for the Pedersens to dine out. Going to a restaurant generally meant Jim was in the dog house.

"Can't a guy take his wife to dinner and give her a break?" There was a long pause. "Okay, you got me. I forgot my anniversary. Not a word. Just meet us when you get here and help save my butt, got it?"

Graham shook his head with a chuckle. "Are you sure about this, Pete? Wouldn't you do better on your own? You could romance her, take her out to Lanzi's on the Lake. You don't need me kicking around."

A snort from the other end. "I need anything I can get to appease my wife's formidable, Italian temper. Come on, Graham, please. I'm begging you. Be a buffer. Otherwise, I'll probably end up on your couch. Come with us and I might live."

"All right. I'll be there in about five minutes. Keep the knives away from her." Graham disconnected and shook his head.

Somehow, Jim could always make him smile. Dubbed Scottie and Pete in elementary school, they did all the firsts together: the first date, the first beer, and the first but last cigarette which made them puke their guts out. They'd been there for life's highs and lows. Jim's shoulder was often the only thing holding Graham up.

Applebee's was relatively quiet. Graham checked his reflection in the mirror over the visor, made sure his clothes were presentable, and gave himself the regular pep talk—*You can do this! You can do this*!

He stepped inside and Jim was at his elbow, grabbing hold and directing him to a table. "What took you? I'm dying here."

Jeanie sat at a booth in a cute, little dress that was fire-engine red and suited the flash in her eyes. Graham was about to slide in across from her when Jim gave a sharp jerk of his head. "Happy Anniversary, sweetie. Are you going to let my buddy live past today or should I pay my respects to him tonight?" He dropped down next to her and kissed her cheek.

Jeanie gave her husband a look that could kill a lesser man, but had only smiles for Graham. "We'll have to see about that. I'm thinking of having the date tattooed on his arm. Maybe that will cure the problem."

A waitress came by to take their order. Graham gave in and ordered a beer. He figured that they would be there for a while. The amber liquid was cool going down and the buzz felt good. It worked quickly, making him start to mellow as the conversations around the room rolled over him. His eyes drifted closed and his body went loose for the first time that day.

"Hey, come back to us, Graham, before you fall over." Jim called out from across the table. Graham opened his eyes with a start to find Jim staring at him intensely. His friend cleared his throat. "I'll be right back. Don't you two run off together."

Jeanie reached over and laid a hand on his arm, giving it the slightest squeeze. It was a reminder. They were there for Graham, every step of the way. She followed her husband's retreating back on his way to the bathroom then gave her attention to Graham. There was concern in her eyes. "Graham, are you sure you're up to dinner? We'll understand if you're too tired."

He put an arm around her shoulders and leaned against her for a moment. "Jeanie-girl, I'm too tired for anything. Most of all, I'm so tired of being stuck in my head. I'm really glad Jim called although I'm sorry he forgot your special day. You know he means well, honey. He's never been good with dates. Growing up, he forgot his mother's birthday so many times that I ended up reminding him the night before. I even bought a gift one year to keep him out of trouble."

Jeanie tilted her head with eyes slit in suspicion. "Have you been doing the same thing with my birthday? I have a gift or two that Jim wouldn't have dreamed of, not in a million years." She nodded at Graham's innocent shrug. "Uh-huh, I thought so."

Jim slid into the booth and tapped the table. "Hey, love birds. Enough snuggling. When I said not to run away together, that didn't mean you could make the moves on my wife."

With a wink, Graham gave Jeanie a kiss. "Sorry, Jeanie-girl. It won't work for us. Even though the poor guy can't remember important dates to save his life, I have to step back to save mine."

Their meals arrived at that moment and they dug in. The more time that went by, the more Jeanie softened . A couple of laughs later and her hand was in Jim's. She gave him a goofy grin. He was forgiven.

Graham let his eyes wander around the room and his body tensed as he saw Sarah's picture tacked on the wall, the flyer staring him down. He couldn't get away from her. Biting off a curse under his breath, he slammed back his beer and swiped his hand over his top lip. "Should have waited for her that day," he murmured under his breath.

Jim reached across the table and snagged his arm. "Stop it right now. You can't change what happened and you have to stop blaming yourself. Life happens, Graham. None of us ever knows what will be next."

Graham leaned his head on his hand. The long day and two beers were catching up. Jeanie slid closer and put an arm around his waist. Their companionship, so badly needed, made him ache. "When did you get so smart?" He murmured.

"Years of practice. I think it's time for you to go home or you'll be asleep at the wheel. Do you need me to drive you?" Jim eyed his friend closely.

Graham shook his head, set his money on the table, and gave Jeanie a kiss on the cheek. "I'll be fine. Thanks for the invite. You two kids have a good night." He stood up and stepped over to Jim's side of the table, leaning down to whisper in his ear. "I'll try and remind you next year. I had a bit on my mind this time around." He gave Jim a wink, a crooked smile, and walked out.

The night was clear and the air nipped at his skin. *Winter's breathing down your neck.* He started his truck and cranked the heat. It warmed the small area quickly. With a sigh, he soaked it up for a few minutes, reluctant to head home to his empty place. He started to drive and his truck brought him to Pleasant Avenue.

It rolled to a stop outside the darkened Gingerbread Cottage and he looked up at the Andersons' top floor. A light burned in Lila's window. It had every night since she'd been staying with her grandparents, like the light that was shining in Graham's window on Pleasant Lake. It made him hurt, picturing the little girl inside.

Staring up at her window, his mind replayed the many evenings spent with Lila and her mother. Those were the best nights. Sometimes they had dinner at home or came back from a day spent together, Lila's warm, small body a pleasant weight in Graham's arms. Such a small burden to carry upstairs, set her down on her bed, and slip off her shoes. Drop a butterfly kiss on her forehead and those little arms would come up around his neck. "G'night, Crackers," she'd mumble. His dream was to make Lila his own, to have the privilege of tucking her in every night, and the luxury of knowing Sarah was waiting for him downstairs.

Graham bowed his head against the steering wheel, sorrow's weight pushing it down. His voice broke with the whisper of a prayer. This time it wasn't for himself and it wasn't for Sarah. It was for Lila.

OCTOBER, FOLLOWING THE BLUE LINE. It flashed in his mind each time he closed his eyes, remained when he opened them again. Graham's finger traced it on the large map on his wall, marking the boundary line that enclosed some six million acres. His hands had skimmed the rainbow of pushpins countless times. He'd covered a respectable amount of space. So much more remained.

Graham opened his eyes, glanced at the clock. 2:00 AM glowed an angry red. It burned, staring up at the ceiling, only seeing the grid. The area was too vast, the hours in a day too short, and Graham was too small. The grandness of the

Adirondacks, once a glory to him, was now a torment. Time was sand, spilling from an hour glass, running through his fingers with no way of stopping it.

Couldn't stand it. Couldn't lie still. Had to get out of bed. A skim of Lila's painting with his fingertips, like a man without sight, a kiss planted on Sarah's photo on the night stand, and Graham was up. A sweatshirt tossed across a chair would do for a coat; he wouldn't be cold for long. Graham shrugged into it and headed into the night.

Feet pounding the pavement and breath forming a cloud, Graham pictured Sarah with every beat of his heart. It was the last time again. He could smell her, a blend of apples from her shampoo and springtime, see the sky caught in her eyes, watch the sun in her hair. She was warm, standing next to him, alive. *God, let me find her, let me find her, let me find her today.* The words were a litany.

The skies opened up and a hard, cold rain came pounding down. "Not the sign I was looking for," Graham muttered through gritted teeth.

Let it come, soak to the skin, chill to the bones, freeze the images within. Enough was enough. He turned back and hit the shower, blistering hot, full blast, fighting a chill that worked its way down to the bone.

Graham grabbed a blanket, his first cup of coffee, and sat down by the large window overlooking the lake, eyes drawn to Sarah's candle burning brightly. The rain petered out, leaving the lake like glass. Warmth slowly seeped into his bones with the coming of the dawn. The trees on the opposite shore were a blaze of red, yellow, and orange when struck by the sun's first rays.

His favorite time of year, it used to steal his breath, but that had been taken from him as well. The cover of fall foliage made it more difficult to search and harder to find any evidence on the ground. He was anxious for the season to come to a close, bringing all the leaves down so that the woods could bare their secrets. He'd have a small window of opportunity before the snow fell.

The sound of tires rolling in his driveway had him up and headed to the kitchen. Jim had pulled in and was leaning against his bumper, thermos of coffee in hand. Graham shrugged into his coat and walked outside. "Why am I seeing your ugly mug this early in the morning?"

Jim straightened his long frame and brought himself to his full height, good humor still intact. "Hey, I'd watch it if I were you; quite a few people think we look like we could be brothers. I was up early and thought it looked like a fine day to give you a hand." He went to Graham's passenger side and climbed in.

Graham shook his head and slid behind the wheel. He took a long swallow of coffee, eyes on his friend. "Are you still in trouble with Jeanie?"

"Truth be told, after making up with my beautiful wife, in our bed and out of it, I couldn't sleep. I couldn't get my mind off of you. I'm worried that you're in trouble. I thought you could use some company. Where to today?"

Graham had stood at the map after his shower, closed his eyes, and stuck a pin in it. Why not? The odds were the same, no matter the method. "Kane Mountain. I was there a few weeks ago with Lila and over the summer. I don't know why but it has a hold on me. Hell, I don't know where I should go. You probably think I'm crazy."

Jim shook his head, gave his friend a brotherly pat on the shoulder. "Crazy over Sarah. You're giving all you've got, using all you know, to find her. Most people would have thrown in the towel and moved on by now. If Kane Mountain has some kind of pull on you, trust your instincts."

Graham nodded, the ever-present tension easing a little, and glanced at his friend. "Thanks, Pete. I don't know what I'd do without you in my corner."

Jim shrugged. "Don't worry about it. I'll be calling in my favor when the time comes." They were quiet for the remainder of the drive. They'd been friends for so long, it wasn't necessary to fill the silence.

The road leading to the Kane Mountain trail had no activity. Most of the homes were seasonal camps. People were still in bed in the few that were year-round residences. Graham eyed one little cabin with envy, followed the trail of smoke spilling from its chimney. He visualized a couple in retirement tucked under the covers, longed to be sharing a bed with Sarah.

The truck rolled to a stop in the small parking area at the base of the mountain. While Graham climbed out and locked up, his best friend assessed the pack on the ranger's back. He shook his head with a rueful grin. "I'm sure there's nothing to eat in there. Good thing Jeanie sent reinforcements. I've got chocolate."

The parking area marked the point of departure for several trails—one to Kane Mountain, one to Pine Lake, and the last to Indian Lake. Graham did not choose any of these. Rather, he went against the grain and forged an unbroken path through the woods for a good distance before veering left. The incline started taking them up, the chill easing a bit with the passing of time and exertion. Graham's eyes were constantly scanning back and forth, on the look-out for anything out of place or not quite right.

Jim started to puff a little bit, but was too stubborn to stop. Graham didn't slow down, although he looked back from time to time to make sure the police officer was still with him. The crisp air, heavy with the scent of the leaves and pine, made his senses sharp, taking him back to the many adventures of childhood. He didn't break stride or his focus. There was no pleasure. The push to move on overrode all else.

"So, why did you take us in this way and not use the marked trails?" Jim asked, grateful when they paused to take a drink from their thermoses.

Graham shrugged, a crease forming between his eyes. "There's no particular rhyme or reason anymore. In the beginning, I covered one particular area as thoroughly as possible. I thought about doing that all over again, tackling one segment of the preserve in two week blocks of time, but I just can't stomach it. Now, I'm just going by my gut and to be honest, I'm not even sure about what my gut is telling me anymore. I'm not sure about anything."

They continued up, the slope becoming steeper and more difficult. Graham had to grab a tree from time to time to pull himself up and caught Jim once when he tripped. The sunlight filtering through the explosion of fall colors would have stopped him in his tracks in the time before. It was the sight of a man on his way down the slope that made Graham take pause.

The stranger was tall, about the same height as Jim. He had sandy hair streaked blonde and white, pulled back in a tail, and a full beard. His breath was a mist drifting past him in the early morning chill. He stared at Graham with golden eyes, eyes with that startled look like those of a buck taken unaware in the forest.

A heartbeat or two and he visibly loosened. The man gave them a quiet smile. "Morning', officer. Fine day we're having, isn't it? What brings you out so early?"

Graham took stock of the man, seemingly harmless, a local out for his daily walk. He was casual, in faded jeans, flannel, and hiking books. Nothing suspicious in his words or actions, and yet something made his stomach tighten into a knot. "We're just on a routine patrol of the area. Have you seen anything unusual that I should know about?"

The man shook his head, calm in his words and manner. "Just the sunrise. Otherwise, all's as it should be and always is out here in the wild. Have a good day, officers." He raised a hand in farewell and continued on down the mountain while Jim and Graham continued up to the peak.

Graham went straight up the tower, Jim dragging behind him and nursing a stitch in his side. "Can you please tell me exactly what you're looking for up here?" Jim bent over, hands on his knees, and worked on catching his breath. He'd climbed the fire tower many times but never in a minute sprint.

Graham pulled out high-power binoculars and was scanning the area intently. "I…I don't know. Lila and I were up here in the summer and saw something red, something that didn't belong, way off in the distance. I haven't been able to find anything again." He studied the view for a few minutes longer then handed the binoculars to Jim with disgust. "I don't see anything except leaves."

Jim took a turn with the binoculars. "Sorry, bud. I've got nothing." He handed them to Graham and they headed back down. They ended up sitting on the porch of the old ranger's cabin. Jim dug in his back and handed over a candy bar. Both men munched for a while in companionable silence.

"Anything new going on in Johnstown?" Graham asked after he worked his way through his second Hershey bar. Might as well try to have a normal conversation.

"Nah, the usual. A few drunk drivers, some vandalism, the occasional domestic dispute or a runaway. Nothing to write home about. I've got some good news on the home front, though." Jim stared down into the bottom of his back pack and debated on a Snickers bar.

Graham finished chewing and gave his best friend his undivided attention. There was a new light in Jim's eyes, making the brown even warmer like hot chocolate. It hadn't been there last time he really looked. "What's up?"

The flush shot up Jim's face and he laughed nervously. "Jeanie's pregnant. We're not making any official mention yet, not until the first three months are up. She's got one more month. She's nervous, you know, after the miscarriage. I don't think she'll mind my telling you."

Graham reached over and gave his best friend in the world a bone-cracker of a hug. "I'm really happy for you two. She's going to be all right this time, I just know it. We all need a little good news."

Jim nodded and had to look away, his voice gone rough with emotion. "I hope to God you're right. I couldn't stand to see her hurting like that again. I don't know if I can last through another month." He toyed with some weeds he had picked, pulling them through his hands.

Graham had learned through hard-earned experience how difficult it was to wait. His hand came down on Jim's shoulder. "You can. You'll make it through the entire nine month stretch and wonder where the time went. You've got something to look forward to now." They sat a while longer then took the return trip down the mountain.

They reached the bottom and Graham set off toward Indian Lake, a hike of considerable distance. By the time they'd finished, the sun was about to touch down and there had been no new clues. Graham did not say anything , depression setting in, his shoulders bowing under the weight.

They climbed into the truck and he slammed the steering wheel with the palm of his hand. "Damn it, Pete, where do I go now? She's not in Rockwood. She's not in Lake George. She's not in Speculator. She's not out here. Where the hell can she be? I can't even trust my own instincts anymore."

Jim shook his head. "I don't know what to tell you, buddy. You have to keep going until something tells you to stop, you have a reason to stop, or you don't have it in you anymore. Part of your trouble is you're burning yourself out. You need to take a break now and then. How about having something to eat? I'll come back to your place. I'll even cook. I'm not promising anything special. If you have your grill ready, I should be able to come up with something."

Graham closed his eyes and let out a breath of pent-up frustration. "Sounds good except for one problem. I don't have any food in my house unless you count granola bars and cold cereal without milk." Time was scarce; there was no wasting it on food.

Jim laughed, a familiar sound that had grounded them both over the years. "Well, I've heard of these places called grocery markets. They so happen to have food. How about we go into town and stock up for the duration since you probably won't be back for a while?"

In answer, Graham turned the key and revved the engine. They pulled out with the sun's fire dipping below the horizon as a backdrop for the drive. They were quiet once again, each lost in his own thoughts. Graham wished he didn't have to face anyone and could go home.

They drove into the Price Chopper parking lot and strode inside. Jim led the way up and down the aisles, making careful selections that would be easy to prepare and would last since Graham wouldn't return unless someone dragged him there. They were standing in line, each with a basket of food, while two people were standing by the magazine rack behind them.

The sudden turn in a nearby conversation grabbed Graham's attention and made him forget about being tired. A middle-aged couple was bickering over which gossip rag to buy when the man zeroed in on the his uniform. "See that guy over there? He's that conservation officer that's getting paid to search for one girl. What a waste of the taxpayer's money! Everyone knows—that girl is dead."

Something inside of Graham, tenuous to begin with, snapped and his basket dropped to the floor. Contents spilled everywhere and he got right in the stranger's face. "You might think it's a waste of money now, but God forbid it's someone you know or love. Once it's one of your own, you'll want someone like me…and I'll tell you something else. *She's not dead.*"

He turned and stalked out, the thin hold on his temper finally giving way. He kicked a cart out of the way in the parking lot, climbed in his truck, and slammed the door—hard. He pressed his forehead to the steering wheel and fought for some semblance of calm and reason. Not happening.

Jim hurried out after him, put the groceries in back, and slid into the front seat. "Are you all right? That guy was an idiot. I told him so in no uncertain terms."

"I don't want to talk about it. You know what I want? I want, no, I *need* a drink." Graham started the truck and peeled out, tires squealing.

He was true to his word and didn't say a thing. With grim determination, Graham found the closest bar, went inside, and took a seat. There would be no beer tonight. Whiskey was in order. The first shot went down fast, burning its way to his stomach. The second was faster. By the third, he'd almost forgotten why he'd gone to the bar in the first place. Another hit and he might forget who he was.

8

JIM STEERED CLEAR OF ALCOHOL AS THE DESIGNATED DRIVER. Satisfied that Graham wasn't going to fall off his stool, he went in search of a quiet spot to make a phone call. The hallway to the bathroom was the best choice. He dialed and heard someone pick up on the other end. "Hey, honey. I'm sorry it's so late. We went to the store after the day's search because Graham had no food and we ended up in a bar. He's having a rough time. I'm really worried that he's about to come unglued."

They talked a few more minutes before Jim returned to the bar room. Graham was leaning forward with his head propped on the bar and his eyes closed. Six shot glasses were lined up in front of him.

"Hey, Scottie, time to head home. I'll drive." He swung Graham's arm over his shoulder and helped him up off the stool. His friend stumbled over his own feet as they made their way out to the parking lot.

"Pete, we don't need to go. I'm having such a good time…call Jeanie, tell her …you'll be out all night," Graham's words were slurred, his eyes already blurry from the alcohol. He was way over his limit, especially on an empty stomach and little rest.

"No way, bud, no way. I've only been on solid ground for a day after forgetting our anniversary. It will turn to quicksand in an instant with one slip." Jim made sure his friend was securely in the passenger seat and went around.

By the time he put himself behind the wheel, Graham was out, slumped against the window. Jim winced at the sight. *Buddy, you are going to have one hell of a hangover. Boy, am I glad I'm not you.* His mood turned sour at the thought. Who *would* want to be Graham?

The drive home was uneventful. Graham groaned when he was first pulled out of the truck. Otherwise, he didn't utter a sound. Jim made it to the bedroom, dropped his friend on the bed, and removed his boots. He pulled the covers up and turned out the light. Before he left, he made a point of turning on Sarah's candle. Graham would want it that way, not that his friend would be seeing much except the inside of his eyelids—until morning.

HIS HEAD WAS GOING TO SPLIT IN TWO—no doubt about it. The sunlight, much too bright of a light for his pounding brain, was poking at his eyelids. With a deep groan that came all the way from his toes, Graham pulled the blankets over his head. He instantly regretted it. The movement had his stomach rolling like he was out to sea. He threw the covers off, flung his legs over the side, and staggered to the bathroom. He just made it and lost everything.

He laid his head down on the cool tile of the floor, went several more rounds, blacked out, and knew no more. It was dark when he came to. Graham stood up and walked gingerly to the sink, moving his aching head as little as possible. A dousing of cold water and he went straight back to the bedroom, do not pass go. He crawled back into the bed, closed his eyes, and tried not to think about his wasted day. Never again. He would not drown himself in drink. Drowning would be less painful.

In the middle of the night, a terrible thirst grabbed hold and shook him awake. He drank a tall glass of water in the darkness, unable to face the light. There was still a mild throbbing in his head and queasiness, but nothing life threatening. He stepped out into the night and walked down to the dock.

The cold air felt good. He stretched out and stared up at the stars, hoping to get rid of the last of his hangover. The sound of the water slapping against the wood actually made his stomach pitch, then settled and finally soothed him. The cool breeze swept away the worst of it. Graham might live through his stupidity after all. He stayed out on the dock until his teeth started to chatter. When he went back to bed, he slept soundly for the first time in months.

Sunlight announced the arrival of another day. Time to lie still, assess the damages. Only a dull headache and the gnawing of hunger pains. He sat up and put his head in his hands, raking his fingers through his hair. How stupid! One day lost and well into the next.

His cell phone rang while Graham was drinking his coffee and eating a bagel. Thanks to Jim, there was real food in the house. He scowled, sure of who was on the other line, but picked up anyway. "What do you want?"

"Whoa, Pete! I was just calling to see if you were all right. I tried to get you yesterday. You never answered." Jim's voice was patient in spite of Graham's gruff greeting.

"I'm alive. The jury is still out on whether I'm all right or not. I only have one question for my best friend who is also a man of the law. Why? Why did you let me do that to myself? You should have cut me off!" The words were clipped, laced with frustration.

"Hey, Graham, ease up. I went to make a phone call. In the five minutes I was gone, you had managed to take six shots. How was I to know you were trying to top our college days? I bodily removed you from the premises at that point. I'm sorry I didn't make it sooner."

Jim's apologetic tone caused Graham to let up. "It's not your fault. I'm sorry I bit your head off. I have only one request. If I ask to go to a bar in the future, cuff me and lock me up for the night so I can sleep off my insanity, okay?"

There was agreement on the other end, a quick review of the day's plans, and Jim hung up.

Graham finished his breakfast and was finally ready to face the map. He stood in front of it, studying it for a long time. Considering the late start—it was already ten o'clock—he chose Northampton State Park down by Northville on the Sacandaga. It was a popular spot and might be busy with free camping for its last weekend before it closed for the season. He pushed a blue pin, signifying his second visit, into the map and grabbed his coat.

A turn of the key and he was on the road. As he approached the little store in Canada Lake, he realized he'd forgotten his coffee. Had to have coffee if nothing else. He took a pile of flyers from his front seat and headed inside. There were a couple of customers. Otherwise, it was quiet.

"Hey, Mattie. How's it going?" Graham called out with false cheer while pouring a large cup of joe.

A young man of about twenty with dark hair and a beard nodded in Graham's direction. He had an easygoing personality and was quick to offer a joke and a smile. "It's going slow now, but I don't mind that the summer rush is over. How about you, Graham? Any news?"

Mattie saw people from all over the place, some regulars and some just passing through. He made sure to keep his eyes and ears wide open to help in whatever way he could.

A shrug held back that wave of darkness that always hovered close to the surface. "No luck. Anything on your end?" At the young clerk's sympathetic shake of the head, Graham held out the flyers. "Here's a new batch anyway. You never know when a lead might happen."

Mattie waved his money away. "Coffee's on me. Why don't you put a few more up on the bulletin board too? I think the rest are gone and Graham…good luck." He reached out and gave him a hearty handshake.

Graham walked out, heart sinking, while a man brushed past him with hair the color of sand and honey eyes. *Familiar…where have I seen...the stranger from Kane Mountain!* Funny thing—in all the years coming into the store, he'd never noticed the guy before. Now it was like déjà vu.

Graham pushed it to the back of his mind, put Sarah's picture up on the bulletin board, and went back to his truck. He couldn't move for a moment, nearly unhinged by the image in his hands. He closed his eyes. It didn't matter. Sarah's face was there, always there.

He whispered a prayer and traced her picture with his fingers. His hand trembled and came to a stop. "Please…let it be today." He started the engine and pulled away. He didn't notice the stranger from Kane Mountain slipping into the woods.

The closer Graham traveled to Northville, the darker the skies became. The clouds gathered and pressed low on the horizon, an ominous gray that was nearly coal black. Lightning flashed and the thunder rumbled. A brief pause and the rain pounded the ground.

Graham pulled on his rain gear, poked his flyers inside his coat, and stepped out. The warm comfort of his truck would be much more preferable. A strong wind picked up, tugging at his hair and clothes, but it could not stop his rounds at each campsite.

Quite a few sites were full for the upcoming Columbus Day weekend. The die-hard campers loved the free weekend even if the facilities were not in use. Graham stopped at every occupied spot and left a flyer before moving on. No one had any new information, yet many wanted to talk about the case. By the time Graham finished, he was mentally drained by their questions, curiosity, and pity. A scan of the empty sites by the lake revealed nothing.

Graham turned the truck around to head back home. It was already late afternoon. There was no sense starting any place else that day. Against his better judgment, he went to the drive-thru window at McDonald's and ordered a burger and coffee. It instantly turned into a heavy lump in his stomach after his bout with alcohol. The rain came down harder on the way home and matched his mood perfectly.

Caroga Lake was quiet when he drove through, his eye drawn to Sherman's. It was a shame seeing the empty amusement park that had been shut down, the giant carousel, housed within an intricate building, with no one to ride it.

Graham remembered the many times he and his family stopped for ice cream or he went on the little rides. Fireworks on the fourth were a tradition.

He got out of the truck and walked through the heavy rain out to the docks, startling a few geese tucked underneath to ride out the storm. What he wouldn't give to have a place to ride out life's storm. Graham stared out over the lake, but he didn't see the choppy waters or the menacing skies. It was Independence Day with Sarah and Lila.

They bobbed out on the water with a crowd of others, faces tipped to the sky as explosions of light splashed across the darkness. Sparks drifted to meet the reflection in the water. Remains of cotton candy were on Lila's cheeks, gummed in her hair, sticky on her little hands. Graham tossed popcorn in the air and caught it on his tongue while Sarah nibbled on a candy apple.

"Here comes the big finally, here it comes!" In a burst of excitement, Lila was up on her feet.

"No, Lila! Sit down..."Graham called one second too late. The boat tipped, dumping them all overboard into the water. There was applause and good-natured laughter from onlookers while Sarah grabbed hold of Lila, bobbing in her life

preserver. Graham latched onto the boat and pulled Sarah along-side of him. "Everyone all right?"

Lila's response—peals of laughter. Sarah swiped wet hair out of her eyes and got caught up in an attack of the giggles as well. "I guess we're just fine. A little water never hurt."

Others on the lake approached, helped them aboard their motorboat, and towed the flipped rowboat to shore, allowing the three, drowned rats to slosh their way out of the lake.

"Let's go again!" Lila shouted. Graham growled playfully at her, swooped down on the little girl, and hoisted her on his shoulders. They were off at a gallop with Sarah close behind. "Crackers, run faster!" More giggles and mayhem while her mother shook her head.

"I ought to make you walk the plank, you little munchkin!" A sudden drop through the air and Lila was swinging in between Graham and Sarah, back and forth. Graham opened his truck door and everyone piled in, Lila installed in her car seat. Sarah sat next to her daughter, rosy cheeked and breathless from the excitement. Like a family.

It was a night of firsts—the first visit to Graham's, turning into what Lila called their first "swumber party." The girls swimming in sweats and flannels that were too big, tangled in blankets and piles of pillows. Sipping cocoa and Graham building up a roaring fire.

He found pictures in the flames for Lila while she lifted her hand in the air, trying to trace them, until it dropped. She was first to fall asleep, snuggled close to her mother. Graham and Sarah talked quietly for a while and she drifted off next. Graham stared at the fire a while longer and felt a deep contentment that he had never known before. He could get used to nights like this. Waking up, seeing the two of them on his living room floor, it didn't get better than that.

Graham came back to the present, shaking with the cold, the rain pelting him without mercy. All of it, gone. Turning away from the water, he scanned the deserted buildings and rides. It suited his mood, desolate and dark. Unable to stand the direction his thoughts were taking, Graham slid behind the wheel and headed back home.

He'd forgotten to leave any lights on. He went inside and turned on Sarah's candle first, changed into sweats and a t-shirt, and stretched out on the couch. He was avoiding bed, dreams of her, his loneliness. A run through of the channels on TV helped him settle on an old classic. Graham made it until the end and into the next before drifting off to sleep.

He dreamed of Sarah anyway. He was in Rockwood again. The last time with Sarah replayed in his mind and the walk was coming to an end. This time, Graham changed the ending, scooping her up in his arms. He asked her to marry him and they drove away in his truck. He took her home, to his bed for the first time, and they spent the night together.

Graham awoke with his face wet, cramped from sleeping on the couch. He stood up to work out the kinks and began to pace, trying to ease the terrible ache that came with the dreaming. It was like having a sore and having someone pick at it, making it angry. This hurting wouldn't go away or get any better until Sarah came home. It would only get worse.

He went into bed, but sleep eluded him. Two hours later, he was out running in the rain. At dawn, with no reprieve from the storm, Graham shot out his frustration at the rifle range. When he couldn't concentrate on target practice any longer, he drove aimlessly. He didn't know where to go or where he would wind up. All of it felt futile. His brain told him to stay the course. His heart told him it couldn't take much more before it would shatter.

His truck brought him back to Rockwood, back to where his nightmare was born. Graham slammed his door and trudged out in the rain. What the hell was he doing? She wasn't here, there was no sign that she had ever been here, no evidence to explain what happened. If he hadn't been with her that day himself, Graham might have believed it was his imagination except for one thing—the empty car.

The trails didn't give him anything either. Graham even took a few that were rarely traveled. It was a waste of time. Nothing mattered, what he did or where he went. Graham had never had a case with a dead trail and no leads. Why did this case have to be the one without hope?

Empty handed again, he returned to his truck and sat inside for a long time. The rain drummed on the roof and lulled him to sleep. When he awoke, there was a darkening in the sky and the rain came down even harder. Much more and Graham would have to build an ark. What he wouldn't give to sail away from his life.

He started the truck and drove with no particular destination in mind. Within minutes, the Gingerbread Cottage and the Andersons' house stood in front of him. He pulled into Steve and Sandy's driveway, uncertain if he should get out. He wasn't the best company.

Graham's decision was made for him when Lila ran out of the house, her blonde hair streaking behind her while her little feet barely touched the ground. He climbed out of the truck and she was in his arms. "Crackers, ew! You're all wet. What ya doing out in the rain? Nana says I shouldn't play in the rain or I'll catch cold. You don't wants to get sick. Come in and get dry. Nana said you could."

He pressed a kiss to her cheek and held her close. His head was busy from her chatter. "So, how's Lila my lovely? Do you like school?"

Lila scrunched her face in a frown. "I'm not crazy about that place, not without Mommy. I keep looking for her across the hall and she isn't there yet. What you been doing, Graham?"

Graham shrugged. "The usual. Let's go say hi to Nana and Pop Pop." He set her down when they walked inside.

Steve was sitting in the recliner in the living room watching the news while Sally was cooking something sure to make everyone's belly happy. It looked like a normal evening for a normal family. They were really good at the charade.

Steve was up on his feet when he heard Graham's voice. "Evening, Graham. What brings you here?" He stared intensely, searching for anything amiss, and offered his hand for the usual handshake.

Graham accepted the offer and found a smile. "I had Lila, and all of you, on my mind. I heard once that you can't always have happiness, but you can always give it. That's what I'm trying to do tonight. Let me know if it's working."

Sally walked out from the kitchen to give Graham a hug. She stood back and brushed his hair from eyes. "Hello, Graham. I just overheard what you said. It would make us all very happy if you'd join us for some dinner. You can be the guinea pig for my new dish."

Lila's eyes were wide. "Nana, Graham's not a guinea pig. He's too big. Can we get one though? Joey at school brought one for show and tell and it had a wheel to run in 'cept his was lazy and it wouldn't move. I'd take care of it. Please, can I?"

Sally tapped her granddaughter on the nose. "We'll just see about that, missy. Go wash up for dinner." She turned back to Graham and fingered his shirt. "You are absolutely drenched. Come on in the bedroom and I'll find you something to wear while those dry." Graham couldn't help but grin as he followed her. There was no arguing with Sally Anderson.

When Lila came back from washing her hands, she laughed so hard and so long she had to hold her belly because Graham was wearing Steve's striped pajamas that looked like candy canes. "Crackers, you are so funny! Can I wear pajamas at the dinner table, Nana?"

Sally shook her head at Lila's babbling as everyone sat down to heaping plates of spaghetti. "Sometime, Lila. Right now, just dig in." There was quiet with bits of inconsequential conversation in between while they enjoyed the meal and each other's company.

After dinner was over and Graham helped wash the dishes, they all sat down with a bowl of popcorn and watched a movie that Lila chose. Tonight, it was "The Wizard of Oz." She climbed up on Graham's lap, taking the edge off the worst of the pain and reminding him of the most important reason to keep going—for everyone in this house that was counting on him.

When the movie was over, Lila was rubbing her eyes and yawning. Graham carried her upstairs and tucked her into bed. He read a short story, they said their prayers, and it was lights out. Only the nightlight and the candle in the window were on. Her arms came up and squeezed his neck. "Crackers, are we gonna go hiking this Sunday?"

Graham nodded. "You think about the place and I'll be there." He reached down and stroked her hair, brushing strands out of her eyes. His hand came to a rest on the top of her head. "Go to sleep, munchkin, and I'll be back soon, okay?"

Lila snuggled down in the covers and smiled up at him. "'Kay. Love you, Graham." Her eyes were already closed.

Graham caught his breath and felt his heart squeeze. "Love you too, Lila my lovely." He went downstairs, thanked Steve and Sally, and said his goodbyes. Walking back out into the rain, he looked down and shook with laughter. He was still wearing Steve's pajamas.

"Graham, did you forget something?" Sally called from the open door, his clothes bundled in her hands. She held them out to him and touched his cheek with a loving pat. "You can bring back the jammies another time. We'll see you on Sunday."

Graham couldn't stop smiling as he walked to his truck and looked down at his candy cane stripes. Looking forward to something might help him sleep for one night.

9

STEVE ANDERSON TOOK a little longer each time he made the short trip to the school. Since May it was as if he was a clock, winding down. Stepping into the cafeteria, seeing his granddaughter expectantly watching the door, reminded him that she was the reason he kept on ticking.

"Hey, Ladybug! Ready to go home?" He stood at the door and pasted on a happy face for Lila. She looked at the cafeteria aide for approval to leave, barely held in check from running, and skipped to his waiting arms.

"Pop Pop, boy am I glad to see you!" She reached for him and he picked her up. Hugging each other with all they had was part of their routine. The two stood still, apart from the others in the room. Every day was like a personal reunion again.

Steve's heart lifted to see Lila's smile, a rare commodity. "Girlie, am I glad to see you!" He set her down and they started walking home. "How was school today?" He held hands with his granddaughter and they swung their arms back and forth.

The little girl watched all of the cars driving by, scanning each one intently before turning her attention to her grandfather. Always on the look-out. "It was good. I got to show my picture from Pine Lake and the one I drew for Show and Tell and my friend, Paige, drew pictures with me today. She even made a picture for me. It's in my backpack. And then, I wrote in my writing journal and I wrote, 'I love Mommy and I love Nana and Pop Pop and I love Graham.' Ms. Ashley taught me how to write Graham and I still remember. It's G-R-A-H-A-M."

Her grandfather stopped and put a hand to his head. "Whoa Nelly! You're making me dizzy, girlie!"

Lila tugged on him until they started walking again. Once they crossed the road to their driveway, she ran straight to the Gingerbread Cottage and checked that her note was still on the door. She peeked quickly in the windows. No one was there. It was her daily ritual and it tore at her grandfather's heart.

She walked back to him and he knelt down by her. "I'm sorry, sweetie. There's nothing new to tell you. I've been watching like I promised." Steve stood slowly, suddenly feeling much older, and they walked next door, holding hands again.

Lila pulled on him until he sat on the steps and climbed up on to his lap. She put her hands on his face and looked him straight in the eye. "I'm sorry I made you sad, Pop Pop. I won't go anymore. I know you're watching. I love you."

Steve hugged her hard even as the wind went out of his sails. His gaze traveled to the little, yellow house next door. So empty. So wrong. So painful. He closed his eyes tightly to shut it out. "Ladybug, you can go home whenever you want to and remember—I love you more!"

Lila shook her head. "I don't think so, Pop Pop. I think I love you and Nana and Mommy and Graham the mostest."

She hugged him back, arms around his neck really tight, until he started laughing. A minor tickle attack ensued until Lila was wriggling in his arms and they were both overcome with giggles.

The outdoor antics could be heard all the way to the kitchen. Sally opened the door and walked outside with a big smile. "What's this? Are we having a porch party and no one thought to invite me?" She sat down next to her husband and Lila climbed onto her lap next.

"No, we were just having a talk, weren't we Pop Pop? Can I have a snack please, Nana? I'm really hungry." Lila gave her grandmother a hug and a kiss.

Sally buried her face in the little girl's fall of sunshine down her back, inhaled the scent of baby shampoo and baby powder, grabbing hold of childhood for a moment. One more deep breath and she stood up to carry her granddaughter inside.

"Somebody's hungry, eh? Good thing I made chocolate chip cookies!" Cookies and milk were already waiting on the table.

Lila sprang down and climbed into her chair while Sally lowered herself into the seat beside her. Steve rested his hand on the nape of her neck and closed his eyes. Somehow, they gathered strength from one another, enough to make it through, minute by minute.

"Lila has a new friend. What's her name, Ladybug?" He winked at his granddaughter as he sat down. He took a big bite of cookie and chewed slowly. Funny that he could savor the taste of chocolate and ice-cold milk when his world should have ended.

Sally's eyes lit as she turned to watch her granddaughter's animated face. "Really, Lila? I'm so glad to hear that! What's your friend's name?"

She took a cookie for herself and dipped it in her milk. Steve reached across the table and took his wife's hand. This was good news, a breakthrough for their little bit of sunshine. Until now, their ladybug didn't talk about friends.

Lila got a milk mustache while she drank her milk, impossibly cute as she munched on the sweet treat. "Her name is Paige like in a story book and we drew pictures today. She made me a picture. Look!" Lila dug around in her backpack and pulled the picture out for her grandparents.

Steve and Sally took a good look at the drawing together, nodding in appreciation. "Lila, this is a really nice picture. Maybe Paige can come over some day." Sally took a sip of milk and couldn't resist sticking her tongue out, sporting a milk mustache to match her granddaughter's.

Lila laughed and wiped off her grandmother's lip with a napkin. Sally returned the favor. "I'd like that. Thank you for the cookies and milk, Nana. I'm going to go hang my picture up in my room and then I might make some more pictures." Lila hopped off of the chair, gave both adults a kiss on the cheek, and ran upstairs.

THE WALLS IN LILA'S ROOM WERE COVERED with pictures that she had made. Most of them were of Mommy, herself and Graham. Graham had told her if she could see them together in her mind, then it would happen. That meant making drawings every day for everyone to see. Lila found a perfect spot for Paige's picture and taped it on the wall. She drew for a little while until she laid down on her bed and closed her eyes. The sound of the doorbell had her springing from her bed and running downstairs. Maybe this time it would be Mommy.

Lila scampered to the door before anyone else could get there. She pulled it open and there was Graham. He was holding a pizza box aloft and wearing a smile, even if it was a little ragged around the edges.

"Did a anyone a order a pizza pie? I have an Italiano pizza pie for one a Lila my Lovely. Did I a come to a the right place?" Graham stood straight and tall, still in uniform, like a big, strong tree in the forest.

Lila wrapped her arms around Graham's legs and held on really tight. "Crackers, what are you doing? We didn't order a pizza!" She looked behind her and her grandparents were laughing. "Did we?" They shook their heads, still unable to speak.

Graham waited until Lila let go, scooped her up with one arm, and carried her inside along with the pizza. "I thought Nana might like a night off from the kitchen." He headed to the kitchen table, set the pizza down, along with paper plates, napkins, cups, and a bottle of soda. "See, I thought of everything."

Everyone sat down, laughing and talking at once. Lila watched and listened with a smile that stretched across her face. Graham didn't stay too long because he was tired, but they decided they would hike on Sunday if the rain stopped. To Pine Lake. Where she would find Mommy.

LILA WOKE UP THREE TIMES in the middle of the night before the hike to check if it was still raining. It had poured for days then it was as if someone turned off a faucet and it stopped. The sunshine actually reached inside her room, touched her pillow, and got her out of bed early.

She dressed right away in the clothes laid out the night before then sat down and put on her hiking boots. They were a present from Graham. She had to poke her tongue between her teeth like she did when she drew pictures and try really hard, but she tied both of her boots. Then she grabbed the note she and Nana had made and ran downstairs. "Nana, I'm going next door to put up my new note!"

Sally walked out from the kitchen and covered a yawn. "Okay, Ladybug. I'll be watching."

She touched her hair and opened the door for her, standing watch as Lila skipped to the Gingerbread Cottage and hung up her latest message. They had written it the night before. It explained where Lila would be if Mommy came home. She was always thinking about when Mommy would come home.

GRAHAM PULLED IN THE ANDERSONS' DRIVEWAY to see Sarah's mother standing on the porch, arms wrapped around herself, shivering. It was getting colder, a jab to the gut. Like a prize fighter, he shook it off and went up the walk. The porch railing provided a good spot to lean on.

He propped his chin on his arms and smiled up at her. "Good morning. Where's Lila my lovely?"

Sally tilted her head to the side. "She's over at the house, hanging up a note. Why don't you go see how she's doing and I'll make you some coffee?" She patted Graham's arm and turned to go inside.

Graham tucked his hands in the pockets of his jacket and wandered next door where Lila was peeking in the window. The door had a patchwork quilt of colorful notes and drawings, including the latest addition with a picture. Every drawing, every word was a stab in the heart.

"Hey, Lila. What have you got there?" He stepped up next to her and was rewarded with little arms wrapped around his neck.

"It's a new note for Mommy. See? It says, 'Dear Mommy, Graham and I are hiking in Pine Lake if you need to find us. I love you! Love, Lila.' I wrote all of it by myself and did the picture by myself too. How do you like it?"

Graham knelt down and put an arm around Lila while he read her letter. There was that familiar burning at the back of his eyes. He blinked hard and cleared his throat. "It's perfect, How about we go back to Nana and Pop Pop's now so we can get ready?"

Lila was a nonstop chatterbox for the entire drive. Even though she had seen Graham only two days before, she was buzzing with excitement about the hike. The little girl was filled with a nervous energy, her anticipation too great to contain. Beneath it all, there was something Graham didn't like—anxiety.

Once they arrived at the parking area, Lila was first out of the truck. She darted over to the log book and took her time, tongue clenched between her teeth, to write "Lila and Graham." Graham made sure he had everything he needed in his pack. He took one long, last swallow of coffee and hoped it would have restorative powers. Night after sleepless night was catching up.

"Come on, Crackers! We've gotta get going! What if it rains again? Besides, I wanna get there real soon!" Lila was bouncing up and down in front of him, unable to wait a moment longer.

She hopped from foot to foot, fall leaves crunching with each step. The wind was a little harder and colder than the last time, making him turn up his collar. He cast up another prayer. *Please God, let it be soon. She'll be cold.*

Graham shied away from his thoughts and took Lila's hand, digging out some enthusiasm. "Lila, my girl, I wish I had half the energy that you do. Let's get started."

He glanced around the area out of habit, noting two cars were parked there that morning. A quick check of the log showed that two parties took the Kane Mountain trail. Something still pulled on him each time they were here, something he couldn't explain nor back up with evidence, making him want to climb that mountain. It was a pricking at the back of his brain that poked at him and said, "*Here*."

Shrugging it off, Graham knelt by Sarah's little girl. "Are you sure you want to go to Pine Lake? It's a long hike."

The five year old showed her stubborn streak as her face screwed up into a scowl and she shook her head vigorously. "We've gotta go this way. I told my class that's where we were going and I wanna take a new picture. Remember what a good time we had camping there, Crackers?"

Graham held his hands up and started to laugh. "Of course I remember. Let's go before you run out of wind!"

Lila's tongue never tired for the entire walk. That girl didn't forget anything. He felt a twinge of pain, deep inside, when he came to an important realization. Lila was Sarah's memory keeper.

Except for Lila's bubbling conversation, the woods were quiet after the past few days of rain. The carpet of leaves was damp, muffling their footsteps while the temperature dropped a little further, making Graham glad he'd worn his coat. Winter was creeping in a little closer, stealing the daylight and its warmth, bringing a sense of dread with it. If it was hard now, trekking through the territory in the bitter cold and mounting snow would be near impossible.

Lila skipped around him and took his hand. "Crackers, what's wrong? You've got that line between your eyes again and you looked like you were some place really far away."

Graham shook off the sense of foreboding and smoothed his face with an effort. Here and now—that was all he had. Tomorrow could wait. "Nothing's wrong, honey. You're just wearing me out. I don't know if I can keep up with you!" He sat down on a large rock conveniently placed by the glaciers of the Ice Age that had carved the surrounding mountains. It was an opportune time for a drink.

Lila scrambled up next to him and drank some water too. "Ready, Crackers? Will we be there soon?"

She was off the rock and back on the trail in an instant. She brought to mind the tiny chipmunks scurrying across the path.

Graham slung on his pack and took her hand. No rest for the weary. "Yes, Lila. We're almost there. Let's keep going because 'time's a wastin,'isn't it?"

Lila laughed, making a delightful sound that would be contagious to anyone who heard it. His heart lifted again, made buoyant with gratitude for these Sundays with his little ray of sunshine.

"Look, Graham, look! There's the campers that stay all the time! We're here, we're here!" She broke away and ran forward in her excitement. Graham had to run to keep up.

A motley scattering of campers sprawled along the woods that bounded Pine Lake, from the silver splash of

Airstreams, new and old, to those that had become homes away from home with lawn decorations, additions, and decks. Others appeared to have grown there, merging with the undergrowth and trees. They appealed to Graham the most, a place where he could hide.

"Lila, wait up! You're too fast for me!" The fact that she was so fast scared him.

Disaster could be only seconds away. It was cruel that life had made him expect the worst. The path went a short distance more and ended in the campsite named for the lake that glistened in flashes of blue through the trees. Lila was just ahead of him and came to a halt at an empty site. She stood very still, eyes wide, her lip starting to tremble.

Graham knelt down next to her and put an arm around her. "Lila, what is it, sweetheart?" Her face had gone white and she was shaking.

"Oh, Graham! I thought she'd be here! I made the picture and I've been staring at the photo from our camping trip all the time really hard to make it true. It didn't come true!" Her little face crumpled and she started to sob.

Her words—they cut deep, to the quick. Surely Graham would soon bleed out…yet he didn't. He picked Lila up, carried her to the picnic table, and held her close to his chest. His hand stroked her hair and he rocked her back and forth, whispering words of comfort. No matter what he said, the words were not good enough. None of them brought her mother back.

RELENTLESS. GRAHAM HAD TO BE. FOR LILA. For the next two weeks, he pushed harder, started earlier, stayed out later. His time was consumed in the forest's heart. Scouring the woods, climbing the hills, scanning the horizon. He didn't emerge until Lila's Halloween parade.

Every year, the children walked around the block in their costumes on the Friday before Halloween. The shift from the woods to normal was becoming more difficult. Moreover, it meant a day cut short from the search, but Lila needed him. She needed all of them more than they knew.

It was dawn and the day promised to be fine, a small blessing for a little girl. Graham started his truck and headed for the rifle range, something to get through the day until the parade. No idle time. His cell rang, unusual at such an hour, and he put it on speaker. "This is Graham."

"Good morning, Graham. Listen, we had a call about break-ins at the camps along Green Lake. Since you're closest, could you check it out?" The dispatcher from headquarters gave him the name and address of the person who made the call.

"No problem. I'll take care of it this morning." Graham disconnected and mulled over his assignment.

The road running alongside Green Lake led to the Kane Mountain trail. Kane Mountain, again—inexorable, it kept rearing its head. Was there a connection between this call and instinct? It made his blood pump a little bit harder, brought him wide awake by the time he pulled off the side of Green Lake Road. The mist was rising up, wraith-like, off the lake, the sun burning it off and touching the trees along the shore. A parallel world was reflected in the waters, had Graham lost in it. If he stepped in, would Sarah be there on the other side?

An elderly man sat rocking on his porch and called out, pulling the ranger's attention to the matter at hand. "Boy, you fellas are fast. I'll know to call you instead of the fire department or the police if ever I need someone." He stood up and offered a hand to Graham in greeting. "Boyd Handy's the name. You're here about the break-ins?"

Graham nodded. "Yes, sir. I'm Officer Graham Scott. I live on Pleasant Lake. If I'm home, I'll beat everyone else. What can you tell me about the trouble here?"

He took out a pad of paper and a pencil. The man gestured to the chair beside him on the porch, inviting Graham to sit. Boyd moved slowly, slightly bent with age, leaning heavily on a hand-carved walking stick before lowering himself into his rocker.

An elderly woman, wrapped in a bright, red robe, padded out on fluffy slippers. Her snowy hair was in rollers, tucked in a net. Wire-framed glasses were perched on her nose as she smiled at Graham. "Good morning, officer. Can I interest you in a cup of coffee?"

Boyd nudged Graham's shoulder. "That's my Eleanor and you'd best take it. It's a rare occasion when she offers." He winked playfully at his wife as she stood with her hands on her hips. She wagged a finger at her husband before returning her attention to their guest.

"I'd appreciate that, mam. Black is fine." Graham dusted off his rusty conversational skills.

A few minutes later with a steaming cup by his hand, he jotted down notes while Boyd told him which camps had been affected. None of them were year-round residences and their owners were gone until summer. The elderly man had noticed broken windows and a sliding glass door that was off its track when he went on his daily walk.

Once he'd been given all the information the man had, Graham stood up and drank the last of his coffee. "Thank you for all your help, Mr. Handy. Here's my card with my personal number if you see anything more. Whatever you do, don't try to take matters into your own hands if you actually come across someone. Call me first and if I'm not available, call 911. I'm going to go take a look at those houses and see if I can find out anything more."

Eleanor came back out with her own coffee and a book of crosswords to join her husband. She gave Graham a little wave as he headed down the steps. "Thank you for coming right away, officer. It makes me a little nervous out here without hardly any neighbors this time of year. I don't want Boyd getting any ideas in his head about being a hero. He was in the war and sometimes he thinks he's still there! Not to mention, he still things he's a spring chicken!"

Graham gave a wave. "Just doing my job, mam. I gave your husband my number. Make sure he uses it if anything comes up and thank you for the coffee."

He went on his way and made a thorough check of the homes in question, plus all the rest along the way. The recent rain and falling leaves made it impossible to find footprints and there was no sign of any intruders. Keeping watch late at night or before sunrise—that was the ideal strategy. Maybe he could catch someone in the act.

The rest of the day was without incident, just spinning his wheels. Frustration mounted. He pushed it down and made a quick stop at the costume shop before heading to the Andersons' place. Sally and Steve stepped out, on their way to the school, and both started to laugh, bringing him back from the edge.

"Graham, you are something else! Does Lila know you're dressing up today?" Sally stepped up close and peered into eye holes in the mask that covered his face..

"No, I thought I'd surprise her. I'll tell you one thing though—I will not be wearing this for trick or treat. I'm dying in here!" It was a full body suit and hotter than heck inside, not to mention he could barely see. "Sally, do you think you could be my guide? I'm practically blind!"

Sally offered her arm with Steve chuckling alongside of them and they made the short walk to school without mishap. People were lined up on both sides of the street and around the looping driveway for the neighborhood's big event. Festive, talking, laughing…living. Mr. Vicenza was the grand marshal, dressed like a police officer while all the staff had costumes with a theme of service to others. The kindergarten marched close behind, giggling and bright eyed, bouncing up and down.

Lila caught sight of her family and darted out of line with Ms. Ashley's permission. She looked adorable in a miniature version of Graham's uniform with a wide brimmed hat like the rangers on TV. "Nana, Pop Pop! Where did you find Smokey the Bear?"

"It's me, Lila. Would you like me to march with you?" Graham knelt down so she could look inside the eye holes and see a little of his face.

He hoped she'd say yes and that it wouldn't take too long because he might die inside his oven of a bear suit. Maybe, just maybe…walking by the little girl, a little of the excitement would rub off, make him come alive again…for a little while.

"Oh, yes!" She grabbed Graham's paw and pulled him over to Ms. Ashley. "Ms. Ashley, can Smokey come with us? He's perfect for my conversation officer costume and he's someone who gives a service. Please, Ms. Ashley, can he please?"

Lila looked up at her teacher with those big blue eyes so like her mother's and Melissa was a goner. "Yes, of course, Lila, and it's *conservation* officer, honey, not *conversation*; that means talking. Join our line, you two."

She moved on to check the rest of her class and the march began. By the time it was over and Lila had joined her class for their party, Graham was certain he was going to have heat stroke. How did people wear these things at games and all day for work? He couldn't get out of it fast enough. He dropped down on the Andersons' porch steps and let the cold air revive him while Sally brought out a tall glass of ice water. Graham thanked her and drank it down in seconds.

Steve joined him on the step and patted the younger man's back. "You're a good sport, Graham. You and Lila made quite a pair. You'll probably be in the paper."

"Anything for Lila. Next time, I think I'll be a ranger too—that will be easy enough!" Graham closed his eyes and allowed himself to relax, let his guard down.

He soaked up the sun, the breeze, a bit of normal. Sally sat down on the step below her husband's and leaned back against his legs. They visited for a spell and then it was time to get Lila.

Graham and Lila went out to the back yard for a little while. Steve had raked large piles of leaves, perfect for jumping into the middle and throwing in the air. They made up a new game with Graham swinging Lila round and round and giving her a toss so that she landed on a cushion of leaves. She had leaves in her hair, attacks of the giggles, and asked for him to do it again…and again. Lila's laugh was still with him when he went to bed that night and helped him to fall asleep.

HALLOWEEN. SUNDAY. A FAMILY DAY FOR GRAHAM AND LILA. Why not make a day of it? The sky was that clear, hurt-the-eyes blue, the air crisp, and the leaves in full color for their last hurrah. A few weeks more and they would all be down. Graham watched the scenery flash by on the drive into town. *Push the search to the back of your mind. It's Lila's day.*

"Where we going today, Crackers?" Lila was endearing in jeans, work boots, and a flannel shirt just like Graham's and her Pop Pop's. Her grandfather had taken her shopping, she informed Graham. Nana had braided her hair in two braids and she looked like Laura Ingall's from that old show, "Little House on the Prairie." Cute as a button.

Graham glanced her way and gave her a wink. "It's a surprise. I'll give you some clues. It's some place with wagons, things that grow on trees, things that grow on the ground, and there are animals." The wait was short for Lila.

"We're going to the orchard and the punkin' patch, right? Mommy loves the punkin'patch!" She bounced a little in her seat in anticipation. It was only about fifteen minutes outside of town and they were at a farm in the country. Ready, set, go to explore the whole place from top to bottom.

GRAHAM WATCHED LILA CLOSELY while they rocked on the hayride around the farmer's fields and up a hill to look out over the trees. The acres of land below were brushed in browns and gold. They had done everything like last year and he had a feeling that the little girl was there now. She looked so sad, staring out at the countryside without really seeing it.

Recognizing her heartache, his own worsened. He pulled her up onto his lap and rested his chin on her head. "Are you having a good time today, Lila, or are you sorry I brought you here?"

Lila sat up straight and tilted her head so she could look at Graham. "I'm really glad we came, Crackers. Can we go get donuts and cider when we're done with the ride?" The donuts and cider were her favorite. Graham had let her in on a little secret: they were his favorite too.

"You bet. Hang in there a little while longer." The wagon circled around, rocking them back and forth, and came to a stop. Graham hopped down and put his hands around

Lila's waist, setting her down beside him. She put her little hand in his and they went to the counter for their treat.

Joe Miller, the owner of the farm, gave both of them a wink. "Your money's no good here, friend. You two are my millionth and millionth and one customers. Your treat's on me."

Lila gave Graham a wide-eyed stare. "Did you hear that? Do you think we'll win anything else?" She sat down on a bench and took a big bite of donut. Sugar ringed her mouth and made her downright adorable.

Graham munched on his own little piece of heaven. "I think he was teasing, sweetie. The cider and donuts are complimentary if you pay for a wagon ride."

He licked his fingers, just like a little kid, to get the last of the sweet goodness. Lila licked her lips. She looked too cute, poking her tongue out in a big circle. Why not copy her?

The little girl giggled, especially when Graham looked at her, cross-eyed. She took another big bite and waited until her mouth wasn't full. "What's complmentry?" Her tongue tripped over the large word.

"It means free, like hugs and kisses," Jeanie Pedersen had stepped up behind them and overheard their conversation.

She made a point of giving Lila and Graham one of each. Jim was next, scooping the little girl up in his arms and running off with her. They could hear her peals of laughter carrying over the grounds.

Graham motioned to the seat beside him for Jeanie. He put an arm around her shoulders and leaned his back up against the picnic table. "It's nice to see you two on this fine day. Are you going to pick your apples and pumpkins or buy them at the stand?"

Jeanie straightened her legs out in front of her and rested her head on Graham's sturdy shoulder. "Oh, we have to pick, of course. Jim says they don't taste right unless you get them yourself. I've pointed out that the ones from the stand come from the same place and the farmer's workers picked them by hand, but you can't argue with the man. It's good to see you out and about."

Graham stared out at the fields and some bright red mums caught his eye along the edge. Sarah would have loved to have that pot of flowers. Maybe he'd buy some for Sally. "Lila and I have our day together every Sunday. We have been since she started school. She really needs it, you know?"

Jeanie rested her hand on his. "I know. You need it too." She paused for a moment, trying to find the right words. "I'm so sorry. Usually, when someone is going through a tough time, you tell them it will be all right. I wish I could tell you that, Graham." Her dark eyes were filled with a sadness that echoed his own.

Graham gave her a shrug and a crooked smile. "I believe it will be all right, Jeanie. I have to believe it or I wouldn't be able to get up every morning. Enough about me. Jim told me your news. I hope you don't mind, honey. He's so excited and so am I. Only a little while longer and you can tell everyone, right?"

Jeanie looked up at him and there was a glow burning in her dark eyes, strong enough to make him catch his breath. Spontaneously, his hand closed tightly around hers. "Only a few more weeks. I can't wait, Graham." They were both quiet, watching Jim gallop across a field with Lila on his shoulders. "He's going to be a wonderful father."

Graham rubbed his thumb across her hand and his voice went deep with emotion. "Yes, he is and you will be an amazing mother."

They sat together in companionable silence, watching Jim practice his skills with Lila while Jeanie daydreamed of the future. Graham closed his eyes for a blink and said a little prayer to bless Jeanie, Jim, and their little one. His next prayer, as always, was for Sarah.

10

"CRACKERS, I'M TIRED AND WANT TO GO HOME. Don't conversation officers sleep?" Lila's feet dragged and her eyes were drooping.

Her ranger's hat hung on her back and her candy sack was about to slip through her fingers. They had been around two city blocks and that was enough for her, especially after her afternoon at the orchard. Fresh air, being on the go, overdosed on excitement, and she was done in.

"Of course we sleep," Graham told her and picked her up for the remainder of their walk. It was a white lie. He barely slept, but that didn't count as a generalization for everyone. He wore his uniform, just like Lila's, and they made a cute picture together. She'd been a little disappointed that he didn't wear his bear suit again. That was quickly forgotten in the anticipation of trick or treating. Now the fun was over and it was off to bed.

Sally opened the door at Graham's knock with a warm welcome. "How are my forest rangers tonight?" She took the bag of candy and Graham stepped inside. His side-kick was fading fast. She barely lifted her head when they were met by the glow of the hallway.

"Tired, Nana, really tired. I wanna go to bed," Lila mumbled into Graham's shoulder.

He took her upstairs to her room and set her on her bed. She flopped flat on her back while he fought with her laces and slipped her boots off her feet. Lila was like a rag doll when he sat her up to take the hat and its string off of her neck. She dropped right back onto the pillow with her eyes closed. "'Night, Crackers. Love you."

"Good night, Lila. Sweet dreams. I love you back." He sat by her bedside for a while, watching her sleep. His eyes caught a photograph of the three of them by her bed. He stared at it for a moment and rested his hand on top of her head. "Sweet dreams, Sarah. I love you too." His words were a whisper and a prayer.

Sally stood in the doorway, her eyes wet with unshed tears. "Come on downstairs, Graham. I'll get you some coffee if you'd like." She waited for him, turned off the light, and wrapped an arm around his waist on the way down.

Graham gave her a poor excuse for a smile when they reached the bottom. "Sally, I'm going to pass. It's been a really long day and I haven't been sleeping…well." *That was an understatement. Try hardly at all.* He found Steve nodding off in his recliner and gave the older man a quick hug and returned to Sally. "I'll talk to you soon, sweetheart. Have a good night."

She kissed his cheek and held on tight. "You really made today special for Lila. Good night, Graham. You go on and get some rest." She waited until he was in his truck and turned off the outdoor light. It marked another night without Sarah, another night of waiting.

The drive home. Nodding off at the wheel, almost in a ditch. It was stretching him too thin, walking this tightrope that was about to snap. Heart hammering, hands gripping the wheel until his knuckles were white, Graham screeched to a halt in his driveway. Head pressed to the wheel. Breathing in deep. Saying a prayer of thanks for a disaster averted.

Straight to bed, do not pass go. He didn't even take off his clothes. Graham kicked off his boots and crawled under the covers in blessed darkness. No fighting it this time. Empty the mind. Don't think about anything. Let sleep take him down.

The sound of his cell phone, an annoying buzzing, pulled Graham back up out of a haze of jumbled dreams. He fumbled around in the darkness and hit it on his nightstand, sending it flying and crashing to the floor. Cursing, he went down on his hands and knees and felt around on the floor, following the sound. "Graham Scott here." He squinted at the number on the screen, but didn't recognize it.

"Graham, this is Boyd Handy over on Green Lake Road. Somebody just broke into my house. I scared him off with my hunting rifle, but he's out there somewhere and Eleanor is frightened." The elderly man's voice was gravelly with sleep, anxious with a shortness of breath.

Graham glanced at his clock. It was three AM. He had figured something would happen at a time like this. "All right. Stay put and don't do anything. I'll be right over. Did you call 911?" He stood up and felt around for his boots. One good thing about falling asleep in his clothes. No time wasted getting dressed.

"No, because you said to call you first thing. You want me to call them too?" The breathing on the other end became heavier, a warning sign that the strain might be too much for the older man.

"At such an hour, it might not hurt for me to have back-up for extra security. Stay calm, Mr. Handy and make the call. I'm already on the way." He hung up and peeled out of the driveway. He patted his side. His gun was under his coat in its holster with ammunition in his pocket. Hopefully, he wouldn't need it. Regardless, he would be ready.

Boyd Handy had all the lights on and opened the door immediately the moment Graham pulled in the driveway. His wispy, gray hair was standing up on end as if he'd been running his hands through it and he looked rather pale. "I'm glad you're here. Come inside and I'll show you where he came in."

He huffed and puffed on the way through the house and led Graham to the back deck where the sliding door had been popped off its track.

Graham looked outside with his flashlight; there was nothing. Whoever had been there was long gone. He turned his attention to Boyd. "Mr. Handy, I want you to sit down. Are you feeling all right? I don't like your color and you're breathing pretty hard."

Eleanor joined them and sat beside her husband on the couch. She gripped his arm, eyes wide with fear. "Boyd has a bit of a heart problem. He's not supposed to overdo it. Tonight was too much for him. Maybe we should call the ambulance."

Boyd waved a dismissive hand at his wife. "I don't need an ambulance. It just startled me is all. Would've given anyone a scare." He sat very still in an attempt to calm himself.

Graham assessed the older man carefully, noted his color coming back and his breathing becoming more regular. "You're right about that. I'm going to see if I can follow the intruder's trail. You said it was a man. Did you see his face?"

Boyd shook his head. "No, he had a winter hat that covered it. He ran as soon as he saw my gun. You sure you don't want to wait for the police, have more than one of you out there?"

Graham lifted his coat to reveal his holster. "I should be fine. When the police get here, tell them all the details and let them know I'm out in the woods and armed. If I don't come out, they'll know what to do. Lock up and stay put. Try not to worry." He put the glass door back on its track, locked it, and slid a heavy chest in front of it. "That ought to keep you."

He slipped out the front door and around back. It was easy to follow the trail. An amateur could've managed. It was muddy in the area behind the house where Boyd had raked out the leaves. Once into the woods, it became more difficult. In broad daylight, it would have been simple to pick up on broken twigs and other disturbances caused by someone in a hurry to get away.

Darkness slowed him down, but he had a good flashlight that cast a wide span of light. Graham's experience and knowledge worked hand in hand to guide him in the right direction. Turning back for a moment, he was relieved to see the flash of blue and red lights in front of the Handys' home. He felt more comfortable knowing someone was with them. There was no concern for himself—he could hold his own.

Working his way in, he became lost in concentration. Each step brought Graham closer to the fire tower on Kane Mountain and lit a flicker of hope. Kane Mountain kept bringing him back and now there was an intruder added to the mix. What if there was a connection to Sarah? That slim chance was enough to make him move faster. He crested the top and flashed the beam to the tower. It was unlikely anyone had climbed it. Only a short time had passed and the tower was a trap with no way out.

Graham panned the area, but couldn't see anything. He turned his flashlight off and paused, let the night settle around him. There was a noise, a slight shuffling, from the direction of the ranger's cabin. As if with a will of its own, his hand reached under his jacket and pulled out his pistol. The cool weight was reassuring.

Taking great care to walk without a sound, he picked his way toward the cabin. Controlling his breathing, Graham slipped with stealth onto the porch and crept beneath the window to the open doorway. *Take a deep breath and let it out...slowly. Keep your cool.* Getting carried away by emotion was how accidents happened.

A figure darted out of the doorway and Graham stuck out his foot, sending him flying. It was definitely a male judging by his voice as he let out a string of curses. Graham replaced his pistol and was on the stranger's back in an instant, knee pressing him down onto the floor, arms yanked behind his back.

"I'm Officer Scott for the Department of Environmental Conservation and I believe you are the mystery intruder from Green Lake Road." He pulled out his cuffs, on reserve for occasions such as this one, and slapped them on. Once satisfied that the situation was secure, he stood and pulled the suspect to his feet. Graham turned him around and yanked the winter hat off his face, shining his flashlight in his eyes.

"Jeez, mister, can you turn that thing down? I didn't hurt no one. I was just looking for some food, that's all. I didn't get nothing." It was a teenager, probably about sixteen, with greasy blonde hair, pale blue eyes that were the size of saucers, and a face covered in dirt.

Graham dropped the arm holding the flashlight, disappointment welling up. Just a kid; definitely not a likely suspect to have taken Sarah . "You nearly scared an elderly couple to death. The man who owns the house you broke into tonight has a heart condition. If anything had happened to him, your breaking and entering could have become murder."

The boy gulped and shook his head. " I would never hurt anyone, officer, honest. It's just my old man kicked me out of the house and I ain't had hardly nothing to eat so I've been going to the camps around here to get something and then sleepin' up here. I didn't know what else to do."

The kid was shaking. Graham sat down on the porch and pulled the teen down next to him. "What's your name?"

He took out his pad and pencil kept on hand for notes and waited, trying to fight off the wave of depression that could flatten him if he let it. He had wanted, very badly, to find his way to solving his own mystery. Had thought this might be it. Empty handed…again.

"Bobbie Clark. Listen, you can't tell my old man. He'll get after me for telling, beat me real bad. He has before and I'm not going back this time. I've just been trying to get by. I didn't think those people would miss a can of food here and there. I didn't mean to scare that old man." His voice broke and he was on the verge of crumbling. He was just a kid.

Graham pinched the bridge of his nose. His head had started to pound the moment he lost hope of any clues about Sarah. "Okay, calm down, Bobbie. I'm going to get you help and we won't let your father hurt you. Let's head back before they send out the dogs."

It was only half in jest. If Graham hadn't come back by dawn, an army of conservation officers and other members of law enforcement would have alighted on the mountain with search dogs to assist them. He'd seen it too many times in other efforts and the initial search for Sarah was still fresh in his mind.

Half way down, Graham released the cuffs after Bobbie stumbled several times. He held onto the kid's arm and felt the boy's trembling. By the time they made it out, the sky was lightening to gray with the approaching dawn. Graham loaded him in the waiting police car, filled the officer in on all the details, and reassured Bobbie that they would take care of him.

A weary goodbye to the Handys and his green, conservation truck was back on the road. There was no sense in going home to bed. It was the start of a new day and his head was too full to let him rest.

11

ON RAINY DAYS, THE FOREST SLEPT, lulled by the drops hitting the ground, the wind like a living presence with its humming. The animals were tucked away in their homes and Kane with them, snug in his woodland stronghold. When the skies let loose, it felt good to stay in, be cozy. A time to work with his hands, building or carving, to turn things over in his mind. To sit at the foot of Caroga's bed and hang on to the last scraps of her time. To be still and watch Sarah.

Sarah was restless in the storm. Kane could see it wearing on her. The weather must have had a soothing effect on his sister. There'd been very little noise from the next room. As for Sarah, she couldn't sit still. Her feet paced back and forth while she wore a worried frown. It made a little crease in her forehead, one he wanted to stroke and erase. Finally, she sat in the rocker by the window and stared out at the rain. Times like this, she was so like Mama.

"These were the best days with Mama. My father would stay in, pop some corn, whistle real low while he whittled. Daddy…he didn't like being within four walls, needed the open air. He only came in for dinner so I looked forward to spending more time with him when it stormed. As for Mama, she would bake and sing while she worked. Then she'd sit in her rocker and read to us. Her voice was sweet and her smile…it could light up the place, like yours."

Kane looked up from his spot where he was stretched out on the braided rug in front of the fire. He had been daydreaming, watching the flames dance. He stood and took Sarah's hand, wincing when he saw her flinch. "You've done so much for my sister and me. I'm so grateful. I hope this will make you smile." Gently, he set his latest carving in the nest of her palm.

His touch had the opposite effect. Sarah's hand closed with a jerk over the figurine and she pulled away. "I… I don't feel well." She stuttered, face gone white, voice shaking. Before he could say a word, she slipped away, upstairs to the loft.

Kane was at a loss. Six months had passed since he brought her here. Plenty of time to adjust, settle in. He didn't feel like he had to watch her like a hawk anymore, trusted leaving her alone for short spans of time. Attempts at escape had stopped. She'd figured it out. Running was useless because he'd track her down. He thought she would come to accept him, yet her eyes told a different story. Her eyes looked like Daddy's after Mama slipped away, as if she was dying inside a little bit more each day.

What to do? Kane couldn't let her go. Caroga's time was short and the thought of being alone again –unbearable. Finding another human being to stay with him—unacceptable. Deep down, he knew it was wrong, what he had done to Sarah. If it were the other way around and someone had forced Kane to leave his home, to live in that other world outside the forest…unthinkable…and yet he *could not* be completely alone.

How to rectify the situation? Daddy died when he lost Mama, the best part of him. The thought had been brewing in Kane as he tried to come to terms with his sister's approaching death. He longed to have a special bond with Sarah. To keep her. Make her his.

He was afraid. If she didn't cross the bridge that spanned between them and he had to live alone without Caroga, would he die too? It was a chance he wasn't willing to take. Letting Sarah go, even though she was not happy, was not an option. Give her more time. She'd come around.

Kane remained in front of the fire, listening for sounds from above. Nothing stirred. He checked in on his sister, watched the slow rise and fall of her chest. He went through his nightly check of his home before going to bed, dropped the bar to secure the door, and drank a cup of cold water. His appetite was gone, his stomach churning with worry over Caroga, Sarah, the future.

Before turning out the kerosene lamp on the small table by his bed, Kane said goodnight to a photos of his parents. A photographer on Canada Lake made a stop at the store one day.

He captured Ben and Mary when they were young, their infant daughter in her mother's arms, Kane's father resting his hand on the crown of his son's head. All of them together. Soon there would be only one. Kane's eyelids fell shut and he longed to go back to the way things were.

He did not sleep well that night, tossing and turning with worry over Sarah. Hurting. He was not a bad man just lonely, so very lonely. In the wee hours of the morning, in that time when the wilderness held its breath and the darkness met the dawn, Kane washed up. He pulled on jeans frayed with wear and a heavy, chamois shirt. He slipped outside, packed a sack with several of his latest carvings, and made his way to the mountain. Carrying on his father's ritual.

The rain had ceased in the night, but the wet forest floor hid the sound of his footsteps. He was glad for it. Uneasiness still crept up during the morning trek after the encounter with the conservation officer a few days before. Made him watch his back. The ranger said he was on a routine patrol, but what if…?

Kane had come across rangers from time to time while out hunting, on a walk through the woods, or during brief excursions into town. They'd passed him by. He blended in, looked the part of a local, had the advantage of Mama's manners and sugar tongue. His father had taught him well. Be polite, meet their eyes, make small talk, and move on. The sunrise came, steadied Kane's soul, convinced him there was nothing to fear.

Once he came down the mountain, the woods pulled him in, always a comfort. A plan had taken shape. Kane took his time and worked his way toward the outskirts of the forest. The sound of the cars was a low rumble reaching him long before they could be seen. The noise was so loud compared with his accustomed quiet that it made his ears ring.

A little bit further and his foot met the road, a large, black snake winding in both directions. Kane breathed deeply, gathered his resolve, and stepped out of the woods. It was disorienting, feeling stripped bare when he left the shelter of the trees and every fiber of his being wanted to go back home.

The store for Canada Lake residents was a short piece ahead, dropped down in a little hollow by the water. It looked quiet, safe. He did not see the vehicle from the Department of Environmental Conservation parked in the lot as he crossed the road and took the steps. The door opened and a man in the green uniform of the forest ranger stepped out, his expression dark.

Kane recognized the face and it almost made him get sick, right there on the officer's feet. The urge was strong to turn around, rush back to the sheltering wilderness. *Keep a cool head. Don't do anything out of the ordinary.* The man's eyes skittered over him, but he did not break stride.

Just one more step to the familiar confines of the store. Mama and Daddy had come here most often on their excursions. The young shopkeeper, with hair and eyes the color of Daddy's coffee, was bent over a crossword puzzle on the counter. "Well, good morning to you, Kane. It's been a while." He set his pencil down and gave his full attention to his customer.

Kane gave a little dip of his head and emptied the contents of his pack on the counter. "'Morning, Mattie. I'll need a few things and you can do the books."

Mattie skimmed through the carvings, his eyes lit with pleasure. "No problem. Take your time and I'll be ready for you."

He turned to a blank page in a notebook that doubled as a ledger and began making a list of the items Kane made and their tentative value. They had been doing business with one another for many years, starting with Kane's father.

Kane never took long. Being away from the forest left him unsettled. Leaving Caroga and Sarah put him on edge. He quickly filled a basket with some apples, squash, and a bag of sugar. Back at the counter, a small, porcelain cardinal was sitting on the windowsill with a blue jay at its side. Sarah loved the little, red birds at the house and often stopped what she was doing to watch them. The blue jay would make Caroga smile.

On impulse, Kane added both birds to his purchases. Mama had loved pretty things.

Mattie gestured to his notebook. "You brought me twenty carvings, Kane. The work is fine, like it always has been, and I can't keep them on my shelves, they sell so quick. The loons and the bears are a favorite. If you could make more, that would be perfect. I'll give you ten dollars each so with today's purchases, you'll get back $185." He took the money out of the register and handed it to Kane.

Kane looked him in the eye and gave him a handshake as Mama had taught him. "Thank you. I'll bring more when I can, maybe some furniture too. Once I'm hunkered down for the winter, I'll have more time on my hands. Will you throw in a few of those pumpkins out on the porch?"

Bargaining was part of the business deal. Kane could remember haggling over a sale when Mattie was a baby in a bassinet behind the counter and his mother kept shop.

Mattie grinned. "I suppose that will be all right, Kane. What's wrong?" The woodsman had been loading his backpack, tucking his money in his pocket, when he became rigid.

Kane's eyes were drawn to the picture on the pile of pamphlets on the counter. Sarah stared back at him. The ranger lied. That had been no routine patrol. The man wanted Sarah. Kane forced himself to look away, but he could feel her watching him. "That's a terrible shame… about that woman. Do they have any idea about her whereabouts?"

Mattie shook his head. "No. She disappeared about six months ago from Rockwood. Nobody knows anything. If you see something strange, you let me know, okay?"

Kane nodded and thanked him, panic threatening to smother him. Had to get out, get to the woods, where he could breathe. He pulled up short at the door. The ranger was still in the parking lot, head bowed at the wheel. Only when the truck pulled out did Kane leave the store, fumbling with his purchases in his arms, and slipping back into the cover of the trees.

The weight of Sarah's stare came with him, boring an accusing hole in his back as he streaked by. It followed him all the way back to the cabin. He kept glancing over his shoulder, stopping to listen, choosing a serpentine path, taking care not to leave a trail. They were still looking for her. Although no one had stumbled upon Kane's home yet, their scrutiny could bring him down.

The cabin was warm, welcoming. Sarah had stoked the fire and was rocking in front of it, staring intensely into its flames. She stood quickly and set a dish of oatmeal and coffee on the table for Kane. Some of the tension eased. She was here.

Her presence alone allayed his fears. She hadn't left, mostly due to Caroga, but surely she was getting used to him. No one would find her. Since his father built their home, there had been no chance encounters. He handed her his pack and sat down. "There are some fresh apples in there. You might like them with your oatmeal."

Sarah emptied the bag, took an apple, and sliced it into wedges with nimble fingers. She set them on a plate and added a scoop of peanut butter, a luxury from a previous trip into town. The spread in a jar was one of her favorites. Kane would have to remember to get more the next time. Before sitting down, she took a few slices, chopped them into fine bits, and sprinkled them with cinnamon. She pushed them into Kane's dish and mixed them well with his steaming cereal. She'd learned how much he liked the sweet treat, had learned countless things about him. He knew very little about Sarah.

Kane's fingers brushed her hand when he picked up his spoon and a flash of heat traveled straight to his heart. "Thank you. Please sit. Eat before yours gets cold." She was not his servant. That was not his intention. He wanted a partner, like his father had found in Mama.

A nod of the head and she started eating. The quiet pressed down on them. Although Kane's parents had often been unobtrusive, it was a quiet born of being so comfortable with one another that they need not say a word. Sarah's silence was becoming a burden to Kane, stemming from her unhappiness. Would she stop speaking to him altogether, become a ghost in his house? No company would be better than that.

Kane finished, motioned for Sarah to remain seated, and washed the dishes. He set a cup of tea in front of her and pulled a chair up close. Dropping down, he set his hands on his knees and waited while she sipped her drink. He could feel her withdrawing.

Sarah's clear, blue gaze was questioning, waiting. She set her cup down and Kane's hand drifted up to skim her cheek. One tear spilled from her eye and slid down, her body stiffening at his touch. Hurt welled up and Kane let his hand drop.

"I hate to see you so unhappy. I brought you a little something." He reached in his pocket and set the glass bird in front of her.

Something flickered in her eyes and her cheeks flushed. "Thank you, Kane. I love cardinals. You remembered."

She stood and went to the window, setting it on the sill. Perhaps it would draw the real thing and let her watch them every day. She stroked the little figure and stared out at the forest, her gaze turned inward as it so often was.

Kane stood as well. "I'm glad you like it. I'll bring more next time. I've brought back pumpkins too. I thought today would be a good day for some pies. If we work together, it shouldn't be long and we'll have a slice of heaven for our dessert. Mama's recipes never fail." It was Sarah's cue to take down his Mama's recipe book and set out the ingredients.

Kane built up the fire in the cook stove, finding the right temperature from experience. He set out the metal pie pans, brought in a pumpkin, and started the work of gutting it. The seeds were set aside for a tasty snack when toasted. Daddy used to walk around with a pocketful, pop them in his mouth.

"There are more pumpkins out there if you want to carve any. Halloween's coming soon and Mama loved to set some out on our porch. She'd light them at night and then let the animals make quick work of them. We'd stay up late, all of us, eating popcorn and watching the moon because there's always a fine moonshine on Halloween. Tonight would be nice for sitting out, you and I."

Sarah gripped her knife tightly as she sliced apples for her pie filling. Kane could see the white of her knuckles. "Lila loved carving the pumpkin. It was her favorite part of Halloween."

She broke off and her hand shook so hard that she dropped the knife. The tears followed. Sarah wiped them away, struggling to maintain her composure. Her daughter's hold was strong. Kane didn't know how to break it.

Best to keep going, keep a body doing things when the mind wouldn't rest. He pointed to the page that gave directions for pie dough, but Sarah disregarded it. Kane stopped what he was doing to watch her, a bit aggravated that she had not accepted his guidance. "That's not the way Mama did it. You need to try adding a little…"

Sarah slammed her hand down on the table. "I'm not your mama, Kane. I'm making it the way *my* mother taught me! And let me tell you one other thing. You're not your daddy! Don't you do anything of your own choosing that wasn't mapped out by the people who went before you? Can't you take your own path?" Her eyes held a storm and her voice rose to a pitch Kane had never heard, not once in a life spent with soft-spoken people and long silences.

His first instinct was to retreat. Confrontation with others was foreign to him, something he never had to do in his life in the woods. "I found you."

Kane became lost in her eyes, in the spots of red on her cheeks, and the rise and fall of her chest. "And my daddy never did this." He stepped forward, gripped arms that were unyielding, and pressed his lips to hers. It was the first time he kissed a woman other than his mother. Sarah did not give or soften. She could have been made of stone.

"*Don't...ever...do ...that...again.*" She spit the words at him and a fierce fire flared in her eyes, hot enough to burn if he did not let go. The door to the cabin opened and in a blur, Sarah was outside. Kane followed, but needn't have worried about her going far. Of all the unlikely choices, the outdoor shower was her destination.

After a cold dousing, shivering and white, she broke away and rushed inside. There was a rustling of movement in Caroga's room, a quiet fit of coughing, not nearly as bad as most. Distracted, Sarah attended to her as his sister awoke from her nap. A moment later and Sarah came out to the kitchen to get a dish of oatmeal kept warm on the stove, took the time to mince apples very fine with a touch of sugar, and poured tea.

Returning to the bedroom, she did not look at Kane and the wall of ice grew taller, shielding her. His frustration grew. They lived in a small space, yet an ever-widening gap grew between them with each passing day. Kane had come to the bitter conclusion. He could force Sarah to live with him, to care for Caroga. He could not make her believe that she belonged. He could not make her love him.

Odds and ends that were his habit kept Kane's hands busy, got him through the day. Sarah remained upstairs. Sleep eluded him again as he mulled over his dilemma. He'd never had problems sleeping before, never felt constrained in this cabin. Now the walls were closing in. Robbed of his contentment, he resented her for it.

He hit his knees, bowed his head, and prayed for guidance as he'd been taught. The answer came not long before the dawn. He would go to the forest and take her with him. Caroga was doing better these past few days, could be left alone for a few hours. The peace of the wilderness was always freely given and Sarah would find harmony as well.

Kane washed, dressed, and went to Sarah's bedside. He need only stand and wait. She awoke without a touch or a word. "Get dressed. We're going to meet the day. I've already brought Little Sister her breakfast. She's resting comfortably. We'll have time."

With that, he went downstairs. He paced back and forth. Would she deny him? Would he have to use force? The knot in his stomach loosened when she joined him. He opened the door and waved her through, barring it behind them. Sarah waited. The light was dim and she would not be able to find her way without him. She would come to see how important Kane was.

He could not speak to her, still reeling from the revulsion he had seen in her eyes upon waking and felt in her touch the previous day. Kane was undeserving of such treatment, had always been kind and patient. Certainly no monster, he was pleasant to look at and in his ways.

Sarah trailed a few steps behind him. Watching her eyes darting furtively, seeming to shrink in on herself, he had the sense of bird with a clipped wing, eyes raised to the sky in search of escape. As they picked their way through the forest, steps quieted by the carpet of leaves on the ground, his mind pondered his dilemma.

Daddy had no other option. He came to the woods to save himself and Mama came with him of her own will. Kane and Caroga knew no other life. Sarah had not chosen to come nor followed someone she loved. Freedom of choice was the crux of the matter. Then there was the child and the child was everything.

They made their way up the remote side of Kane Mountain, far from the heavily trodden trails, untainted by the passing of so many that did not respect the forest. Kane chose their path both for its beauty and the unlikelihood that they would meet anyone else. His journey to meet the sun had never been interrupted until…his heart thumped painfully in his chest. The forest ranger.

With an effort, he fought down a rush of anxiety. It was only a coincidence. The ranger had merely stumbled upon Kane that day. There was no link to Sarah. Kane's heart slowed and he breathed easy once they crested the summit at the same time as the sun.

Dawn's inferno restored Kane's equilibrium with its waves of color, intense at first, then fading as they spilled over the dark silhouettes of the mountain and the land. He could not be the judge of the woman by his side. Face bathed in light, she was a closed book, unable to be read, giving nothing away.

He forged ahead, taking her down the mountain in another direction that bypassed the marked trail system. The brisk air, the quality of light as it caught the canvas of colorful leaves, and the calming presence of the woodlands steadied Kane. He was comfortable in his skin again when they arrived at his destination, an isolated section of Pine Lake that was uninhabited. It was a place he often went to settle himself since his parents' deaths, alone and with his sister.

A large, flat boulder stretched out along the shore. Kane gestured to it for Sarah and went about finding two saplings. He cut them both down with his father's knife, tied a bit of line to the end of each, and attached a hook. A little bit of digging unearthed two worms and their fishing poles were ready. One for Sarah, one for himself.

He sat down on the rock to drop his line. He did look not at her, would not feel the sting of her reproach. Kane heard her line hit the water and a rustling on the other end. Good—she kept her distance. Kane was not up to being close to her this morning. Being spurned still rankled in the pit of his stomach.

The sun crept higher in the sky, warming their rock on a day that was quite mild in autumn. Kane's hurt eased. He had simply taken Sarah off guard. With more time, patience, and the realization that there was no other choice, she would accept him. A fondness *would* grow between them. They would form a bond, with a strength and endurance like that of Kane's parents. They would create a family of their own, fill Sarah's emptiness.

"Daddy always said…" Kane broke off, remembered Sarah's words about his father, started over. "I love to come here to fish or simply to sit. It's one of my favorite places because it soothes the soul. It will for you too, Sarah, if you let it." He turned to face her, to see its work in her.

Sarah's pole rested on the rock beside her. Her knees were drawn to her chest and her forehead was bowed to her knees while the tears fell like rain. She shook her head, her voice breaking. "You don't understand, Kane! I know you've lost your family and it's hurt you—badly—but you are keeping me from those I love more than anything in the world! It is torture. Nothing will fix it until you bring me back to them. Please, Kane, please…I'm begging you. Let me go. Let me go back to my family. Please." Her body shuddered with silent sobs, all the more painful to watch.

Kane's spirits plummeted. What had helped him had done nothing for her. If anything, her sadness deepened. With a sigh, he untied their hooks and tucked them away in his pocket. He stood and took her arm. "I'm sorry. I can't do that. I *will not* be alone. The sooner you stop fighting it, the easier it will become." She shook her head but Sarah went with him because she had no choice in the matter. Kane's power over her was too strong.

They'd been walking about a half hour when they heard voices and laughter. Heavy footsteps approached. Outwardly calm, Kane's pulse began to race. A young couple in their teens came into view and became animated upon catching sight of others.

"Thank God! We are so lost! Can you tell us how to get to the Pine Lake campsites? We left there this morning and got all turned around." The young man, practically a boy, was open, with wide, brown eyes and dark hair in a crew cut, eager to prove he could get them out of trouble.

His girlfriend, with a riot of red curls and moss green eyes, wore a big smile, obviously relieved. "We thought they'd have to send out a rescue party. Can you help us get straightened out?"

Kane gave Sarah's arm a squeeze, hard enough to keep her quiet. Her skin had gone white and he could feel her quivering, a rabbit trapped in a snare. "Sure. Just head in that direction, keep the sun at your right and in about a half hour or so, you'll be there."

He heard Sarah's sharp intake of breath and dug his fingers in deep while giving the strangers a pleasant smile. They gave their thanks and quickly went on their way.

Closer. The outside world was encroaching. Had to get home! In a flurry of movement, Kane took the trek back to the refuge of his cabin. Sarah had to run to keep up. Curse those kids! They'd given her a location, bearings, something to latch on to. It did not matter. She would not find her way on her own nor would he allow opportunity for escape.

The cabin appeared as if rising up out of the forest floor and Kane felt Sarah wilt. Once inside, he let go and dropped the wooden bar in place. He pressed his forehead against the heavy oak, taking comfort in its solid surface.

Breathing hard, blood rushing in his ears, he heard soft footsteps behind him. Sarah would not be going anywhere with one exception— to her loft. Kane checked on Caroga to find her sleeping, built up the fire, and sat before it. He picked up a piece of wood and began to carve until his nerves calmed and his heart steadied its pace. Home was safe and had balance.

Kane would have to keep a close eye on Sarah, be more careful than ever. When his work was done, he sat by his sister's bedside. She slept fitfully. More and more, her days passed in slumber and the significance stabbed at his heart.

He leaned over her and stroked the hair from her forehead, tucking it behind her ear. A tiny smile formed on her lips, like when she was a child. Kane straightened her blankets and noticed one hand held something tightly. Glancing at it carefully, he saw the blue jay peeking out and the sight made his eyes sting. As surely as Caroga would not let go of that bird, he would not let go of Sarah.

12

THE SUNRISE SET THE HORIZON ON FIRE, announcing the arrival of another day. Graham met it head on, on the road for the next leg of his search when his cell phone rang. A quick scan of the number and his stomach churned. It was the district office. He hit the speaker and steeled himself. "Graham Scott here."

"Graham, it's John. I need you to come in this morning. There's a matter of vital importance and I would prefer to meet in person." John Christopher was the regional director. Graham had only dealt with him on crucial cases such as a high profile hiker that was lost a couple years ago. The last time they had seen each other was when Graham implored him to be placed full time on Sarah's case. "When can you get here?"

"I can make it in about an hour. I'm on my way." Graham hung up, his insides twisting as he mentally scrolled through the reasons they wanted him. Two were most likely: they were taking him off the case or they had found Sarah and would not tell him over the phone. The latter had him ready to pull over and lose his latest cup of coffee, but he stayed the course until he reached Albany.

Graham detested the city, any city. The crowds, the noise, the filth…everything pressing in on a person until it was hard to breathe. Anytime he had to go, his main intention was to get in and get out as quickly as possible. Today was no different.

Graham parked and walked inside, going against every instinct that told him to turn around. Set on heading straight to the director, he was forced to make a last minute detour to the bathroom to splash cold water on his face and to breathe deep, the sink holding him up when his legs wouldn't. Nerves as steady as they'd ever be, he forged ahead and knocked on a heavy door made of hardwood. "Come in," a voice called.

John Christopher stood upon Graham's entrance and approached his officer with his hand extended in welcome. In his late fifties, he still maintained the toned body of an outdoorsman after years of being a ranger himself. His hair had grown gray and his face was lined, yet there was the strength of a younger man in his handshake and compassion ran deep in his brown eyes. "Graham, how are you holding up?" If appearances said anything, the answer was obvious.

"I'm holding my own. Why did you need to see me, sir? I know this isn't a social call." Might as well get to the punchline. He sat down in a cushioned chair by a window while the director sat across from him and propped his elbows on his knees.

"Graham, I have difficult news. I think you have a right to know about it and make your own decision. A young woman disappeared the night before last in Old Forge. She matches Sarah's description and her resemblance is strong. I wanted you to hear this from me first and not on the news. Here's her picture." John reached over to his desk and picked up a color photo.

Graham's body went cold when he saw the blue of her eyes, the fall of blonde hair, the easy smile. She could have been Sarah's sister. He swallowed hard and his hand gripped the edge of his chair. "Who is she?" His mind was spinning so fast he had to fight to keep it together.

"Her name is Caroline Richards. She's 25 and has lived in Old Forge all of her life. The night of her disappearance, she went out with friends and never came home. She still lives with her mother, who called it in. It became an active investigation after the first twenty four hours. The area police shared the case with our department when they saw how much she looked like Sarah. It's possible the two cases are linked." John laid Sarah's picture next to Caroline's, driving his point home.

Graham was up on his feet, a hand raking through his hair as he turned toward the window. "What—you think it's some kind of serial case out there?" He would not say the word killer, would not even allow himself to think it.

John stood and laid a hand on his shoulder. "It's a possibility we have to consider. I'd like someone to go up to Old Forge today to talk with the local police department, interview the family, and help organize the search efforts. You are my best candidate. You know the lay of the land, you're honed by experience when it comes to a thorough probe, and you know all the ins and outs of Sarah's case. I realize you're spread thin, you're on edge, and you may not have the heart for this. It's your decision and I won't fault you, whichever way you go."

Graham turned around and met John's eyes. "I'll do it. It has to be me. Thank you for consulting with me before making any decisions." The rest of the meeting was brief. Sensing the ranger's eagerness to leave, John gave him a folder with pertinent information and wished him luck.

Graham's legs held out until he reached the bathroom. This time he dropped to the floor while his stomach heaved. He laid his cheek against the cold tile and waited for his heart beat to slow. No matter how he tried, he could not erase the girl's image from his mind. Sarah's picture went with it, hand in hand. It was inevitable. Another woman, ripped from her family. Another family, drowned in anguish. It had to stop.

The nightmare wouldn't end if he remained on the floor, wallowing. Graham did what he always did. Picked himself up again. Rinsed his mouth, mopped his face with cold water, walked outside. He took deep gulps of the cool air, thankful for its bite. A glance at his watch told him it was only eight AM. If he took the thruway, he would make good time to Utica, move on to Old Forge in a reasonable amount of time.

It was quiet in Old Forge. A small, seasonal town, it thrived in the summers and winters. Autumn was a slow interim with the occasional tourists and leaf peepers making their way through, a favorite for Sunday drivers. Otherwise, most of the businesses, selling the quaint or rustic, were shut down during the week, hoping for a rush during the holidays and the approaching snowmobiling exodus.

Graham noted one major detail that was out of the ordinary any time of year—law enforcement making an appearance in force. State troopers, local police from the outlying areas, and environmental conservation vehicles were evident in all directions. He could feel his heart pick up the pace and had to fight the shakes. This was how it began with Sarah.

The first stop was easiest. Graham went to the local police station, consisting of two units, and met with the sheriff. Everything known to date was laid on the table with the additional insights of a local man who personally knew Caroline Richards. Another link was forged between the cases—people involved in the investigation, driven by their own acquaintance with the victims.

Sheriff Meyer was not romantically involved with Caroline, but he had been a regular customer at the diner where she worked. She was one of his own, a member of the public he had chosen to serve and protect. She mattered to him. Graham left with the sheriff's assurance of full cooperation as he made the environmental conservation officer the lead contact for the search efforts.

Graham's next stop found him parked on the road, staring at a house he did not want to enter. It was small and white, something out of a story book. Another Gingerbread Cottage. He'd never forget meeting Sarah's parents that terrible night.

He had to dig deep for his courage, wiping sweaty palms on his thighs and counting to ten with each breath until he found the strength to get out. He squared his shoulders. Made it to the door. Gave it a firm knock and wished the ground would swallow him whole.

"May I help you?" A small woman with frosted blonde hair stood at the door, looking up at him with eyes that would have been a riveting blue if they were not blood-shot and red-rimmed. She wore her bathrobe and slippers even though it was approaching afternoon.

"Mrs. Richards?" Graham croaked. At her nod, he cleared his throat and continued. "I'm Officer Graham Scott. I've been placed in charge of organizing the search efforts for

Caroline because it's my specialty. I always work closely with the families involved and hope you might have time to talk this morning." He kept his tone easy, did his best to be warm and open, to offer her a sense of confidence he did not feel.

"Please, call me Barbara. Come in." She opened the door wide, stepped aside, and shut it behind him. She led the way to the living room where they both sat on the sofa. "Can I offer you coffee or tea?" At his refusal, she stared down at a tissue that she fiddled with in her hands. "I…I thank you so much for coming to meet with me. I just don't know what to do. My husband died several years ago and Caroline…she's all I have. When she didn't come home…" She broke off, the words stuck in her throat.

Graham laid a reassuring hand on hers until her fingers stilled. *Give her what she needs.* "I know how difficult this must be for you, Barbara. I want to assure you that we will do everything possible to find Caroline and bring her home again. What can you tell me about Caroline that can help me to better understand her? When I need to find a missing person, that person is more than a name to me. I really want to know as much as I can about her. She matters to you. That means she matters to me."

Barbara picked up a photo album that was lying on the coffee table and handed it to Graham. "I've been looking through this all morning. I made it for her birthday this year and chose a picture that was a highlight for every year of her life."

While Graham began flipping through the pages, the woman next to him drifted off to the past. "Caroline has always been the light of our lives. She's curious, active, loves to perform. She's always been very outgoing and popular too. She sang in the church choir, was in all the plays in high school, had her head in the clouds about becoming an actress. She went to college for performing arts and even did an internship in New York City, but nothing permanent came up. After struggling to make ends meet in the city for a few years, she took a break and came back home. She found a job at the diner and she's been sending out her resume all over the place. I know she's really hoping for a break. Caroline has always tried to make the best of it." Her words trailed off and she stared into space.

The face in the album, so like his Sarah's, tugged at Graham's heart. He pulled his eyes away and looked up at Mrs. Richards. "Barbara, was Caroline seeing anyone? Any problems with anyone and do you think she would leave on the spur of the moment if she was unhappy?"

She drew herself up straight and her eyes became ice. "If you're suggesting she would run away without a word and put me through such worry, I can assure you she would not. She had no enemies in this town; she was well-liked by everyone and drew a regular crowd at the diner. As for boyfriends, she went out from time to time, but there was no one steady in her life. I think she was afraid to get too attached when she didn't plan on staying long. She wouldn't want to hurt anyone. That's the kind of person my Caroline is."

Graham forced a smile and gave her hand a squeeze. "I'm sure you're right, Barbara. I'm just trying to look at all the possibilities. I'm also trying to make any connections with another case I've been working on recently. It's for a young woman who disappeared in Johnstown."

He opened the folder he had brought with him, kept his hands steady, and laid out two pictures on the table. Both were on flyers to aid in the search, one of Sarah and the other of Caroline. "Her name is Sarah Waters and she has an unmistakable resemblance to your daughter."

The woman beside him inhaled sharply and skimmed both photos with her hand. "Oh my God! I've seen the other girl's picture in the grocery store. The first time I saw it, I thought about how much she looked like Caroline. I don't know how I could have forgotten about her until now. Do you think Sarah's disappearance and my Caroline's have something to do with each other, that maybe the same person…" She couldn't continue, her words cut off and eyes wide.

Graham stared at the pictures in front of him and was appalled when his eyes began to sting and his throat to close. Not now. Had to keep it together. For Barbara Richards, the wound was fresh, raw, and frightening in its intensity. He needed to be there for *her*. "We really don't know yet, Barbara. I know it's terrifying and I don't want to go there myself, but we have to be realistic and consider all possibilities."

It was Barbara's turn to offer comfort, her hand holding his and her voice gentle. "You know Sarah don't you? She's not just another face. She matters to you like my Caroline does to me. You're here for both of them." There was no judgment, only kindness.

Graham's eyes closed tightly and his jaw worked silently for a moment before he found the words. "Sarah is my life as Caroline is yours and I promise I will do everything in my power to help you." He stood up abruptly and gathered his materials. "I've taken enough of your time. Here's my card. Please call me anytime you need to and I will keep in touch. Thank you for meeting me."

He couldn't look her in the eye, his hold on his control was that tenuous. He made it to the door, thought he was in the clear, when an arm came around him and held on tightly.

"Thank you, Officer Scott, for caring. I'll say a prayer for your Sarah and you say one for my Caroline, all right?" Barbara stood beside him and looked up at him with hope in her eyes that had not been there before. Graham gave her a nod, unable to say anything more and walked out the door. Her trust hurt.

.

THANKS TO THE ASSISTANCE OF SHERIFF MEYER, all law enforcement officials on the case were gathered in the parking lot at the high school. Everyone stood attentively before Graham, awaiting their orders. Packets of information, concerning Caroline and Sarah, had been distributed and the possible connection to the cases had been made a focal point of Graham's opening remarks. That potential link sparked a new-found energy for the ranger as well as an increased sense of urgency.

"Striking while the trail is fresh is key. I'd like area law officials to be thorough in canvasing the neighborhood, all acquaintances, people from the diner, anyone that might have seen her and work your way out into the outlying areas. We're looking for anyone who saw her after her friends said good night at the bar. Environmental conservation officers will be taking different segments of the forest in this area with a gradual fanning out if we need to expand the search."

Graham took pause as officers murmured to one another, waiting for silence. "Remember that Caroline is your focus at this time, but be aware of anything that should come up about Sarah or any other similar cases. We may be looking at multiple victims. That's it for now. You have my card if you have any questions. Feel free to contact me at any time. You can also get in touch with the regional director's number in your packets if I am not available. Sheriff Meyer is a liaison as well. I thank all of you for your efforts and dedication. Good luck."

Everyone dispersed, each with their own destination and task. Graham had chosen to begin with a marked trail on a stretch of forest near the bar where Caroline had last been seen. It was just as good a place as any and he had to start somewhere. He said a prayer, as he always did. This time it included the names of two women—Sarah and Caroline. "God be with me today. Let me bring them home. Please." He walked into the woods and resumed the task of dissecting the Adirondacks one step at a time.

THREE DAYS. It had rained for three days, straight. Any longer and Sarah would go out of her mind. *She had to get out*! It was bad enough feeling that the cabin would crush her. Having Kane there for the duration was going to push her over the edge. The weight of Caroga's illness as it dragged on was heaping more on her shoulders…and yet, Sarah sensed the end was near. What would Kane do then?

Acting had been something Sarah loved to do. It was part of why she did so well with speaking, storytelling, and songs while teaching kindergarten. Playing Kane's meek housemate was the greatest challenge of her life. The intervals when he would leave her alone with his sister were what made her abduction bearable, a time to plan her escape. Outings with him made it more tolerable. She was in the open air and …maybe…just maybe she would get away.

Caroga was resting quietly after a sponge bath. Sarah had cleaned every surface of the cabin, rubbing the wood with a lemony polish that Kane's mother made. The floors had been scrubbed and swept. Dishware went into the basin of soapy water repeatedly only to be dried and put away. Clothes were washed in the same basin, wrung out, and hung over the fireplace. Frenetic in her efforts, anything to keep her hands busy, nothing could stop her mind.

Kane didn't help any, stretched out on the rug, staring into the fire, driving her crazy. She picked up the cook book and looked for something challenging to make, but didn't have the patience for any of it. She wanted to throw it at her captor. Scream. Stomp her feet and tear at her hair. Unable to do any of those things, she paced from window to window like a lion in a cage. Exhausted from searching for some sign of hope, Sarah dropped down in a chair and bowed her head, pressing her palms into her eyes.

On these rainy days, missing Lila became a weight so heavy like a stone tied to her neck, ready to take her down into murky depths. Surely it would kill her, not having her baby girl in the next room, not having her in the classroom across the hall every day, not seeing Lee's smile and expressions in that little face or hearing his laugh live on in her. To not feel those little arms wrap around her neck and have butterfly kisses pressed to her cheek. It was like an amputation of the heart and how could one go on without a heart?

Kane had been rambling for some time. Sarah tuned him out until the instant he touched her, making her feel physically ill. She looked down to find a carved ladybug in her hand. Lila loved ladybugs. Fearing she would actually throw up or start shrieking and never stop, Sarah jumped up. "I…I…don't feel well."

She ran upstairs and buried her face in her pillow. Hot tears came and she couldn't stop them. When would this end? Dying would be better. Sarah wouldn't know what she was missing.

It was one of those nights that felt as if sleep never came. If it did, it was too brief to be restful. She stared up with dry eyes, trying to memorize a little spot on the ceiling. Something to hold on to, keep her sanity. Her mind played out every possible scenario for escape. She hit a wall every time and its name was Kane. As soon as she heard him leave in the morning, Sarah was out of bed. She dressed, washed, and went downstairs for something to nibble on.

More pacing, following an invisible track on the floor. She would go. She would walk out that door and run as fast as possible. She would go as far as her feet would carry her and would not stop until she found help or died alone, lost in the forest. Sarah made it to the door, hands pressed against the warm, solid wood.

Taking deep breaths, she gathered her resolve and stepped out. She streaked across a carpet of leaves, the crunching beneath her feet so loud she was afraid the whole world could hear her. A glance over her shoulder stopped her in her tracks. The sun was rising. A shift in the light and the cabin would be gone. Kane would return and it would be over. The mountain man could follow her clumsy trail with ease. He'd proven it time and again in her past efforts.

Tears running down her face and heart pounding, Sarah cursed him for chipping away her confidence a little piece at a time and replacing it with fear. She went back inside and did what she had done every day—prepared his coffee and breakfast. In her imagination, it was for Graham.

All too soon, the cabin door opened, letting in a rush of cold air and the perfume of autumn, pulling Sarah back to the present, her prison. Kane came bearing gifts. Infuriating! To appease her with apples! As he sat down to his meal, Sarah's hands were busy while her mind raced. He had traveled out of the woods to bring things back. Others were not too far away. It could be done. Sarah could find her way out.

Kane invited her to sit and eat. *So courteous.* A bitter pill to swallow when he denied her the most important human right: her freedom.

He even cleaned up, served her tea, let her sit. He approached and sat closely beside her. The closer he came the more her skin crawled. A gift of a glass cardinal was placed before her. "I hate to see you so unhappy. I brought you a little something."

Trinkets! The gall of the man to think pieces of glass could buy her affection! Placing it on the window sill, it took every ounce of self-control not to smash it on the floor, watch it shatter. It was a symbol of her life, the little creature of nature trapped in glass within four walls, like Sarah.

She faked pleasure while her insides were writhing. "Thank you. I love cardinals. You remembered." It was eerie. He remembered every bit of her she had shared, forcing her to be sparing.

What came next…unthinkable. She should have seen it coming, been prepared. He was a man after all. He had desires, like any man, even if he had not acted upon them. Kane stepped forward, put his hands on her arms, and pressed his lips to hers.

Fury, white-hot only an instant before, turned to an ice so cold it could root the man to the spot. "*Don't …ever…do…that…again.*" God help her, she'd kill the man or herself, let the house burn to the ground in the night around them, before she allowed him to make physical advances again.

Out. Sarah had to get out and away from him. She shot out the door, went to the bathhouse, through the inner door to the outdoor shower. Her clothes dropped to the floor and she pulled the cord from the tank, raining cold water down on her head. In the late spring and summer, or on an unseasonably hot day, the water warmed enough to feel pleasant.

Not now. It was shocking, making her fold in upon herself. She scrubbed until her skin turned red and raw, pulled at her hair, tried to wash away his touch, his nearness. Feeling like ice ran in her veins, wishing to be numb, Sarah stepped out to find a towel waiting on a hook. She dressed and walked out. Kane was waiting. Always waiting. Following her. Her shadow. Once inside, Caroga's fit of coughing pulled at Sarah. She cared for the ill woman, brought her food, and retreated to the loft.

A fitful sleep pulled her under until Kane awoke her. Another day. Trapped. "Get dressed. We're going to meet the day. Caroga has been better and there is time," he informed her. Sarah chose to follow or so she would make him believe, slipping a small paring knife in her pocket from the kitchen. Maybe there would be an opportunity to use it.

Kane was displeased as he waited for her. She could see it in the darkness in his eyes, hear it in his sharp tone. She dressed quickly and stepped outside. It was still dark, the night on the brink of giving in to the dawn. The air nipped, creeping up under Sarah's clothes , a reminder that winter approached.

How could she survive the time of ice and snow, trapped alone with Kane?

The sunrise on the mountain was nothing short of amazing. Sarah itched for a camera to add it to Lila's photo album, another "sunny-up." A new beginning and a hope, not a sundown and close of another day. They walked for a long time. The glory of the trees in full autumn regalia, the escape from four restricting walls, and the quiet was a balm. Maybe today would be the day that she could make a break for it. Take him by surprise, plunge the knife in his heart, but what of Caroga? Sarah didn't even know the way back.

Kane was unsettled. His eyes darted from side to side, he kept looking behind him, and did not linger. Usually, they would amble with pauses for wildlife lessons or to watch the world go by. Today, he was on edge. A chink in his armor?

The forest gave way to a lake on a quiet, isolated patch of land, the view of the surroundings blocked by trees. Kane gestured to a stone by the shore and went about the business of making fishing poles. He handed one to Sarah and found his own spot, keeping to himself and leaving her to her thoughts. Memories of camping with Lila and Graham washed over her like the waves lapping against the shore.

The campfire flickered on Lila's face, her daughter tucked in under Graham's arm while he helped her to build a s'more. "Crackers, it's all sticky!" The little girl squealed as he licked his finger after wiping marshmallow from her cheek.

She took another bite, scattering crumbs all over his lap and christening him with her newfound nickname.

"They're supposed to be messy. That's what makes them taste good." He grinned and lifted his chin toward Sarah. "What about you, Mom? The S'More Shop is still open. We make the best, don't we Lila?" He gave her a little tickle and had her belly laughing.

Watching him with Lila, seeing those green eyes shimmering in the flames did something to Sarah's inside, something good, long missed since Lee's passing. They held promise like finding precious stones at the bottom of a stream.

She shook her head and lifted her hot dog on a stick out of the flames. "No thank you. I'm still working on my dog, diggity dog."

After the fire died down, Graham made a quick patrol of the perimeter before making sure they were all tucked in. He laid down in his sleeping bag across the doorway to provide a sense of security. Sarah couldn't fall asleep right away. She lay awake, listening to the sounds of the woods and animals at night.

It was a sweet comfort to have Lila by her side with her feather breath brushing Sarah's cheek and her little hand resting on her mother's neck. Knowing that Graham was there, sure, steady and strong like the mountains around them, lit

Sarah with a warm glow. She could hear the sound of his breathing, soft and regular. "Good night, Crackers," she whispered softly. She drifted off with him on her mind, her last thought of the night.

The sun was reaching in through the open windows and laughter slipped in with it. It was a blend of fairy notes and deep, low tones. Sarah stood and looked outside. Graham and Lila were at the bottom of a slope, standing on the shore of Pine Lake with homemade fishing lines. Lila had a little sunny spinning in the sunlight. Sarah nearly had to close her eyes, blinded by the light on her daughter's face and it's reflection in Graham's.

"Sarah! Come down here and get a picture of this prize catch. I think it's a record breaker!" Graham had caught sight of her standing in the window and waved to her.

Shrugging into a sweatshirt and pulling her hair up in a ponytail, Sarah grabbed her camera and picked her way down to the fisherman and girl. "Oh my, Lila! What will you do with such a fine sunfish?"

She gave her daughter a hug and knelt down to get a picture of the twosome side by side. Lila's grin was wide enough to split her cheeks and Graham's wasn't far behind. She took the picture and Graham offered her a hand up, sending a thrill running straight to her heart. They stared into each other's eyes and it was suddenly hard to breathe.

The edge. She had been standing on it, her back against a sheer, wall of rock since Kane stole her life. There was no way to reach the top, the bottom was too far. Sarah felt as if she was about to go over when a rope was tossed her way. Young voices. Nervous laughter. The crunching of leaves, unbelievably loud in the quiet of the forest. Two teenagers rounded a bend, relief blooming on their faces.

"Thank God! We are so lost! Can you tell us how to get to the Pine Lake campsites? We left there this morning and got all turned around." The boy could have been a young Graham, dark and sincere.

Sarah felt Kane's hold on her arm tighten, the message clear; she would regret it if she spoke out. Her heart pounded. *Now! Jab him in the arm, make him let go and run to them, tell them!* His fingernails dug into her skin and she lost her courage. Besides, he might hurt them. There was no way he'd meekly let them all walk off into the sunset.

Kane sent them on their way, making haste to get home and Sarah nearly went over the brink. Had to hold on, just a little longer. He had brought her to Pine Lake! A place she knew, so close…close to Graham and home! Hope burned bright. Escape. It could be done, but when?

13

GRAHAM HAD JUST STEPPED OUT OF THE SHOWER when the phone rang. He wrapped a towel around his waist and left a trail of footprints on his way to the living room. A chill set his body to trembling as he picked up the phone, rivulets of water running down his neck from a tangle of wet hair. "Graham here."

"Hey, buddy, listen, I pulled a guy over on Main Street around midnight because he was driving erratically, all over the place. I figured it was a typical DWI. When I opened the door, the stench of alcohol just about wrapped it up until I had him get out of the car. He had a bloody pocket knife, plus blood on his shirt." Jim Pedersen was short of breath, his words almost incomprehensible in his rush to spit them out.

An icy prickling rippled down Graham's spine. "So, what does that have to do with me? I know it's rare to have some excitement for you guys in town, but couldn't this have waited until later? We could have had a beer or something." He was starting to shake in earnest. *Clothes would be nice right about now.*

"Graham, he had blonde hair on his clothes and he said something about a girl, that he didn't mean it. They didn't get anywhere with an interrogation because the guy was so drunk.

Nothing he said made any sense. Gibberish, that was it. He's just coming around after sleeping it off and we'll try again. I thought you might want to come in and see him."

Graham had to sit down, his legs suddenly gone weak. He propped his head on his hand and willed his heart to stop racing. "I'm getting dressed and I'll be right down. Thanks for calling, Pete."

He disconnected and sat very still. What if this was it, the end of the line? Nearly seven months of desperate searching could all come down to one drunk. "No, I don't believe it. I would know if something happened to her, I would feel it." He spoke out loud, practically shouted the words in an attempt to find his conviction. He dressed, downed a cup of coffee with a hand that still trembled, and climbed into his truck.

Graham couldn't remember the ride to Johnstown or how he got there, only that he prayed fervently the entire time. Lost in his own thoughts and attempting to avoid the darker places in his mind, it was like coming out of a fog when he pulled into the parking lot at City Hall on Main Street. The moment he stepped out of his truck, his legs were like jelly. He had to lean up against the side of his vehicle. He steeled himself and pushed off.

Jim stepped forward the moment he entered the station and gripped Graham's arm, outwardly calm. He had his poker face on. "Come on in here. We've got a two-way mirror and you can listen in. Don't get your hopes up. The guy's a mess. His name is John Roberts. I ran a check and he's clean. We've sent the evidence off to the forensics lab in Albany and they're putting a rush on it. Until then, trying to get something—anything—out of him is all we can do."

His friend gestured to a small room with a table and chairs against the wall. A large window allowed them to watch the unfolding scene in the interrogation room. Graham sat down and leaned on the sill, intent on the suspect and officer engaged in questioning. A cold sweat popped up on his forehead and it was a wonder everyone couldn't hear the thundering of his heart while he waited to find out if Sarah…He couldn't even finish the sentence in his mind.

An officer sat on one side of a table while a disheveled man sat on the other. The latter's dark hair was greasy and unkempt, stubble covered his face, and his clothes were rumpled. There were dark, rust-colored stains on his shirt. Graham's eyes were repeatedly drawn back to them.

The suspect was clearly agitated. He kept running his hands through his hair and he was crying. "I'm telling you, I don't know what happened. I was drunk, so damned drunk. I can't remember anything." He broke off, incoherent, and mopped at red-rimmed, bloodshot eyes.

The officer, Clark Matthews, was also chief of police and presided over the most serious cases. This one would be going beyond local jurisdiction. He would do his part to lay the groundwork. A member of the force for twenty five years, he tolerated no nonsense as was clear in his demeanor. A snowy crew-cut, clean-shaven jaw, and stern eyes of a stormy gray were an outward representation of his authority.

He used the weight of experience and his manner to bear down on their suspect. "You were well over the legal limit of alcohol in your blood. That is the least of your worries. Tell me about the blood and the blonde hair. Someone else was in the car with you. Who was it, John?"

The man appeared to crack with the chief's words and his face caved in. "I…I don't know! She never told me her name! I didn't mean to hurt her! Oh God!" He covered his face with his hands and great sobs shook his body.

Graham's palms begin to sweat and he wiped them on his legs. Suddenly light headed, he gripped his knees and dug his nails in. *Breathe in…breathe out.* Whatever the outcome, he needed to see this through. This could mean the end of the road…for Graham or for someone else waiting for a loved one to come home.

Officer Matthews bided his time until Roberts began to settle down. When the crying quieted, he spoke in a low, soothing voice. "I know you didn't mean it, John. Let's go back to the beginning. What were you doing earlier in the evening before we pulled you over?"

Roberts leaned on the table, his hands threaded in his hair, his breathing ragged. "I was out…at a bar, just into Dolgeville…I don't remember what it's called. I had a few and then I got in the car. I pulled out and I was still thirsty so I grabbed my bottle of whiskey in the back seat. I had just taken a good swallow when I saw a girl walking along side of the road. She had her thumb out so I stopped." His jaw started to quiver and he swallowed hard. "You don't think I could have something to drink, do you? I'm still really thirsty."

Officer Matthews signaled to another officer standing guard by the door. A moment later, a steaming cup was placed on the table. The chief slid it in front of Roberts and straightened in his chair. "Take a moment and pick up where you left off when you're ready."

If only he would get it over with! Graham closed his eyes and fought a wave of nausea that hit when his mind turned to the girl. Who was she? Was it Caroline Richards? Dolgeville was a long stretch from Old Forge. He didn't believe it was Sarah. She would never hitch a ride because it was too dangerous. But the nagging question, "*What if?*" had Graham on the edge of his seat, ready to jump out of his skin.

Roberts took a big gulp of coffee then let his breath out slowly. He started to rub at his legs and the words came tumbling out. "I opened the door and asked her where she was going. She told me she didn't care as long as it was away. I offered her my bottle and she drank some. There wasn't much left and we finished it off in no time. I drove up to the liquor store on Main Street here in town and bought some more and we kept drinking. She was really loose, laughing and then she was crying, going on about getting out of here. She was acting kind of crazy, you know what I mean? I don't know how long we drove. It's all mixed up, like a dream. Maybe it was a dream…I wish it was a dream!"

He stopped and his fist came down on the table, making the coffee splash over the side. A shaky breath later and the words tumbled off of his tongue. "She had to go to the bathroom and we were way out with only the woods so I stopped. I walked in with her. I didn't want to leave her out there alone in the dark, you know? I turned around to give her privacy. When she was done, I tried to put my arm around her." His face turned red and anger laced his tone. He sipped at coffee to calm himself.

"What happened when you tried to put your arm around her, John?" Officer Clark's voice was steady and calm, betraying no emotion. He could have been asking his suspect to tell him a bedtime story. He took a swallow of ice water and waited several seconds before trying again. "Tell me, John. What happened next?"

The other man's eyes narrowed and his hand shook, forcing him to set the coffee cup down as his jaw tightened. "She pulled away from me and looked at me like I was a scumbag or something. I hadn't done nothing to deserve that! I was good enough for a ride and for some booze, but not to touch her. I took out my pocket knife…I just wanted to scare her." He broke off, visibly shaken. What little color he had drained from his face and he picked up the coffee cup again only to spill it all over his lap.

"What happened when you tried to scare her, John? Think about it carefully." Officer Clark leaned on the table, the picture of calm. Graham knew he had to be seething underneath that composed exterior.

"She ran away from me and then she tripped. I pulled her up to her feet and she fought to get away from me…and then…and then…she fell…on the knife. Dear God….I didn't mean to do it….there was so much blood…I got back in the car…I had to find…the police station…get help….I drank some more…to steady my nerves, but I couldn't forget the blood…God, my ex-wife told me drinking would get me in trouble. I didn't mean it!" His head fell into his hands and he was sobbing inconsolably.

In the adjoining room, a chair crashed to the floor in Graham's haste to get to his feet. Back and forth, back and forth, he crossed the small room while his heart raced. If he didn't keep moving, he was going to go in that room, put his hands on that man, do the unthinkable. At any moment he could explode with the questions crashing inside his head.

Jim tried to prevent a meltdown. "We don't know who it is, Graham. Maybe it's a runaway teen or a housewife who had enough. There's a chance it's Caroline Richards. It could be anyone."

"But it could be Sarah. No matter who it is, Pete, there's a girl out there who's been hurt. We have to do something about this and the guy's giving us nothing!" Graham broke off and stood still when he heard steel in the police chief's next words to his suspect in the next room.

Clark Matthews had moved to the other side of the table and was now beside John Roberts. The chief leaned forward with his elbows propped on his knees and locked his gray eyes on the cowering man beside him with an intensity that would have quelled most.

"John, this is very important. I need you to tell me where you left the girl. We still may be able to help her and you can avoid a murder charge. Where is she?" His voice had dropped down low and was hushed, intimidating as it pressed down on the alcohol-impaired man sitting beside him.

Roberts shook his head from side to side and dropped his face into crossed arms on the table. "I don't know! I drank so damn much that I don't remember where I went. I just know there were woods, nothing else. I'm sorry! I'm so sorry! I didn't mean to hurt her! You've got to believe me!" He continued to cry like the broken-hearted. They would be getting nothing more for the time being. Officer Matthews glanced at the two-way mirror and shook his head.

"I need to get some air." Graham bit the words off and stepped out of the room, intent on making it outside before he lost it. He hit the door and took in great gulps of a cool gust of wind. Fearing his legs wouldn't hold, he leaned against the sturdy brick wall and braced his hands on his knees before he folded.

Jim was not far behind, accompanied by his police chief. He spoke with Officer Matthews in hushed tones. The older man waited, allowing his officer to join his best friend. "Are you all right? What can I do? What do you need?"

Graham straightened and did what he always did—pulled it together. "I need to put together a search team." He nodded to the chief who was immediately at their side. "Clark, I need your help. Call your people and I'll get in touch with mine. Let's meet in a half hour at the Fulton County Sheriff's Department. Daybreak's coming and we need to get a move on. She's out there, she's been hurt, and there's the slightest chance she's alive." If there was one thing Graham could do, he could search. It was about the only thing he had left in him.

With the first rays of dawn creeping over the horizon, teams headed out in all directions. Some hit the arterial, heading both ways, others were on 67, while other crews split up either west or east on 29. Graham chose the stretch of forest between Dolgeville and Oppenheim, as good a guess as any and the place where John Roberts began his night. Perhaps he ended it there as well.

Several other conservation officers and state troopers fanned out on both sides of the road with Graham trudging ahead in the lead. He was trapped in a nightmare that would not end, the same scene looping repeatedly. The hours crawled by, the air grew colder with a wind that bit at their skin and hinted of snow. Darkness fell and Graham continued, pushing on until he could do no more for the night. He'd been awake and on edge since about four in the morning. It was nearly eleven when he made it home and dropped in to bed with his clothes on. He was out when his head hit the pillow.

SOMEWHERE ON THE EDGE OF CONSCIOUSNESS, a loud banging pestered Graham. It was accompanied by insistent shouting. He drifted in a sleep-induced fog, trying to make sense of his dream because all of that racket had to be a dream. He cracked an eye open. The noise didn't go away.

It was just past midnight. Lucky him, he'd been granted an hour's worth of rest. What couldn't wait until morning? His stomach protested from lack of sleep and his head throbbed. As for his body, it had forgotten how to cooperate and wouldn't even move. A few more minutes, that was all he needed. His eyes drooped shut and he started to go under again.

"Scottie! Open up! It's Pete! I've got to talk to you!" Jim stood at the front door and used his best, crowd-control voice. "Come on, *come on*, Graham. Get up!"

"What the hell is going on?" Graham growled as he yanked the door open, squinting when the outdoor light hit. "You couldn't come see me in the morning? I've been in bed for about an hour and I'm whipped. What's so damned important?" Something he saw in Jim's eyes stopped him cold. His body went weak, a chill washing over him. "What is it, Pete?"

Jim motioned to his cruiser. "Get in and I'll tell you while we're on the way." He hurried back to the car and sat in the driver's seat.

Graham stood in the doorway, frozen. If he didn't move, it wouldn't be real. He wanted to close the door, go back to bed, shut out the world. He did none of those things.

Instead, he inhaled deeply, let it out, and gently closed the door behind him. He walked around to the passenger side and sank down into the seat, pulling the door shut with a bang that was loud in its finality. "What did they find?"

Jim stared at the steering wheel, his knuckles white. "They found a girl, Graham, about a half hour ago. It was too late. She's dead. They haven't identified her yet." He didn't lift his head and his voice went hoarse.

Graham stared at his friend hard enough to burn holes through his clothes until he could find his voice, marveling that it was steady. "Where is she, Jim?" His gaze was unwavering while he hung by a thread of nerves for an answer that somehow he already knew. "Tell me."

Jim spoke in practically a whisper. "Rockwood."

Graham braced his hands against the dashboard and sucked in air because all of the sudden it was hard to breathe. "Take me there."

He closed his eyes. It didn't help to shut out his imaginings. Time to face whatever truth was out there. After all of the heartache, the desperation, the endless searching, it could all be over tonight. Graham started to pray on a twenty minute drive that was over in a blink.

Police cars and EMT vehicles swarmed the parking area at the Rockwood State Forest. Blue, red and white lights flashed, officers milled about, and a news crew was on the scene. The car rolled to a stop and Graham stared straight ahead, unmoving.

"You don't have to do this now. It can wait until she's at the coroner's. Buy yourself a little more time." Jim gripped his arm. "You can take as long you need. You don't have to go in there at all. Let someone else take this on."

Graham pulled away and opened the door, following the flow of people traveling through the main entrance into the woods. Jim flanked him and did not break stride. The further they walked, the more Graham's soul sank. Roberts said the girl with him had needed to go to the bathroom. They would have stayed on the fringe of the forest… unless she ran. The further they went in, the more unbelievable Roberts' story became.

It felt like an eternity had passed, taking them deep into the forest's heart when the night exploded with floodlights, a crowd of people doing the painstaking job of collecting evidence around an area cordoned off with yellow, caution tape. Graham's feet wouldn't move forward and the beat of his heart became sluggishly slow. Pain streaked through his chest. Maybe he would have a heart attack and save himself the trouble.

In the middle of the commotion, lying still in a sprawl across a carpet of leaves, was the body of a girl. Her face was turned away, but a spill of blonde hair flowed into the flaming yellows and oranges that surrounded her. Jim held onto Graham's arm, a source of comfort and strength.

Graham took one, deep breath, counted to ten, let it out. His feet went back into motion, carried him under the tape, closer. He nodded to the medical examiner collecting data. "Can you turn her over, please?"

The examiner nodded and set his logbook down. Gently, as if handling something incredibly fragile, he slowly rolled the body over until her face was tipped to the sky, empty, blue eyes staring without life. Graham heard the blood rushing in his ears and his heart kicked into gear, thudding hard enough to hurt.

The face. It was so like his Sarah's. For one agonizing instant, he thought it was her. A quick scan of her body revealed something that did not belong—a heart tattoo on her bare shoulder.

After the initial shock, there were other small differences as well. He nodded once to the man at his side and stumbled away from the lights and watchful eyes. In the cover of darkness, his legs gave out and he began to heave, his body shaking.

Jim clamped a hand on Graham's shoulder to steady both men. "Hang in there, Graham. Easy, buddy, easy. It's not her. You know it's not Sarah."

The heaving stopped, but the shudders didn't and sobbing took over next. "God help me, I thought…at first…she looked just like Sarah and God forgive me, I'm…glad…it's not her." Graham let the weeping have him until all that remained was an empty shell, brittle enough to shatter at the slightest touch.

Jim waited, patient as the mountains, until Graham's breathing slowed and the tremors stopped running through his frame. It was as if all the strength had bled out of him. He was very still, kneeling on the ground with his forehead pressed to the cool forest floor. "Can you stand? I want to get you out of here."

Graham nodded and pushed himself up off the ground, let Jim help him to his feet, and leaned on him on the way out. Stumbling like a drunken man, his thinking process wasn't much better. Everything was a jumble with flashes of Sarah, Caroline Richards, and Caroline's mother colliding in his mind.

Caroline slept behind him on the forest floor and he had failed her. What about her mother? He made it to the car and dropped in the seat. Had to shut down for a little while. "Take me home...please."

Jim started the car and pulled out without a word. He glanced from time to time at his friend beside him on the drive back to Pleasant Lake. Graham stared blindly straight ahead, a fine tremor running through his frame. They arrived at the cabin without mishap. Jim got out of the car, walked around to the passenger door, and offered a hand. Graham brushed it aside.

Twenty steps. That was all it took to reach his front door. He counted them on the way. It helped him to make it that far. Graham turned and slung an arm around Jim's shoulders. "Thanks, Pete, for being there again. I don't even know how many I owe you." He felt a pat on the back on his way in the door, staggered to his room, and fell into bed. He knew no more.

14

SLEEP DIDN'T LAST. IT NEVER DID. The dreaming took him, back to the vivid scene in Rockwood from a few hours ago, only this time the girl lying on the forest floor was his Sarah. "Stop! Please, God, make it stop!" Graham shouted as he sat up in bed and tugged and scraped his hands across his face.

Why couldn't it let him go for the last few scraps of darkness? Was that really too much to ask? He stretched out once more, buried his face in the pillows, and pulled the covers up. It was pointless. Sleep would not come for him. He looked out the window, saw the horizon begin to catch fire, and watched the clock. Six o'clock. Might as well get up.

The shower scalded Graham's skin, yet wasn't hot enough to reduce his memory to cinders. His mind would not quiet until he took care of his responsibility for the day. Swiping at the steam on the mirror, he stared into the face of a stranger. *Who am I kidding? There will be no rest until I find Sarah.*

The coffee, while as strong as he could swallow, was unable to take away his bitterness. Searching through the laundry for clean clothes might give a fresh, outward appearance. That didn't make wearing the uniform any easier.

Graham had a duty to a mother whose daughter would never come home.

The road couldn't stretch long enough that morning. With each passing mile, clouds gathered and thickened in accordance with Graham's mood. The day grew dark. The highway was clear, allowing time to pass quickly, and all too soon, he was parked in front of Barbara Richards' home.

Graham stepped out of his truck and the sky opened up as if in mourning, pouring fat, cold drops on his head. A quick glance at his cell phone confirmed that it was 8:30. The date jarred him, something important about today, something with Lila at school…a Thank You Luncheon.

His eyes slammed shut and he leaned up against his truck, hopeless and helpless to stop his life from spinning out of control. Letting Lila down was the worst, but he barely had a grip on himself. One wrong move and it would be over. Cursing life in general, Graham dialed the Andersons' phone number.

"Hello, Graham. How are you this morning?" Sally's voice reached out to him. It always managed to soothe, something cool pressing on a burning hurt. Graham shied away from its touch. He didn't deserve it.

"Good morning, Sally. I'm not so hot actually. I'm really sorry. I won't be able to make it to lunch today. I had a really rough night; they found Caroline Richards and I'm in Old Forge now. I have to go talk to her mother." His voice shook and he could kick himself for that too. *Sally doesn't need your problems. She's got enough on her own plate.*

"They found her... Did it...did everything turn out as you hoped?" Sally's voice trembled slightly and then there was silence. He could picture her standing there, holding on to hope. This search had hit home for the Andersons. What happened to Caroline could happen to Sarah.

Graham cleared his throat. He couldn't lie. They would see the news all too soon. "No, Sally, I'm sorry to say it didn't go well. That's why I'm here and I don't know how long I'll be. Once I'm through here I think that it will be it for me. I'm really done in."

Water ran in rivulets down his face and neck. A chill had come over him, causing a fine shiver to run through his frame. He waited and heard sniffles, a soft sighing. When would it stop?

"I understand, Graham. You take care of yourself." The phone disconnected.

It took time to collect himself, gather his nerve, walk down the path. It was raining in torrents, drenching him, yet his feet dragged. He stared at the heavy oak door, miserable. His hair pressed against his head, water ran down beneath his collar, and his clothes stuck to his skin. He raised a hand to knock when the door opened, catching him off guard.

Barbara Richards took one look at the disheveled officer on her doorstep and wrapped her arms around him. "Thank you. You didn't have to come. They've already told me…it's over." Her voice broke and her body began to shake with her sobs.

Graham's arms came up around her with a will of their own and he could swear his heart split down the middle. His throat filled and he did not trust himself to speak, not yet. He waited it out and held on tightly to the quaking woman in his arms.

He dug down deep and searched for something to say, some small comfort. "I…had to come." He cleared his throat and continued. "I thought you'd want to know something. I listened to the suspect during questioning, the one who picked up Caroline, and I don't think he ever meant to hurt her. I truly believe it was an accident. It's little consolation. Everyone worked hard to find her and we deeply regret the outcome." His voice died out at the end.

Mrs. Richards pulled back and laid a hand on Graham's cheek. "I know you did your best. Every day, I'll pray that you and Sarah get your happy ending. Now if you'll excuse me, I really need to go lie down. Thank you again for coming to see me. It means a great deal to me." She gave him a quick hug and slipped inside.

Graham stood on the steps in the rain. His body would not stop shaking. Time to move on. He climbed back into his truck, cranked the heat, and began to drive. There was no particular destination in mind. No searching. Shaken to the core by Caroline Richards' death, he couldn't take any more, not today.

The rain picked up in intensity, cutting down visibility to the point of having to pull off to the side of the road several times. It didn't matter. There were no urgent calls to the wilderness. Caroline's case had come to a close. As for Sarah, the trail had been cold for too long. People had given up. Graham leaned his head back against the headrest and listened to the hammering of the rain on the roof with his eyes closed. Despair rolled over him, heavy enough to drag him down and keep him down.

There was lull in the storm and an eerie silence. The only sound, his harsh breathing filling the cab of the truck. Who knew how long the reprieve would last? With a sigh, Graham returned to the road. Over an hour passed and brought him to the cemetery in Ephratah. It was small and quaint, a place where generation after generation slept on a hillside beneath a canopy of trees. No one else was there in that tranquil setting. It brought no peace.

Graham wiped palms that had become sweaty on his pants and climbed out. His father's stone, a simple slab of granite with the words 'Beloved father and husband,' was sheltered beneath an old oak, glorious in a burst of yellow. He did not like coming here. It did not comfort. This place was only a morbid reminder that his father, his rock and foundation, was no more. But right now, he sought something, anything, to help pull him through.

The ground was wet from the storm and a bitter wind swept around the stones, strong enough to send leaves skittering along the path and make him stumble. Oblivious of the dampness and the dirt, Graham sank to his knees in front of his father's grave. He reached up and traced the letters and the dates. The barely healed crack in his heart grew wider.

"Dad, I know it's been a while. I'm sorry. I've had a lot on my mind and I don't deal well with being here. I know you're really not here. All things considered, I'd really rather not think about graves right now." A rush of pain stopped the words, threatened to wash him away.

"If you have any pull up there, Dad, I could really use some help right now, something to keep me going. I need to know I'm doing the right thing. Give me a little light…please. I know we're supposed to be strong, even when we are tested, but Dad…I think I've been tested enough." Graham bowed his head and waited.

His cell phone vibrated in his pocket. Sally Anderson's number flashed on the screen and his heart sank with a bad feeling setting in. He cleared his throat and picked up. "Sally, what's up?"

"Graham, Lila wasn't in the cafeteria at the end of the day when it was time to pick her up and they can't find her. What are we going to do? First Sarah, now this. I can't take it if anything happens to Lila and it will kill Steve." Her voice was creeping toward hysteria.

His feet were already carrying him to the truck. The engine revved and kicked into gear. "Sally, I'm on my way. I'll meet you at the school." He hung up and glanced out the rear-view mirror at his father's headstone. "Not the answer I was looking for, Dad." The tires spun, kicking up gravel and he was back on the road.

It was time to shove down the panic and drive—fast. He punched in Jim's phone number on the way. "Hey, Pete…I'm doing. Listen, Lila's missing. Will you meet me over at the school? Right. Be there in about five minutes." He hit town doing sixty miles per hour and barely slowed at the school parking lot. A police cruiser pulled in at the same time.

"Scottie, you just can't get a break right now, can you? Bring me up to speed." Jim matched his stride with Graham's as they ate up the sidewalk with their pace. Graham could come unglued at any moment.

"Lila wasn't in the cafeteria at the end of the day when it was time to pick her up and they don't know where she is." Graham spoke between clenched teeth. Angry, God he was angry at the hand fate kept dealing. Had he wronged someone in another life? It seemed the only logical explanation for such a debt to pay.

Sally and Mr. Vicenza were waiting in the lobby; both looked relieved at the arrival of reinforcements. Graham gathered Sally in and held on tight. She was trembling as he met the principal's gaze. "Where are we right now?"

"We've searched the building several times. No luck yet. She is so little that it's possible we've missed her." The words hung unspoken in the air, *"And it's possible she isn't here."* Mr. Vicenza was clearly shaken. He had never lost a child in a lengthy and colorful career. Now was not the time to start and definitely not with this child.

Jim gave a curt nod. "All right, here's what we'll do. I'm going to hit each classroom, tell all the teachers and any other staff to do another search. Is it all right with you if I have your secretary make an announcement on the loudspeaker?" At a nod of approval, he was off without further discussion.

Graham stood still, forehead creased in thought. "What about the playground? Has anyone checked outside? Also, did you call her classmates? She might have walked home with one of the other children." Possibilities and nightmares—a vivid imagination, strained to the limit—brought up a flood of scenarios.

Mr. Vicenza nodded to each proposal. "Yes, the custodians have been over the grounds and my secretary is calling through the entire list of students in her class. We've had nothing yet."

Graham turned to Sally and put an arm around her shoulders. "What about the house? Did you look there? She might have slipped out and gone to the wood shop or in her room." He could see her wilt and the tears welling up.

"I…I didn't because I didn't want to alarm Steve. He's taking his afternoon nap and doesn't even know about any of this yet. I guess I had better." Her jaw trembled and Graham could feel her shaking harder.

He gave her a light kiss on the forehead and spoke with a confidence he did not feel, hoping his green eyes were tranquil for Sally. "It's going to be all right. She hasn't gone far, I'm sure of it. Go on home, try not to wake Steve, and take a look around." As she turned to leave, he called after her, "And Sally, don't forget the Gingerbread Cottage." Her face went whiter, if that was possible, but she nodded and went out the door.

Graham started to pace then came to a stop. "What about the Nature Trail? I know it's closed right now, but did anyone think to look back there? Lila loves the outdoors." His heart squeezed at the thought of the little girl and all of their adventures in the woods. *Please, God, let me be right. Let her be all right. Please.*

Mr. Vicenza shook his head, dark eyes troubled. "No, I didn't consider it because it's taped off and I've been very stern with the student body that they should not go back there until the work is completed. Some areas aren't safe."

There was that feeling deep down in his gut, telling him to go to the trail. Graham turned to the principal and gave him a reassuring pat on the back. "I'll go back and check it out. I've got my cell phone if I need any assistance or find anything. Why don't you give Jim a hand in here, all right?"

Mr. Vicenza was off like a shot in his haste to help in any way while Graham hit the back door at a run. His heart began to trip and it was hard to catch his breath at the thought of yet another search. If they didn't find her…He sprinted the rest of the way.

He slowed to a walk, making a conscious effort to control his breathing, beat down the panic, and ducked under the yellow tape that formed a make-shift gate across the entrance. The sight of it brought a flash of last night's findings to his mind. Graham viciously slammed the door on that image and picked up the pace.

"Lila! Lila, it's Crackers! Honey, if you're out here, please answer me!" The sense of déjà vu was strong. Replace the name and it was back to the beginning.

Urgency, made his heart erratic, pushed him to run, cursing the thick undergrowth badly in need of thinning and trees that got in the way. The leaves rustled under his feet and he called out again. It sounded like a stampede coming through. No response.

The trail wound around a bend where planks were laid down over a swampy area. Graham pounded across the wood, his foot breaking through a weak board and sending him to his knees. He bit down on some colorful words and got up again, limping in pain from a wrenched ankle. The sun was dropping low in the sky, bringing the anxiety level to red alert.

A short distance further pulled him up short at a bridge that went to the right. All of the boards had been stripped from the bridge and only one thick beam spanned the creek. Up on a hill on the other side was an observation deck. Graham squinted, focusing on a spot under the deck. There was something bright red. What was it about the color red?

A lady bug coat, one that Sarah had picked out in the spring, was tucked in a ball in the corner. Lila, making herself very small. Graham closed his eyes for a moment, lightheaded with relief, and said a prayer of thanks before moving to the beam. "Lila, honey, stay right there. I'm coming."

His ankle throbbed, badly enough to bring tears to his eyes, and threaten his balance. He hit his knees and crawled to the other side. It wasn't dignified. Graham didn't care. He climbed the hill, his ankle fighting him every step of the way until finally he found himself beside Lila.

He sat down beside her and held out his arms. "Lila, I'm so glad you're all right, honey. You scared the dickens out of us." His voice broke and his vision blurred; she was the best thing he'd seen in a long time.

Lila climbed into his lap and began to cry. "I'm sorry, Crackers. I know I'm not supposed to come back here. I just wanted Mommy so bad!" She cried harder, taking in great big gulps between sobs and hanging on, hard. Her face was smudged with dirt, there was a tear in her tights, her pretty dress had mud stains, and the hem was wet. It had been rough going.

Graham stroked her hair and murmured reassurances, rocking her back and forth. He pulled out his cell phone and dialed Sally's cell. She picked up on the first ring. "Sally, I'm with her on the Nature Trail. She's all right, just very upset. I'll bring her out once she's calmed down. Would you please call to the school to let them know? Thanks, Sally. I know…I know…yes, she really is fine. Bye." Eyes closed, he rested his chin on Lila's golden head.

They sat that way for a long stretch, the sky turning purple, pink and red with the sundown. Eventually, Lila's crying stopped until there were only snuffles and an occasional hiccup. Her little body was limp, a warm, damp weight against Graham's chest. He brushed a strand of hair away from her face and smiled down into those big, blue eyes, so like her mother's. *Hold it together—a little bit longer. You can lose it in private.*

"So, you want to tell me about it? What happened to make you run away? Something had to make you do what you've been told you never should do." He was gentle but stern. Lila needed to understand how serious this had been.

"This afternoon…we had a thank you lunch to say thank you for the people we love because Thanksgiving is coming soon and everybody's mommies and daddies came today. Nana and Pop Pop came, but it's not the same, Crackers, it's not! Everybody else had a mommy or a daddy. Some had both and I didn't have any!" Lila's lip started to quiver and the tears were close to the surface. She stared up at him reproachfully. "I thought you'd come and surprise me."

"I'm sorry, honey, I really wish I could have come. I had to help find another girl." He held on tight to Sarah's daughter while Caroline Richards' face floated to the surface of his mind. So close…what if it had been Sarah last night? Put Lila's close call on top of everything and Graham felt weak.

She looked up at him with wide eyes, her little face too serious for a child. "Did you find her?" At Graham's nod, she hugged him tight. "I'm so glad, Crackers. That's okay you didn't come then. It's just it was so hard without you and Mommy. I saw all those mommies and daddies and I couldn't stop thinking about them all day and at the end of the day, I ran out here 'cause I thought maybe Mommy would be here. You said she could be anywhere so why not here?" Her face caved, bringing the tears with it. "But she wasn't here, Graham. When is she gonna come home?"

Graham's throat thickened as he held her. "I don't know, Lila, but I have to believe she will and you need to believe it too, with all of your heart. Keep saying to yourself, 'Mommy's coming home.' That's what I do." He gave her a shaky smile of encouragement.

Lila nodded solemnly. "All right, Crackers. If you can do it, so can I. I got thinking about something today when everybody came to school at lunchtime. Can you be my daddy since my daddy died in the war? You're like a daddy to me and I'd really like to call you Daddy and you could come to all the special things like you already do. Could you please, Graham?"

Graham's heart swelled near to bursting. Lila's request was bittersweet. It was exactly what he had dreamed of being when they became a family. "Lila, I would like nothing more but I can't be your daddy until Mommy says it's okay. As soon as I find her, I'll ask her, okay?"

This time, Lila smiled. "'Kay, Crackers. You found that other girl and you found me so I know you'll find Mommy too. Can we go home now? I'm hungry and my tummy is grumbly." She stood up and tugged on Graham's hand.

Graham took both her hands in his and held her firmly. "Yes, but one thing first. Lila, promise me you will never do such a thing again, okay? No matter how bad you feel, running away is very wrong. You worried a lot of people. Everyone at school was looking for you, Jim came from the police station, and Nana and Pop Pop were afraid. When Nana called me, it scared me so much, Lila, especially since your mommy's been gone. If anything happened to you too, I don't know what I would do. I love you so much. Even though I am not your daddy, I feel like you are mine." Unable to say more, he pulled her into a fierce hug.

Lila's voice was muffled against his chest and she was crying all over again. "I'm sorry, Crackers. I won't ever do it again. I promise, pinky swear."

Graham scooped her up and carried her out. Mr. Vicenza, Jim, and Ms. Ashley were all waiting in the gazebo beside the trail entrance. They all came forward to give Lila hugs, to laugh and cry, and touch her, reassuring themselves she was all right. It was a brief reunion. Graham had to get her home.

He held her close and wouldn't let go all the way to her grandparents' house where Sally and Steve sat on the porch steps, arms around each other. Without a word, Graham set her on their laps and stepped back. His heart was too full to speak. The fairytale ending happened—sometimes.

HE DIDN'T LINGER WITH THE ANDERSONS. Too raw, too worn down. Sally and Steve had seen the news reports. They knew Caroline Richards' fate. They didn't force the issue of making him stay. Lila was so tired, she fell asleep on the couch while the adults drank coffee.

Steve gave him a hug when Graham pushed his cup aside and stood to go. “Son, don’t give up and don’t blame yourself. I can see it in your eyes. I know you did everything you could for that girl and you have gone beyond human limits for our Sarah. Go home and get some rest. It’s got to get better. That’s what I tell myself every day.”

Graham found a ghost of a smile to hide the fact that he’d been brought down so low. This could be the day he fell apart and couldn’t pick up the pieces. He had to get out before the Andersons were subjected to that.

“Thanks, Steve. I’ll try and remember your advice. Have a good night.” He went to the couch and kissed Lila’s forehead, making her lips turn up in a little grin. He covered her with a blanket, fingers trembling, and walked to the door where Sally was waiting.

“Thank you, Graham, for always being there for this family when we need you.” She rose up on tiptoe to kiss his cheek and wrapped her arms around him.

He held himself back, couldn’t let down his guard. “If I had been here for the luncheon, none of this would have happened today.” His gaze fell on the little girl on the couch.

She looked like all was right in the world when she slept. How desperately did he want to make that true… for all of them.

Sally pulled back and put her hands on his cheeks. "Graham Scott, you look at me and you listen well. You cannot be everywhere at once. I know that you want to take care of all of us for Sarah's sake, you want to bring her home, and you wanted to save that girl. You are not Superman. You're burning the candle at both ends, young man, and you're going to put yourself out."

Graham gave her a hug and this time he didn't hold back. "Thanks, Sally. I needed a Mom talk and that was just right. Have a good night." He kissed her cheek and headed to the truck, swiping his sleeve over his eyes before he could drive.

15

"JEANIE! WE'VE GOT TO GET GOING, HONEY!" Jim stood at the bottom of the steps, arms laden with the makings for dinner. He tapped his foot and barely refrained from going upstairs and carrying his wife down.

He usually had no problem waiting on a woman. If his wife could put up with waiting for a cop to come home from each shift, Jim could be patient when she was getting ready. Not tonight. Anxiety made his blood pump harder and his heart palpitate. They had to go—*now*.

Jeanie hurried down the stairs, ready to do verbal battle with her husband. "I'm sorry! I'm already plagued with going to the bathroom a hundred times a day even though I'm barely pregnant!" She took one, good look in his eyes and held her tongue. "What is it you're not telling me?"

Jim held the door open for his wife and locked up. He didn't speak until they had pulled out of the driveway. "I just have this feeling that we have to get there, right away. I've never seen Graham the way he was last night after we saw

Caroline Richards' body. I'm really worried about him, Jeanie."

He resisted the urge to curse, gripping the steering wheel tightly while another wave of rain came crashing down. Why did Pleasant Lake have to be thirty minutes away? Urgency pressed the pedal to the floor.

GRAHAM STEPPED INTO DARKNESS. A clumsy fumbling for a light switch and his keys dropped on the table by the door. Shrugging out of his coat, the couch caught it and he wandered into the kitchen. He should have something to eat, couldn't even remember the last time he *had* eaten. A glimpse in the refrigerator proved to be fruitless; it was empty. It didn't matter. He wasn't hungry anyway.

What Graham really needed was something to make him forget it all for a little while. Beer wouldn't cut it. Dealing with a dead girl and a missing child called for something strong enough for sweet oblivion. Tucked far to the back was a bottle of unopened Southern Comfort, the sole item in his liquor cabinet. It had been a Christmas gift from someone at the Department of Environmental Conservation. Graham had been waiting for a special occasion to break it out. Or a moment of crushing weakness. He could be strong again tomorrow.

The rain resumed its drumming on the roof, pushing him to open the bottle and take a swig without the benefit of a glass. He walked to Sarah's picture and her eyes had a hold on him.

They seemed to be filled with reproach. His hand hovered in hesitation to light her candle. It hurt too much.

It had been seven months. What were the odds that Graham would ever find her? Another swallow of alcohol burned its way down to his stomach, making his head spin a little. The windowsill gave him something to steady his balance and he turned the candle on anyway. It was the only thing he'd managed to do for Sarah.

There was a rumble of thunder, lightning flashed, and raindrops bounced hard off the surface of the water until it looked as if it were raining up. The lake called to him, drawing him out onto the deck. A few more swallows propelled him onward, weaving his way down to the dock. The harsh wind caused a fit of shivering. His coat was in the house, on the couch. Graham didn't care. He really didn't care about anything at the moment.

Graham made it to the end of the dock, tipped his head back for a long gulp, and threw the half-empty bottle into the lake. He stood and stared out into the darkness, the mountains a looming shadow, still keeping their secrets. How much longer?

The road he had traveled, beginning seven months ago in Rockwood and making a full circle back again, seemed too long. He just wanted it to end. Swaying back and forth, the gloomy, cold waters were inviting. Their embrace reached out.

Hypothermia would come quickly, like going to sleep. To sleep and not dream, to let it be. To end it. Just make it stop. A moment's pause and he stepped off the edge.

The water was ice, stealing his breath, making his insides hurt. Graham let his air out in a trail of bubbles and sank down deep, praying it would be quick, when one face flashed in his mind. "*Lila*," a voice whispered.

His feet touched bottom, gave a desperate kick, and fought his way to the surface. It was too cold. His limbs didn't want to cooperate. It was a long way back to the top and Graham wasn't sure he was going to make it.

JIM STOPPED THE CAR AND JUMPED OUT. He didn't even bother with the food in his rush to get to the door. Jeanie grabbed the bags and was not far behind. He pounded until the windows rattled. There no answer. Jim peered inside.

"The light's on, but I don't see him." He suddenly became aware of his wife's heavy load. "Jeanie, you're not supposed to be carrying all of that! Give me those." He took the bags away from her and tried the doorknob. It was unlocked.

They stepped inside and Jim set things down on the kitchen counter while Jeanie walked through the house, calling Graham's name. A quick run through the rooms revealed nothing. She came back to the kitchen, hands up in confusion. "He's not here, honey. Where could he be?"

Something odd about the living room caught Jim's eye as he glanced at the picture window where Sarah's candle burned brightly. "Look, he left the front door ajar a little bit. That's strange. It's too cold to let the heat out."

He walked to the door and pulled it open, allowing them a clear view of the dock below and Graham's tall, slim figure stepping off the end. "Oh my God! He just went into the lake! Jeanie, get some blankets!"

Jim ran down the lawn, slipping and sliding on the wet grass and leaves. After a frantic scrambling across the dock, his feet pulled him up short when he came to the end. He peered into the depths of an instant twenty foot drop-off, wishing for a flashlight, when he caught a glimpse of ghostly white.

He dropped flat onto his stomach and reached into the water, almost pulling back at its frosty chill. Heart slamming against his ribcage, a bird trapped inside and smashing against a window, his hand plunged deep. Jim stretched as far as he could and fished around. He only grabbed hold of water.

"Graham, don't you dare do this to me, do you hear me?" Jim shouted and shoved his arm in again, all the way to his chest. If this didn't work, going in would be next.

There was a swish of hair like seaweed, a clammy face, and his hand hooked under Graham's shoulder. One desperate heave brought him above the surface. "Graham Dylan Scott, what the hell were you doing?" Another tug and he managed to haul his best friend up on the dock.

While Graham sputtered and coughed, Jim turned to see Jeanie standing on the deck, hugging a blanket to her middle while tears streamed down her face. He waved to her and called out weakly, "He's all right. He's a stupid idiot, but he's all right." Jim slumped down on the wood, drew his knees up to his chest and leaned his head on them. "I'm going to ask you again. What the hell were you doing?"

Graham still lay flat on his back, gasping and shaking until his teeth chattered. "I had a little too much to drink. I was trying to clear my head."

Jim clamped a hand on his best friend's shoulder and dug his fingers in, hoping it hurt. It would only be a fraction of his own hurting. "*Don't lie to me*! In all these years, we have never lied to each other. Don't start now! You were trying to kill yourself, weren't you?"

Jim's eyes were accusing, his words dagger-sharp. His chest heaved and his head pounded in rhythm with the beat of his heart. He waited for his friend to answer when all Jim wanted to do was hit him. Knock some sense into him. Shake him until his teeth rattled out of his head.

Jeanie approached Graham first, wrapping him in a blanket. His hand, as if weighed down by a stone, slowly lifted to brush her cheek, fell again. "Thank you, Jeanie-girl." She squeezed him, hard, and moved on to throw a blanket around her husband. Jim was shaking until his jaw clacked together and Jeanie wasn't far behind.

Jim kissed her cheek, maintaining self-control, barely. "Honey, why don't you go inside and warm up dinner? I need a minute with Graham. Thanks, baby." He waited until she was out of earshot. Turning back, he saw his friend still had not moved except for the tremors from the lake's bitter chill. "Graham, it's time for you to drop the search and get some help. Look at yourself, look at what almost went down tonight. If I hadn't been here, it would be over."

Graham managed to drag himself to a sitting position and look Jim in the eye. "You're right and I'll always be grateful you were here when I needed you most—again. It wasn't how it looked…I mean, it was, at first, but… then I thought of Lila and I tried to come up, honest." His head dropped onto his knees.

Jim crept over to his friend and saw how he shivered. Pity welled up, forcing him to share a blanket and wrap an arm around him. "Graham, I'm glad that you decided to come up, but what brought you to the point of going in? You have people who care about you. I know that you have been going through hell. Don't you realize we'd be going through hell if anything happened to you?" His voice choked on the last. He'd come damned close to losing his best friend tonight.

Graham leaned his head against Jim's shoulder. "I'm sorry, Pete, so sorry. I wasn't thinking. It's just been so hard…first Caroline and then Lila. It was too much. I started drinking. It messed me up. Almost the instant I hit that water, I snapped out of it, really. I won't ever be that stupid again. I promise."

Jim pressed his friend's arm. "Don't you dare, got it? You've got somewhere to turn no matter how hard it gets." They were silent a moment except for the sound of Graham's ragged breathing. "Come on into the house. Jeanie's making something good and it will warm you up."

He stood and helped Graham to his feet. When his old friend began to sway, Jim was there to catch him. The distance from the dock to the door seemed nearly insurmountable. Both men were exhausted when they crossed the threshold.

Jeanie met them at the door and gave them both a bear hug, ending with Graham. She took his face in her hands and her dark eyes lashed out. "Don't you ever pull something like that again, do you hear me? You made me ten years older and I was old enough already. Go take a hot shower before you catch pneumonia!"

Her voice was fierce enough to make him go without argument. She watched him leave and turned to join her husband leaning against the mantle, absorbing heat from the fire. Jeanie walked up behind him, her arms wrapping around his waist, and pressed her cheek to his back. A shudder ran through his frame and he turned around to lean his forehead on hers.

"He scared the hell out of me, Jeanie. If we didn't come tonight, he would have killed himself. He says it won't happen again, that he was messed up from drinking, exhausted, but I don't know if I believe him. What are we going to do?" Jim stared into his wife's eyes and waited for her to toss him a lifeline.

She kissed him and held on tight. "What we're already doing— be there for him." Jim sighed heavily and closed his eyes, letting the warmth of his wife's arms and the fire ease the cold that had nothing to do with the lake and everything to do with a near brush with death.

GRAHAM LET THE HOT WATER RAIN DOWN on his body until the last of the chill slipped out of his bones. He toweled off, then pulled on soft, flannel pajama bottoms and a heavy sweatshirt to join his friends in the kitchen. Jeanie had set the table and dished out bowls of homemade soup. Jim poured drinks while his wife placed grilled cheese sandwiches on three plates.

Graham tried for some enthusiasm, however lame the effort. "Wow, this is really nice, guys. You really didn't have to do this."

Jim pointed to a chair and stared his friend down. "Yes, we most definitely did. Sit down and start eating. A big part of your problem is you're not taking care of yourself. It sounds to me like you need a babysitter to tell you what to do. You probably haven't eaten, you aren't sleeping, you've been through a traumatic experience, and you never take time for yourself. You're getting some. *Now.*"

He sat down and ate his own meal, joined by Jeanie. It was a quiet dinner, without their normal give and take. Everyone was too shaken from the night's events.

Graham ate everything on his plate. It took only one look in Jeanie's eyes to see the flames of her temper barely banked, ready to flare at the least provocation. Add to that the fact that she was pregnant and he wasn't taking any chances. When he was done, he dropped a kiss on the top of her head.

"Jeanie-girl, that was just what I needed. A good meal goes a long way." He went to the sink, filled it, and started to wash.

Jim came up beside him and gently pushed him aside. "Don't worry about these. That's what we're here for. You go relax, all right?"

He nodded to the living room while Jeanie assisted in the clean-up efforts. They made quick work of straightening the kitchen and walked out to find Graham stretched out on the couch, on the brink of sleep.

"He's so tired. How long can he go on, Jim?" She pulled a quilt over Graham's body and tucked a pillow under his head. There was a little space by his legs, enough to sit for a moment and rest an arm on his back. She rubbed in gentle, soothing circles. A few more minutes and he'd drift away.

Jim sat down in the recliner that faced the sofa. "I don't know, I really don't, but he shouldn't be alone tonight. We should stay and keep an eye on him."

Graham cracked one eye open and spoke in a low murmur, his words slurred with fatigue. "You don't need to stay. I'm going to sleep. Scout's honor. I wasn't in my right mind for a blink earlier tonight. You helped me find my way back again. All I'm going to do is stare at the inside of my eyelids. You've already done enough. Go on home, take care of that baby on the way."

Jeanie took his hand in hers, her lips trembling. "Are you sure, Graham? We really don't mind. We'd do anything for you, you know that don't you?" She turned to Jim to back her up.

Jim knelt down by Graham's head, pressed a hand to his neck, and leaned in close. He spoke in almost a whisper. "It's no problem to stay. I'm afraid to leave you alone. I will never forget watching my best friend take the plunge into those frigid waters and never want to see such a thing again."

Graham reached out and pulled the man that was like a brother close. “I’m sure.” They didn’t give up easily but his exhaustion was convincing. After packing everything up, they headed out into the rain and Graham went to bed. Close…it had been too close tonight. If it hadn’t been for Lila, Jim, and Jeanie…they were his lifesavers. He’d been drunk. He’d nearly drowned. With a full stomach, the tide of exhaustion took him down.

That night, he dreamed… again. The images were vivid, like watching a movie. It was that last time with Sarah in Rockwood.

They were walking and Graham knew what was coming. He tried to make the time stretch, but the sun continued its relentless streak through the sky, getting closer to the horizon. He felt Sarah in his arms, solid, warm. Relived that kiss, the kind a man could die happy to have once in a lifetime. Tried to make it last, hold on, turn back the projector .

It was as if someone grabbed him by the nape of the neck, forced him to climb in the truck, and drive away. Even as his hands pounded the wheel, the truck would not turn around. The rearview mirror held Sarah’s image , the sunlight forming a fiery halo around her hair, hitting her sweater as he watched her figure recede. Her sweater…he had forgotten how bright it was, her favorite color red, like Lila’s ladybug coat.

The scene shifted. It was no longer Rockwood. Instead, he was on the fire tower on Kane Mountain. This time, it was not a replay but rather something that hadn't taken place, at least not yet. He was staring through the binoculars and he could hear the echo of Lila's voice in his mind. "Look, Crackers! There's that something red again! What is it, Crackers?"

Graham scanned the area, back and forth, turned up the intensity and saw it—a flash of red, strangely familiar, snagged in a tree. Something he'd seen before. He looked again, sharpened the focus and suddenly, it hit him—that something red belonged to Sarah, had been there, all along, waiting for him to find it.

16

LILA GOT UP WHEN THE SUN WOKE UP. It was Saturday and she had something important to do. She had to help Graham. Lila had the feeling that he was in trouble. When she looked in his eyes yesterday, it scared her because it looked like Crackers felt bad, really bad, worse than Lila felt. When he picked her up, he was shaking. From the beginning, Crackers had told Lila that she had to believe that Mommy was coming home. After seeing Graham yesterday, Lila thought that maybe he needed some help believing too.

Her jeans, flannel shirt, and boots from the pun'kin patch were waiting on the chair where Lila neatly set them. She needed work clothes for today. She got dressed, washed her face, and combed her hair. Humming all the way downstairs, Lila skipped into the kitchen and came up short to see Pop Pop getting a cup of coffee. "Pop Pop! It's early! What are you doing up already?"

Pop Pop scooped her up and gave her a hug, topped off by an Eskimo kiss with a rub of his nose. "Oh, I woke up early, sweet pea, and Nana was really tired this morning so I thought I'd let her sleep in for a change. Why are you so bright-eyed and bushy-tailed this morning?" He smiled and there was a sparkle in his eyes that Lila hadn't seen in a long time.

"I've got plans today, somefin I have to do, but first I has to make some breakfast. Do you want some breakfast with me, Pop Pop?" She leaned in really close and pressed her forehead to Pop Pop's while she waited for an answer. He just had to have breakfast with her!

"All right, Lila Ladybug. I'd love to have breakfast with you." Pop Pop laughed and it really sounded good to hear that sound again. It made Lila feel all sunny inside. He put her down and sat at the kitchen table with his cup of coffee.

Lila pulled the stepstool over to the refrigerator and took out the milk. It was really heavy and she had to use two hands. She almost dropped it. Next, she took the cereal out of the cabinet and two bowls from the dish dryer rack. She poured two great, big bowls of frosty flakes and tipped the milk jug until the cereal went all the way to the top. Then she carried a bowl to Pop Pop with her tongue between her teeth to get it there without any spills. Lila carried her bowl next. A little sloshed over the sides, but she made it and sat down next to Pop Pop. "Would you like a nanner in your cereal, Pop Pop?"

Pop Pop picked up his spoon with a smile. "No, thank you. This is perfect, just perfect." He started eating, crunching with every bite. Lila smiled back and started to eat her own cereal. They didn't have to talk. She was just happy to sit with Pop Pop.

When he was done, Lila picked up their dishes and set them in the sink. She filled it up and added soap. Pop Pop cleared his throat behind her. “Lila, thank you for breakfast. Now, what’s your plan for the day?”

Lila finished washing their dishes, wiped her hands on the dishtowel, and climbed down from her stepstool. She walked back to Pop Pop and set a hand on his knee. “Pop Pop, I need to go decorate the Gingerbread Cottage for Thanksgiving ‘cause Mommy’s coming home. Will you bring me over there, please?”

The light in Pop Pop’s eyes went away, a candle blown out. “But Lila…” He seemed to get smaller, like air going out of a balloon. He couldn’t look her in the eye and cleared his throat. Lila climbed up into his lap and turned his face her way. She stared at him, hard.

“No buts, Pop Pop. Crackers says we have to believe that Mommy’s coming home and we’re all making it pretty hard on him by making him believe all by himself. He was feeling really bad yesterday, I could tell. I think he’s getting tired of being the only one who believes. If we all believe extra hard, it will come true. I just know it, Pop Pop. B’sides, I know you go over there every day to check on things. You don’t even have to stay. What do you say, Pop Pop?” Lila took his hand and tugged on it, bringing him toward the door.

There was a big sigh that sounded like it came all the way from his toes, but Pop Pop put on his slippers and his robe, took down the house keys, and followed Lila as she scampered across the lawn to her house. It was really cold and she could see their breath making clouds in the sky like the smoke messages the Native Americans used to send. It was so cold that Lila did a little dance while waiting for Pop Pop to open the door. The moment it opened wide, she scooted up to her bedroom to see if Mommy was there. It might be like a spell in a fairytale that had finally been broken.

Mommy wasn't there. Lila checked each room. She stood in front of the mirror in her room to talk to the girl in the mirror and try to get her out. It didn't work. To really bring Mommy home, she had to do more than pretend. She had to believe, with all of her heart. She had to picture it over and over and say it too. If she was s'posed to picture Mommy coming back, what better way than to make pictures?

Lila took out her paints and started with a water color on the great big paper on the easel in her bedroom. She painted the sundown and the trees had pretty colors even though the leaves were almost gone. Next, she made Mommy and painted her favorite red sweater. She painted herself in her lady bug coat and blue jeans. She couldn't forget Graham and she put him in his conversation officer clothes because he would be wearing them when he found Mommy.

She pulled the picture down and started another. While she worked, she could hear Pop Pop poking around downstairs, turning on the faucets, flushing the toilet. He must have turned up the furnace because her room was getting nice and toasty.

The sun reached inside Lila's bedroom and stretched higher across the walls. Pictures were on her bed and all around on the floor. Next, Lila took out her crayons and did the picture in crayon. She wanted to make sure she believed in every way. She still had chalk and colored pencils to go.

"Little Ladybug, I'm going to go over to change my clothes and bring us some lunch. Don't you go anywhere!" Pop Pop called up the steps.

Lila went out to the railing to look down. "Okay. I'll be right here. I love you, Pop Pop!"

She blew him a kiss. He pretended to catch it, put it on his cheek, and blew one back. Lila went back to work. She switched to chalk and finished with colored pencils until she had used the last sheet of paper on her easel. Next, she took tape off of her desk and started hanging up her drawings. Every room in the house, every door, and every window had a picture. The last picture went over Mommy's bed.

Lila stood and stared up at her work and spoke out loud. "Mommy's coming home for Thanksgiving. Mommy's coming home for Thanksgiving. Mommy's coming home for Thanksgiving."

She clicked her heels together like Dorothy did. Lila didn't have ruby slippers on, but it couldn't hurt. She walked slowly around Mommy's room and touched her favorite things like her jewelry box, her china doll in the rocking chair, and a picture of the two of them nose to nose with their eyes closed when Lila was a baby. Lila went to the closet next and pressed her nose to Mommy's clothes. They smelled just like her.

"Mommy's coming home for Thanksgiving! Mommy's coming home for Thanksgiving!" She said it really loud because she was sure that would help make it come true.

Lila turned to step out of the closet and there was Mommy's red bathrobe hanging on the door. It was thick, fuzzy, and really warm. A lot of times after a bath, Mommy would let Lila step in next to her and she would close her robe around both of them so they would be really cozy. Lila buried her face in it and breathed really deep. It smelled like Mommy's cuddles at bed time. She pulled the robe down and brought it over to the bed. She climbed up and hugged it close, like it was Mommy, and put her nose right in it.

"Mommy's coming home for Thanksgiving," she whispered and closed her eyes. It almost felt like Mommy was really there when Lila fell asleep.

STEVE STEPPED BACK INSIDE the Gingerbread Cottage and pushed the door shut, shivering with a blast of November air that followed him in. Winter would be here soon, a thought that depressed him more with each passing day. He couldn't stand the thought of his girl being out there in the cold.

He tried to shake off the gloom that was never too far away and went to the kitchen table. It was a bright, sunny place, like his daughter. He set out lunch and dropped into a chair. Pressing his forehead to clasped hands, Steve prayed because it was the only thing left to do. "Please, God, bring this trial to an end. If not for my sake, then for the sake of a mother and a daughter, please bring our Sarah home."

He didn't know how much time went by. Eventually he stood and wiped the tears away. A cold drink of water came next although Steve wanted something stronger. He stood very still and listened intently. That was strange. There was no sound from upstairs. Earlier, there had been papers rustling, the tap of little footsteps, humming. Now there was nothing.

His heart began to flutter painfully and he rushed from the kitchen. "Lila! Are you all right, Ladybug?"

He took the steps two at a time, his gaze falling on the pictures that lined the wall on the way up. There were more pictures on each door and in every room, but no Lila. He was short of breath and on the brink of a full-blown panic attack when he opened Sarah's bedroom. The tears came back at the sight before him. Curled up in a little ball, clinging to her mother's robe, Lila slept with a giant poster above her head. Three smiling faces that belonged to Sarah, Graham, and his granddaughter, beamed over her like a blessing.

Steve made his way to the bed on shaky legs that barely held. He stretched out across from his little slip of sunshine and reached out to touch Sarah's bathrobe. It was warm and soft, like his daughter. He rested a hand on Lila and her little mouth tipped up at the corners, making his heart smile. His eyes drooped shut and he caught his breath again. Why not take a rest for a piece and leave the world outside?

GRAHAM SHOT UP STRAIGHT IN BED, wide awake, breathing hard like he'd been running. Jerked from a solid sleep, he felt like he'd taken another dip in the frigid water of Pleasant Lake. His hair was dripping with a cold sweat and he was shaking. His dreams were still with him and had not faded with waking. If anything, they were clearer.

The flash of red on Kane Mountain and Sarah's sweater! It was not a coincidence. There was a reason that Kane Mountain kept rearing up, calling him to make the climb again. It held the answers. He and Lila had been given the key, back in the summer soon after Sarah vanished. It was simply a matter of finding it again to unlock the secret.

He sprang out of bed. Filled with a nervous energy, he could not be still. It was only three o'clock. He needed daylight to follow his lead. There was no way Graham was going back to sleep, no sitting around, waiting.

A glance out the window showed the first snow of the season had fallen in the wee hours of the morning. It didn't stick to the road. He pulled on sweats and a heavy sweatshirt, a knit cap, and hit the door. Time for a run.

Graham's feet pounded the pavement and the words, *Kane Mountain*, repeated themselves in his mind with every step. A shower followed his run, so hot it could have peeled the skin off of his body. He didn't feel it, too mired in a maze of thought. He dressed carefully, in layers, making a point of wearing his uniform.

It would be official business today. He took out his pack and ran through a thorough checklist. Cuffs. Ammunition. Flares. A first aid kit. Rations of food. Water. Satisfied, he took one sweep of the cabin and headed out the door.

Sunrise was getting closer, but not close enough. He drove to the Pine Tree Rifle Club to kill some time, shooting repeatedly at the same holes in his target. There were no distractions. He didn't even hear anyone else come in as he aimed with deliberation and fired. Bull's eye, right between the eyes.

"YOU'RE HERE AWFULLY EARLY, AREN'T YOU?" Jim called out as soon as his friend emptied his clip. He stepped up. Stared. Graham had fired off a hell of a lot of rounds; Jim had watched.

There were three, focal points on the poster that held the shadow of a man: the forehead, between the eyes, and in the chest. No shots strayed from those targets. Graham had become a true marksman. His accuracy made the hair stand up on Jim's neck.

Graham reloaded his weapon, set the safety, and put it in his holster. "I've got to go."

He pulled on his coat and headed for the door. Once outside, he flipped up his collar against the bitter fingers of air that ran across his neck. His stride didn't break until he hit his truck.

Jim followed close behind, shivering as soon as they met that nasty chill. "Whoa, whoa, whoa. Where are you going? It's five in the morning. How about a cup of coffee before you go back into the woods?" It was a Catch-22, a combination of relief to see Graham out and about and a lack of trust born from a duel with the icy waters of the lake.

Graham was in the truck and had the motor running. "I don't have time this morning. As soon as there's first light, I'm going in. I'll have to take a rain check. Have a good one, Pete. I'll talk to you later." He started to pull his door shut when Jim braced his arm against it.

"At least tell me where you're going. I'm sorry, Scottie, but after last night I'm worried about you. You scared the hell out of Jeanie…and me. Neither of us barely slept. All things considered, I think you owe me an explanation about what you're up to today." The heat in Graham's gaze nearly burned him down to the ground.

"I'm on my way to Kane Mountain. I've got a hunch. I have to check it out and it's got to be now before it's too late. I'll keep you posted." He was curt, not wasting any more time.

Jim felt his stomach knot. He didn't know why, but he didn't like the idea of Graham going up there alone. "Wait a minute. You've already been up there several times. What's one more day? I can't get off today—they were short staffed and I'm covering for someone. Give me until tomorrow and I'll go with you. The temperature has dropped below normal, it's nasty, and the path is going to be rough after the snowfall. If you were telling anyone else what to do, you'd tell them not to go alone. Do me a favor and wait for me to come along, be your faithful sidekick."

Graham clamped his hand down hard on Jim's shoulder. He looked him in the eye so there would be no misunderstandings. "Pete, you know I'd like to have you at my side, but it has to be today. It's just a gut feeling. You're going to have to trust me on this one. You know where I'll be. I'm not going anywhere else. You can come and get me when your shift is over. I promise to be careful. I have to do this."

Jim nodded once and stepped back. "All right. I'll be there as soon as I can. Whatever you do, don't do anything stupid."

The only answer was the slamming of the door and receding taillights. Jim sat down in his cruiser and closed his eyes. "Please, God, keep an eye on him. You pulled him through last night. Please get him through today."

He started the car and pulled out. Every instinct told him to follow Graham and join him on the mountain. However, it was not an option. He had a duty to his town as well as his best friend. A drive through the immediate area was reassuring. All was as it should be. His car seemed to have a mind of his own. Next thing he knew, the cruiser pulled into his own driveway.

Jeanie was awake, watching from the kitchen window when he walked in. "What brings you here on this wintry day?" She looped her hands over his neck and gave him a kiss. Her smile was warm, but she looked tired with dark circles under her eyes.

"Just a routine patrol, Mam. I wanted to make sure all was in order. How about another one of those kisses to tide me over for a while?" He dipped his head and was rewarded.

His wife sank against Jim with a sigh. She was soft and smelled of something sweet, one of those lotions women wore to madden men. It made him want to forget about work and go back to bed. Now there were two places he'd rather be.

He gave a low groan. "Why did I decide to be noble and take someone's shift today of all days?"

Jeanie pulled back and studied her husband closely. "What's wrong? You hardly ever stop home when you're on the job."

She waited. She knew him well and had learned to be patient. He'd get around to whatever was bothering him eventually. It might be slow and painful, but she always made time for him.

"It's Graham. I saw him at the firing range. He's on his way up Kane Mountain, says he's got this hunch or something. I've got a hunch of my own and I can't shake it. He shouldn't be alone up there. He said he couldn't wait and that was that. I don't like it, Jeanie."

Jim turned away and leaned on the windowsill. His eyes turned to the backyard, staring blindly. He didn't see anything except the grim determination on Graham's face that morning.

Jeanie hugged his waist and pressed up close against her husband. "You just have to have faith. Get up there as soon as you can and in the meantime, try to keep busy. Let me make you a cup of coffee before you go." She brewed him a fresh cup, set a homemade muffin on top, and walked him to the door.

Jim reached out to cup her cheek in his hand. "Thank you, Jeanie-girl. I don't know what I would do without you. Go back to bed and try to get some sleep. I know you're worried too so I'll give you the same advice: keep the faith. I'll check in with you later." Jim stole one more kiss and headed back on the road.

LILA WOKE UP TO FIND POP POP sound asleep on Mommy's bed. He'd forgotten to take his glasses off and they were digging into his cheek. She wriggled forward and took them off. Pop Pop was nice and warm so she tucked herself in really close. She had just closed her eyes again when she felt a hand on her hair.

"Hi. Would you like some lunch, Ladybug? It's waiting on the table. I came to get you and you had turned into Goldilocks, sound asleep in Mama Bear's bed. You looked so comfortable that I had to try it and here I am, snoring away." He smiled down at her and Lila smiled up at him.

"Okay, Pop Pop. Did you see all my pictures? Do you think they look pretty?" Lila pointed to the one over her head. "This one's my favorite, but I like them all and I know that Mommy will too. I think Graham will really like it the next time he comes over." She frowned all of the sudden thinking about Graham. Her tummy felt all flip floppy and she was afraid.

Pop Pop lifted Lila's chin so that she had to look right at him. "What's the matter, Ladybug? Those eyes of yours look worried and you are too young to do the worrying. You can leave that to the grown-ups."

She slid in closer and hugged her Pop Pop really hard. "I feel bad about Graham, Pop Pop. He's working all the time and when he isn't, he's sad. I want to make him feel better. What can we do, Pop Pop?"

Pop Pop hugged her back, but not too hard. She could still breathe. "I'm sure that Graham will be all right. He's had a lot to worry about lately, Lila, but we're all here to help him feel better. He'll be back soon and you'll see for yourself."

Lila sat up with a big smile. Pop Pop knew everything! "'Kay, Pop Pop! Let's go have lunch. Piggyback!"

She waited and he put her on his back, galloping her all the way down to the kitchen. She was lucky she was still little enough for piggy back rides. They sat down and Lila ate everything on her plate. All this believing was hard work!

GRAHAM ROLLED TO A STOP in the parking area below Kane Mountain. He turned off the headlights, sat back, and waited. He was used to it. He'd done a lot of waiting these past seven months. Gradually, the sky lightened from slate to a milky gray and the first streaks of color painted the sky. They were dark, deep purples, fading to pink, and the sun was a flame on the horizon.

His feet found solid ground and his breath was caught by the dawn, splashed across the fresh snow. Amazing. Too bad he wasn't here to enjoy it.

Shoulders squared, it was time to hit the trailhead. He had made a decision on the drive. If today was a bust, he would take Pete's advice, take a break before losing his mind. If the dream was right, it would all be over soon and Graham would be normal, a conservation officer. No more, no less.

He stood at the bottom, gazing up, mind centered on the snippet of red that he and Lila had seen once before. A bright flash of color in his memory, he held on tight, not letting anything else get in the way. This was it. Time to find out.

He took a deep breath and started up a trail that had become treacherous with snow, ice, and mud. A grim smile made his face hurt. Couldn't expect it to be easy. Nothing ever was anymore.

17

KANE HATED WINTER. THE DYING SEASON. They'd buried Mama in winter…Papa the following. While it was still autumn, the bitter chill and snow were already creeping into November, a time for farewells. The geese flew overhead, filling the mornings and evenings with their raucous calls to one another, writing a "v" in the sky. The animals scurried about in a last minute flurry before the land wore its cold cloak of white. The trees were clinging to the last of their finery .

Everything was letting go. It was a reminder that all living things would go to their final sleep. He would lose Caroga soon, teetering on the edge between fall's glory and the deep freeze. There was no doubt.

The brief lull in her illness had ended. The evening he and Sarah returned from Pine Lake, the fits of coughing came back with a vengeance. He'd been up all night sitting by her bedside, waiting for the next attack to steal her away. She still held on. How much longer?

A loathing for the season had him in its grip, fearsome in its intensity, born of loneliness and isolation. Kane felt it keenly, a gaping hole that was widened by the woman who lived under his roof, but had built an unsurpassable wall around her heart. He fought his despair with a frenzy of preparations to survive being locked in ice and snow—figuratively and literally.

Long, hard, back-breaking work to tire the body and a mind that had become too busy. Felling trees. Chopping and stacking wood. Storing as much as possible. He had to do it now, get as much done before the weather turned on him. But today, everything came to a halt. The focus was on his sister.

The first rays of dawn approached. Thankfully, Caroga slept, exhausted from her horrible night. Kane pushed his way outside into the crisp morning air. He had to escape the truth that stared at him with hollow eyes and sharp cheekbones from his sister's pillow all night long.

He walked around the cabin. Repairs needed to be made, shutters replaced, cracks filled to hold back drafts. From a distance, on a small rise, he studied it with a critical eye, making sure the place was well-concealed. Kane cut fresh, pine branches to fill any gaps and piled more stones around the bottom. A final inspection and he was satisfied. The cabin blended well, disappearing into the landscape.

His father had been brilliant in his choice of location and design. Ben Johnson had the eye of an artist. When he came to the woods, he saw the natural lay of the land and built his home in accordance. A large boulder and tumble of rocks, left from the glaciers of long ago, kept one side of the cabin in shadows. The rest was tucked beneath several deciduous and evergreen trees, their trunks hugging the walls while their boughs dropped down to provide cover for the roof. Ingenuous.

Kane leaned against a boulder, his body weary, strained to the limit. His mind was in turmoil, caught in the grip of anxiety. A constant companion, it gave him no rest. He had always been at peace with himself and the world around him contained within the wilderness. This was his place. No one had ever stumbled upon him or given him cause for concern.

"*No one stole a girl like you did.*" An insidious voice whispered within his mind. It had been repetitious, becoming louder and more insistent with each passing day since Sarah's eyes stared out at him from the picture posted in the store in Canada Lake. The voice would not be silenced and brought with it a paranoia that had him looking over his shoulder. The sensation that eyes were watching his back at all times couldn't be shaken.

Contentment. Kane had known what it was, should've managed on his own, left well enough alone before it was ripped away. It was too late now. The girl had spoiled him and there was no going back. Heart heavy, he went back indoors to hear a harsh fit of coughing …worse than in the night.

Stepping into the room, his eyes were drawn to a bloody mess of blankets on the floor. A startling amount of crimson appeared on the cloth held to Caroga's mouth. Kane pressed Sarah's shoulder as she held his sister close, both women shaking with the force of the attack. "Leave us. Please." His voice was hoarse with anguish.

With a nod, she wiped tears from her face and retreated. He took her place, cradling his sister like she was a baby. Fitting somehow—Kane held her the day she was brought into this world and would do the same on the day she left it.

"Shh. Easy. Easy now, Little Sister. Let go. It is okay to let go." He fought to keep his voice steady, say the words that formed a terrible emptiness within. To ask her to stay, to watch her suffer, to leave her in pain, was wrong on any level. Too selfish of him to ask. The crack in his heart widened.

The coughing finally died out and she patted his arm feebly while Kane gently wiped her mouth. "I'm…sorry….Big Brother. I…love…you…more…than …anything." Her breath was becoming more and more shallow with each word, a terrible wheezing that made him cringe.

"I love you too, Care. Say hi to Mama and Daddy." One final sigh and she went limp in his arms, a lone tear slipping down her cheek.

Kane began to rock her back and forth. The silence swallowed them both until his cry of despair broke through. His sobs, harsh and overpowering, could not be contained. He set her down when there was a feather touch on his shoulder. Turning, blinded by his tears, he fell into Sarah's arms. She held him like Mama used to do.

HE KEPT VIGIL THROUGH THE NIGHT, dry-eyed, staring into the darkness. Beside him, Caroga slept peacefully at last. A tide of emotions welled up, sorrow, confusion, rage. Sarah had comforted him until he calmed and left him to his grieving. What to do with her? Her reason for being there was no more.

Kane should go upstairs, tell her she was free, open his door and send her in the right direction, yet he could not move. In the morning, he would need to bury his sister and make a decision about the woman in the loft. For now, his mind was a kaleidoscope.

"*Let her go.*" It was the unyielding voice of his father. Kane knew he should obey, but it simply could not be done. His life would be stark without her. If he let her go, the authorities would track him down like an animal. Take him from the forest. Pen him in prison, a fate worse than death. He would die there.

In the early hours of the morning, long before his usual trek to greet the dawn, Kane began preparations. He warmed water on the stove and filled a basin. He stripped the blankets from Caroga's bed. With hands that shook, he lifted her and removed her nightgown.

So light. She was so light, whittled down to next to nothing. He bathed her, washed her hair with homemade soap, braided it, and slipped Mama's dress over her body. All the while, Kane felt eyes on him. Sarah was hovering, holding herself as if she might break.

Broken. That's what Kane was and he needed fixing. What could possibly fix this? He wrapped his sister in a soft, supple deer skin because she had loved the animals so. Shrugging into his coat, he gathered Caroga into his arms and the weight of his sorrow nearly brought him to his knees.

Sarah stepped forward as he began to sway and took his arm, offering support. He closed his eyes for a moment, took a deep breath, and clenched his jaw. "Get your coat and the shovel outside. We will bury her today at the dawn."

Stepping out into the early morning chill, Kane smelled snow in the air. The darkness was slowly merging with the daylight. He set out, Sarah trailing behind him, the only other sound her sniffles and muffled crying. He cast a silent prayer to God, Mama, and Daddy. *Show me the way.* His mind was cruel, replaying the past.

The first snowfall blanketed the land, not nearly as cold as the ice that ran through his veins seeing Mama drop in the kitchen. It happened that morning, in the middle of the mundane, making coffee, oatmeal, and cornbread for their Thanksgiving feast, a life ended in a blink.

Daddy caught her before she could hit the floor, but the life had already left her eyes. She looked fragile, as if she might shatter at his touch. Hours later, when his father staggered away to prepare for her burial, Kane crept forward and took her in his arms. A cold and waxen figure, hard as stone, that woman was not his mother.

When his father returned, haggard and aged beyond belief, Kane stood and wrapped his arms around the older man. "What can I do, Daddy? Let me help."

His father pulled away, jaw tense, eyes dead. "She's my wife. I'll do right by her."

Ben Johnson lovingly prepared her body and tended to her hair. He pressed a kiss to her forehead, silent tears splashing down, before wrapping her in the wedding quilt that had graced their bed for over forty years together. Made with her own hands, it would go with her to her final sleep. Thanksgiving was a day of mourning that year.

The day was very like when Kane's parents had been buried. Sarah could have been a wraith or a shadow, trailing behind him. The chill outside deepened, matching his heart. The journey was long, far into the forest's heart, bringing them by a burbling creek that Mama had loved.

Kane's family used to take picnics. Since their deaths, it had become too painful. Two pines grew close together, some of their branches bending in such a way as to form what looked like a heart. Beneath their span were two wooden crosses, carved with his parents' names, their dates, and the words "Beloved Wife" and "Father of My Heart." His legs gave out and he dropped to his knees, laying his burden in the shadow of the crosses as the first light of dawn crept over the horizon.

Kane pressed his forehead to the ground and felt a flicker of movement as Sarah knelt beside him. At first, he could not speak, the lump in his throat too hard to swallow. Eventually, the words forced their way out in a voice that was not his, raw and worn ragged. “Honor them. Only you and I know that they are here. They should be remembered on this day that their daughter joins them.”

His words stopped him, making him tremble. Who would bury him and mark his place? Who would remember him? He reached inside of his pocket, pulled out a rosary, and placed it over Sarah’s shining, curtain of hair, a shield that kept her face from him. “This is Mama’s. Take it and wear it. May it give you her peace and strength.”

Very carefully, he unwrapped his sister and placed another rosary, his own, over her head. The tears came once more as he looked on her face one last time and pressed a kiss to her forehead before covering her again. Kane bowed his head, clamping down on the pain or he would not be able to do this. Hands pressed to his knees, taking deep breaths as the vapor rose up from his mouth and drifted away, he forced himself to his feet. He began to dig. The tears ran like a river, wetting his beard and his jacket as the memories threatened to drown him.

There had been two burial journeys that winter to this place, scars on his mind that nothing could erase. The wind kicked up, keening in the trees, pursuing them. Kane offered to help his father in bearing his burden, Caroga holding on tightly to his hand, but Ben Johnson refused. Daddy tucked Mama in his arms like a baby. He did not pause or falter, only forged ahead with eyes forward, tears continuing to streak down his face. He would not let Kane dig her grave either. It was his final duty to his wife.

In February, only three short months later, Kane returned. He awoke shivering in the early morning hours. He'd kicked his covers off, restless since his mother's death. His father must have slept in. That had to explain the cabin's chill. Usually, Ben was up several times in the night, stoking the fire, especially when a cold snap had such a fierce hold on the land.

Kane climbed out of bed, hopping from foot to foot as he pulled on long johns, frayed jeans, and two layers of flannel shirts. He reached back to the hair trailing down his back and braided it quickly before securing the tail with a leather band.

He stepped out into the next room, set to call his father for their daily trek to meet the dawn. The sight of him sitting in the chair by the window, unnaturally still, stopped Kane in his tracks. A lantern burned on the table beside him. Kane's feet dragged as he approached to see Daddy's open eyes trained to the east. He did not blink.

Their light, dim since Mama's passing, had gone out sometime in the night. In his hand was a picture of Mama. The son took his father's hand and dropped down on his knees. He remained, eyes turned in the same direction as his father's as the sun's first rays filled the room. Kane couldn't stop crying.

The snow dropped in great flakes like pieces of the sky falling down and his world was crumbling. Caroga walked by his side, but she could not carry this weight. It had been grueling, stumbling through the snows with his father's body slung over his shoulder. Once at the gravesite, he remained on his hands and knees with his head resting on the snow, waiting for the strength to finish the job. Caroga pressing a hand to his shoulder, his saving grace.

It was backbreaking work, shoveling through the layers down to earth, fighting with frozen soil, until Ben Johnson rested beside his beloved Mary. Kane placed the cross he had carved in the ground and stretched out on his father's grave, his breath a sob, cold air burning his lungs, heart threatening to burst.

He had wanted to die there that day, but his sister took his hand and pulled him back from the edge. They walked back home as the sun went down. Both parents, left behind, beneath the snow, in the hard, unforgiving ground. Only Caroga remained…until today.

A pricking at the back of his neck made Kane shrug off the weight of his memories. He turned to see a scurry of movement in the distance, a steak of golden hair whipping in the wind. Sarah would dare flee now and disrespect his sister? Flinging the shovel down he pursued her with the single-minded drive of a predator for his prey.

He caught her easily with his much longer stride, slamming her to the ground. The anger, white hot beneath the coals of his sorrow, rose into a flame of fury. It coursed through his body, so powerful he could barely think. Kane flung Sarah over his shoulder, carried her back, and tied her down.

His body quivered with the effort to contain his rage and he could only bite out the words, "You. Will. Show. Her. Respect."

His anger gave him the strength to finish his gruesome task. Digging, laying Caroga down in that cold pit, and covering her once more, his body could do no more. Kane fell to his knees. Behind him, there was the sound of sniffling and the occasional stifled cry, the soft hiccup of Sarah's breathing. He did not trust himself to look at her. He wanted very badly to hurt her and Kane had never hurt another human being in his life.

Silence pressed down on them and then Sarah's words drifted down to him with a flurry of snowflakes in the air. "Kane, I'm sorry about your mother and father. I'm heartbroken about Caroga. I barely knew her, yet her sweetness will not be forgotten. I know how much you must miss all of them."

Her voice was warm, thawing some of the ice that had formed around his heart, dampening the flames that licked at his heated mind. Lifting his head, he turned to her and watched the tears streaking down her face, making her blue eyes shimmer. "I know what it is to lose someone you love. When Lee, my husband, died in war, I thought that I would die too. There was this empty place inside that I thought would never go away. But you go on, Kane. Time passes. You learn to live without that person.."

Resolute, Sarah drew herself up best she could, restrained against the tree. She met his eyes and grabbed hold of her courage. "Keeping me is not the answer, Kane. I have a place, a life, a family of my own. The pain you feel at the loss of your family—that is what I feel. They live. They wait for me. If you could be reunited with your parents and your sister but someone kept you prisoner, how would you feel? Please, Kane, please…"Her voice broke. "Let me go back where I belong." Her voice broke on a sob and she let her head fall.

Kane closed his eyes and rose to his feet. He approached her and touched her hand. Her urge to pull away with the slightest of jerks was obvious even though she could go nowhere. More fuel for the fire within.

He walked away, spun around, his words knives. "You say it will get better, to let you go, but don't you understand, Sarah? I have nothing! I have no family, no child, nothing!"

Sarah raised her head and tried again. "Give it time, Kane, and you may find someone, someone who belongs with you, someone who chooses you. That is how relationships happen. Venture out of the woods, go where people are, let them come to you. I thought it would just be me and Lila, forever. Then one day when we were hiking, Graham was on patrol and found me. You need to wait for that someone who is meant for you."

Kane suddenly stiffened with the onset of an inner chill. The words were hard to form. He pushed them through clenched teeth. "You say Graham was on patrol. Is he a ranger? Don't even bother to lie. I'll know."

He already knew the answer, as surely as he knew his own name. His heart slowed to a snail's pace. Maybe it would stop, like Mama's.

Sarah's eyes widened and there was fear there. She had made a mistake, her words tumbling out as from a dam that had burst, spilling her secret—a man named Graham. She'd never talked about him before, only her family. That she had kept such knowledge from Kane incensed him, making him wild.

She swallowed hard, licking her lip nervously. "Yes, he's an environmental conservation officer." Her voice was very small.

Kane stepped behind the tree, untied her without speaking and watched her wince with the strength of his grasp as he pulled her to his side. Back to the cabin, they made haste, without pause. By the time they reached it, Sarah was bent over, holding a stitch in her side, breathing hard. Kane had no sympathy.

He shoved her inside, followed her, and barred the door. He took hold of her arm, digging his fingers in deep, and dragged her to the loft. He pushed her until she landed in a sprawl on the bed, his chest heaving with barely banked fury. "How dare you not tell me what I am up against? If they find me, I'll lose everything! You would get to go back to *your* life. I'll lose mine. I will not allow that to happen and you can forget about me letting you go! *I need you! I WILL NOT BE ALONE! You* belong here with *me*!"

He stormed downstairs, oblivious to her crying. He would have to take extra care from this point forward. If it meant staying put, so be it. She would pay for her disloyalty.

Sleep eluded Kane again that night. He cursed his sister for leaving him and the woman above him for stealing his peace of mind. Whenever thoughts turned toward Sarah, he veered away. Memories of his mother and father, Caroga tagging along with him everywhere he went, were the only thing that calmed him. He went as far back as he could remember to their happy times together. Finally, he slept.

The sun pricked at his eyelids and woke him the next morning. Kane groaned inwardly. Caroga was gone. He had missed the sunrise, something he had couldn't remember doing before. His body was heavy and sluggish. He climbed out of bed and scraped his hands across his face. A splash of cold water at the wash basin helped to refresh him. He brushed his hair, pulled it back, and changed his clothes.

He checked upstairs. Sarah still slept. He returned to the kitchen and made his coffee. He was sitting by the window, staring out at the cardinals and blue jays, when she came downstairs.

She nodded to him and placed a kettle on the stove. While she waited for it to boil, she brushed her hair until it was a gleaming fall over her shoulders. Sarah was lovely, the most beautiful thing Kane had ever seen and a balm to a spirit worn ragged. She was graceful in the way she moved, soft-spoken and gentle, like Mama. It took his breath away every morning and every night, watching her. Seeing her in his kitchen, with his mother's rosary still on her neck, he yearned to keep her…forever.

"Thanksgiving is almost here. I'm going to go hunting today. Hopefully, luck will be with me and we'll eat well in a few days." He rose and approached Sarah. His fingers grazed his mother's rosary and then her cheek. She did not pull away, but the shutters dropped over her eyes. "I'm sorry about being so angry last night. I was out of my mind with grief for Caroga."

Kane went to the door and took down his gun. He filled his pack with ammunition, something to eat, and a canteen of water. His father's old, army jacket hung on a hook on the wall. He shrugged into it and slipped a brown, knit cap over his head. "I'll be back as soon as I can."

He walked out and dropped the heavy bar across the door. The shutters were next, each closed tightly and sealed with a bar as well. She would be safe until his return. A prickling on the back of his neck made the hair rise and gave him pause for an instant. He turned and scanned the area, but could see nothing out of place. He chalked it up to being overtired and anxious. Best to push on.

The first snow had fallen, coating everything in white. It glistened in the early morning sun and made nature look like it was dressed up for him. What better timing than today when he needed a successful hunt? He considered it a good sign. Kane watched his breath floating like a cloud in the air, glad for his father's warm coat and the heavy, deerskin pants his mother had made years ago.

The white coating on the ground was beneficial for two reasons; the blanket of snow quieted Kane's steps and it made it easy to follow any animal tracks. He paused and studied the forest floor. There were rabbit tracks veering off in one direction. Bird prints went in circles under the trees. They were too small. He moved on, taking great care to go slowly, quiet his breathing, and become one with the woodlands. His daddy had taught him well to be patient and silent like the animals that shared the wilderness with him. He was rewarded with the larger hoof prints of a deer.

Kane was lost in concentration, focused on the trail before him, when the sound of shattering glass caught him, making him freeze. He had traveled a fair distance away from his cabin, but sound carried far in the woods and his senses were so highly attuned that he could easily distinguish anything out of the ordinary. His heart began to pound and he turned back, moving quickly.

Sarah burst through the trees, eyes crazed, glancing back over her shoulder in her haste to get away. She failed to see a root in front of her and landed in an untidy sprawl, her breath coming out in a rush. She pulled herself to her feet then stopped with a jerk. Kane stood before her. His hands came up and gripped hers. They were like steel, cold and unyielding.

Anger boiled inside of him, hot enough to devour them both. Kane wouldn't doubt it if Sarah could feel its heat on her skin. "You dare to defy me, to break my trust!" He grabbed the rosary around her neck and yanked. It broke, the beads raining to the ground. Only the cross remained in his hand. "You do not deserve my mother's cross. You do not deserve my compassion. It is obvious that I cannot leave you. I *will not* be alone!"

He took her arm, paying no heed to the blood running down it and onto his hand, dragging her back to the cabin. Sarah kicked and pulled at him. She tried to grab his hair. She jabbed with her elbows and screamed. It felt like a little bird fluttering against him.

Kane didn't even try to stop her. No one would hear. He let her wear herself out. He brought her inside and sent her to the loft before dropping the bar inside to secure his home. He began to pace, fighting to calm his breathing, to stop the racing of blood in his veins, and quiet the pumping of his heart. He could never be sure of her again.

Slowly, the adrenalin rush died down and with it, Kane's strength. It was eerily silent up above. Had she escaped again? He rushed upstairs and scanned the small room. Sarah was huddled on the bed, her body shaking with silent crying. She pulled herself more tightly into a ball at the sound of his footsteps.

A cold wind swept over him and he looked to the window. That she had broken it was not hard to believe. How she had managed to climb through such a small space was a wonder.

Silently cursing, Kane went back downstairs and returned with boards, nails and a hammer. He pounded away, banging out his frustration, shrouding the room in darkness. Her punishment was fitting. There would be no view of the outside world and no chance of getting out again. No matter what, Sarah was his.

18

JIM WAS RIGHT. The going was rough, to say the least. The combination of snow, wet leaves, and mud would be a hindrance if Graham was at his best. With his nerves taut and his body spread thin with exhaustion, it was a challenge to stay on his feet. His ankle throbbed angrily from the incident with Lila the day before. Had it only been a day? Everything ran together.

The incline became steeper and Graham found himself making little progress. Two steps forward, three steps back, sliding halfway down and scrambling back up again. Grabbing hold of anything he could get his hands on, twigs snapped off in his grasp and rocks tumbled down the trail. The cold made his fingers slow and clumsy. How could he have forgotten gloves? Tugging his sleeves down, Graham pushed on.

The urgency surged, making him want to scream. If Graham could have run up the side of the mountain, he would have. His ankle gave and sent him half way down again. He remained still for a heartbeat, wet, covered in mud, breathing so hard it was almost a sob. A voice at the back of his mind told him he was crazy. His heart told him he couldn't give up. He went with his heart and pulled himself back to his feet again.

His body fought to bridge the gap to the top while his mind replayed the dreams. What if it was a wild goose chase? Doubts cropped up. He refused to give them credence. The images were too clear, the details engrained in his memory. It was as if he had placed a DVD in the player and could hit replay.

The beginning seemed to be the best place to start. How ironic that his dreamscape had carried him back to the fateful day that turned the key, unlocking the strange turn of events that brought him to the here and now. Graham had returned in reality, retracing their steps, many times in the Rockwood State Forest. Never before had he been able to relive that day with the absolute clarity he had been graced with in last night's dream.

The day unfolded in his mind once again. The light in her hair and in her eyes, the touch of her hand, the smell of her shampoo. His heart filled near to bursting. So close, she was standing so close to him. His fingers itched to reach out, to touch her. Graham waited until they stood by his truck and he was about to leave. The image paused.

He would stop it there this time, before he left, while he still held Sarah in his arms. She was soft and warm. Her sweater was a fiery red like the passion behind her kiss, hinting of more to come when they became one. The yearning was intense, to go back in time, change what came next.

His mind switched to the next dream, the one that never happened, yet felt so real. It was like the other visits to the tower with Lila, Jim, and going solo. Graham was certain it was prompted by that time in the summer when Lila found something hidden in the canopy of green leaves. A red object, out of place, triggering his interest. He had searched intently, had a brief glimpse. The wind shifted and it was lost. Lila distracted him, eager to move on, and they left the tower.

Every trip back, it was the first thing Graham looked for. No luck. In the dream, he knew exactly where to look, could see it as plain as day, found it with ease. Studying it through the lens of the most powerful binoculars, the color and texture jumped out. A revelation. Sarah's sweater from the first dream matched it perfectly. It had to be hers. The dreams and the inexplicable pull of the mountain had brought him back… for Sarah. He knew it as surely as he knew he was Graham Dylan Scott.

His lungs near to bursting, the ache in his ankle was fierce and his body was past the point of no return when he crested the top of the trail. Graham went to the ranger cabin, out of habit, and gave the interior a quick inspection. It stirred him, made him long for simpler times when his job would have been to live in the cabin, watch for fires, and be a guardian of the forest. A time when the world was a safer place.

Graham dropped down on the porch and rested his hands on his knees. A few minutes, that was all he needed, to recoup before tackling the fire tower. *Who are you kidding, Scott? You're afraid of what you'll find at the end of the road.*

What if he was wrong? What if the dreams were merely a trick born out of frustration and desperation? If this didn't pan out, it was a long way down from the tower. He yanked his thoughts away from that path and bowed his head. *God...Dad, anyone who's listening...please be with me. Please let me be right.*

Graham grabbed hold of the post and rose to his feet. A deep breath and he gathered his resolve to walk to the tower. There was a twinge in his ankle, but it held. One more gaze up at the top and he was off, taking the steps two at a time. His quickest time yet had him bent over, hands braced on his legs, while his heart threatened to explode.

Once he could breathe again, he foraged in his pack and pulled out a pair of binoculars. They were high-tech with extremely powerful lenses, courtesy of the Department of Environmental Conservation. He fiddled with the knobs, procrastinating for a little longer. *This is it. Take a deep breath and look out on the surroundings.* His head moved from side to side. He lowered the binoculars and gauged his position on the tower. Changed his stance according to his dream. Looked again. Made an adjustment. Forgot how to breathe.

There it was, that something red, snagged in a low-hanging tree branch. Narrowing the focus and honing in on the object, it practically shouted at him. Something made out of yarn with a texture... *like Sarah's sweater.* Graham tilted the binoculars to peer beyond that something and it was as if his heart slammed to a halt in his chest.

Tipping his head one way and then another, shifting his position slightly as he did, it was like an optical illusion. In one instant, the scene was like any random section of the wilderness with a stand of trees and large boulders. In the next, there was the faintest outline of a building. He closed his eyes tightly, opened them, and squinted, not sure he believed what his mind was trying to tell him.

Maybe Graham had finally gone off the deep end. Staring intently until his eyes burned, his mouth went dry. There was one wall, practically hidden by the giant boulder next to it. A window was covered with shutters that had been chopped from some type of hardwood, the bark giving the impression that they were part of a tree. It was the work of a genius!

Concealed with deliberation, trees hugged the building until they merged with boards that mimicked nature. Heavy bows drooped down over the roof line. A close inspection revealed greens tucked in any gaps. At ground level, smaller boulders and rocks filled the spaces between the trees. Without the aid of powerful binoculars, it was unlikely that Graham would have ever found the place. On every other trip, he had brought an average pair, good for birdwatching. Binoculars had not been a top priority on a search that concentrated on the forest floor.

Conditions on previous visits had not cooperated either. The explosion of greenery in the summer and burst of autumn foliage had been an obstruction. Today, everything fell into place perfectly. The leaves were down on the ground, no longer providing cover, and the fresh layer of snow had settled on the mysterious building, tracing and emphasizing its lines.

Graham's heart kicked into gear again, only now it was a trip hammer, pounding at an alarming rate. His breath came out in a rush and he sucked in air, dizzy from discovery. The implications were mindboggling. The scrap of red, the building—they changed everything.

What kind of person lived out here? If that person had Sarah, what had become of her? New-found hope, a phoenix rising out of the ashes, wavered. It had been seven months. If she had been here, if that something red really was hers, what was the likelihood that she was still alive?

A cold sweat broke out and pain stabbed in his chest. A full-blown panic attack or heart attack in the making. *Get a grip, Scott! Get a grip! You're not helping anyone if you pass out!* The voice in his head had the bark of a drill sergeant. *Inhale, deep. Exhale. Repeat. Get your feet back under you.*

A flash of movement made him zoom in and almost drop the binoculars. It was a man, camouflaged in greens and browns. A long ponytail of sandy and white-streaked hair fell down his back, a thick beard obscuring his face, and a gun was slung over his shoulder. He paused for a moment and glanced behind him. Graham ducked down then stopped himself. The stranger would not be able to see him.

A close study and Graham began to shake. He knew that face. It was the man that he and Jim had encountered on the other side of the mountain only a month ago and again in passing at the store in Canada Lake. Did he have a connection with Sarah?

As the woodsman moved away, Graham continued to observe his progress and fumbled for his cell phone. Had to call back-up, get someone else out here. He flipped it open and inwardly cursed himself out. Service wasn't the issue. There was a cell tower nearby. Stupidity was the problem. In his haste to carry out his self-appointed mission, he had forgotten to charge his phone. He was on his own.

There was no question in his mind. He was headed to that cabin. It would be risky. Sneaking up on such a man, a hermit accustomed to the ways of the wilderness, would be tough. Graham would have to bide his time and let the stranger put distance between them. Then, he'd have to pick up the pace, get in and out before anyone returned.

The sound of breaking glass made Graham shift his focus back to the cabin. It must have been on a side of the building he could not see. He panned back and forth when a splash of shining, blond hair caught his eye. A woman emerged from behind the cabin and started a frantic sprint in the opposite direction of the stranger. Graham zeroed in on her face and this time he did drop his binoculars.

His hand gripped the railing and he fought for consciousness because his head was spinning. That face. He could pick it out in any crowd, had studied it countless times, in photos and in his mind. It belonged to Sarah.

Alive. He sent up a prayer of thanks and scrambled for the binoculars. His cheeks were wet as he raised them and found her again. She must have become disoriented because she had circled around and was heading back toward the cabin. She passed it and Graham felt his heart jump to his throat. In his mind, he urged her to come his way, but she did not turn and in an instant, it was all over.

Her abductor, as Graham now renamed him, had returned, attracted by the noise from a shattering window that was so loud in the forest's silence. He grabbed hold of her, his shouting carrying through the woods, and dragged her back. Sarah didn't give up without a fight. She kicked, punched, and screamed all of the way until they disappeared inside.

It took every last shred of self-control Graham had to stay put. His initial instincts raged to go down to that cabin, barge in, face the enemy, and get Sarah out of there. The rational portion of his brain, perfected by years of experience and expertise, told him to be still, stay calm. He couldn't charge into that man's cabin. The stranger would hear him well in advance, was unpredictable, and on high alert. If he took Graham out, it would be over for Sarah.

Another dilemma remained while he waited. What was the stranger doing to her right now? Adrenalin raced through Graham's system and kicked his heart up a notch. She had survived this long. The man wanted her alive. Graham had to have faith that those feelings had not changed with her attempt at escape. *Please don't let him hurt her. Please God, keep her safe.*

A plan of action was what he needed, not impulse. Caution. Patience. Persistence. Graham would have given anything to have Jim by his side. Together they would easily see this through to completion.

The trip up the mountain could have waited until the next day, as Pete had suggested, but it might have been too late. Anything could happen by tomorrow. The cabin could be empty or the weather conditions might obscure it. Sarah could be…dead. Graham was certain—he was meant to come today.

His mind ran through all the possible strategies, landing on the best hope. The element of surprise was the answer. If the woodsman had any inkling that someone had discovered his home, there was no predicting his reaction. The man was armed. He lived in absolute isolation. He was a survivor. Graham was certain the stranger would not take kindly to any intrusion, especially someone who meant to take something he had laid claim to as his own.

The choice was clear. Graham would have to wait until night, the prime time to make his move. Under the cover of darkness, Sarah's abductor could be drawn out. There was a long distance between the tower and the cabin. It would be best to inch his way through the forest while there was daylight. When he reached the cabin, he would conceal himself and wait until dark to find his way. Find Sarah.

Graham took his time going down the steps of the fire tower. He pulled a water bottle out of his bag and drank it down. He'd had the presence of mind to throw in a granola bar. He chewed it without tasting one bite. It would give him the energy needed to keep a steady head. To psych himself up.

The journey through the wilderness began next. Graham moved with painstaking slowness, grateful that the wet ground hid the sound of his footsteps. The snow on the fallen leaves was beginning to melt, another advantage; his footprints would be harder to find. He went in a zigzag pattern, slipping behind trees and rocks whenever possible.

The cabin's windows had been covered. Hopefully, Sarah's abductor felt a need for privacy with the day's turn of events and would leave them shuttered. If the woodsman did not look outside his windows, he would not see Graham's approach. Regardless, Graham behaved as if he was being watched, striving to remain hidden.

A snail could get there faster. *Where is it? Where the hell is it*? Second-guessing himself, he checked his compass several times to make sure he was still moving in the right direction. In spite of doubt shaking his confidence, Graham pushed on.

The sun shifted in the sky and the distance seemed to stretch on much too far. It couldn't take this long, no matter how slow the pace. He tripped over a rock and fell to his hands and knees. His ankle protested at the abuse and it took a moment to regain his feet. Would he ever get there?

A few steps more and a large boulder, surrounded by an outcropping of rock rose up above him. *Come on, Graham. Go the distance*. He slipped past the rocks and almost walked smack into the side of the woodland house. The place looked like it grew out of the surroundings.

Graham stepped back, amazed at how well-hidden the tiny building was. It was even more difficult to discern once on top of it what with the way the cabin merged with the wilderness. There couldn't be much space inside judging by its size. Perhaps a living area and a cubby hole of a bedroom.

Glancing above, he saw another window that had been covered from the inside, possibly a loft. Everything was buttoned up, snug. Sarah's captor was probably going to sit tight until morning. And then what? A shudder ran through Graham, making him steady himself on a tree. He couldn't wait to find out.

Sarah had come from a part of the building that had been outside his line of vision. He needed to survey the entire area in order to know what he was up against. A slow inching around the building and he backed up to the rock face to peek at the rear side of the house. There was a door and wood stacked within the boulder's shadow.

Barely daring to breathe, Graham got down low, hugged the ground below the windows on the lowest level, and rounded the first corner. There was another door with a heavy bar next to it, allowing it to be blocked from the outside. Beside the door was another shuttered window. A quick scramble by what must have been the front of the cabin and he was on the opposite side.

Scanning overhead, the last remnants of sunlight glinted on another window. This one was broken and a piece of wood sealed it from the inside. Graham's breath quickened at the sight. This must be where Sarah had made her escape. How had she managed to wriggle through that small space?

The drop was too high. She would have shimmied down the closest tree. Streaks of red marked her climb. She was hurt! Graham's fists clenched, itching to break in, but the timing wasn't right. It might be the hardest few hours of his life. He *had* to wait until sundown.

The need to find a secure, hiding place was imperative. He felt exposed standing beside the cabin where the risk of discovery was the greatest. The need to ascertain if Sarah was all right was stronger. Knowing full well that it was reckless, Graham stepped up to the cabin and pressed his body against it. He placed his ear directly on the side of the building and fought to quiet his breathing. At first, the only sound was the thunder of his heart. Eventually, he detected movement inside.

There was a rattling, perhaps of a stove, and heavy footsteps. Graham heard a creaking and a man's deep voice asking Sarah to eat. A moment passed that must have stretched on for an eternity and then there was her response, begging to be left alone. Graham's eyes clamped shut and he said a prayer, of thanks and for strength, before stepping back and considering his options. The most important game of hide and seek in his life was about to begin.

In the end, he settled behind a slab of rock on a gentle rise that overlooked the front of the cabin. If the woodsman came out of either exit, Graham would see him without being seen. Sliding down until he was on his knees, he leaned against the boulder and began the waiting game.

Time dragged and the sun barely budged overhead. The cold and the damp seeped into his clothes until he was shivering uncontrollably. He didn't care. All of the hours of searching, worrying, and wondering came down to this moment. A little discomfort would be a small price to pay to finally have his Sarah back where she belonged.

The hours passed and Graham's body grew stiff. He had to get up and shift his position several times. Otherwise, he'd be unable to move when push came to shove. The forest did not take notice of a stranger in its midst, the wildlife carrying on with the business of survival.

Squirrels and chipmunks were a blur of motion, racing across the ground or from tree to tree. Occasionally, the first would argue, making an unbelievable amount of racket for a creature so small. Rabbits thumped past on their way to their burrows. The chatter and flutter of the birds was a clamor compared to the rest of the wild. Graham watched, listened, and marveled at nature. Its work would go on regardless of the presence of man.

The waiting was excruciating until his patience was finally rewarded. The sun touched down on the horizon while the trees became black skeletons against a sky of pink that shifted to red, ending in a deep purple before the cloak of darkness covered the land. Stars appeared, offering pinpricks of light. The moon was hidden under a cloud and Graham was grateful. The darker this night, the better.

He stood and walked slowly back and forth to work out the kinks. His hand reached under his coat as if by a will of its own and pulled out his pistol. One last check proved it was loaded and the safety was on. A deep intake of breath, a count to ten to steel his nerves, and Graham let it out slowly. *It's now or never.*

19

IT WAS COLD FOR SPRING IN ARLINGTON. The wind blew, the clouds were oppressive overhead, and the sky opened up. Rain poured down on the mourners as if heaven cried with them. Sarah stood in a black dress and shoes, her blonde hair a sharp contrast as it whipped around her face, and her tears fell with the rain. She held Lila, a small, warm bundle in her arms. Her little one was Sarah's only comfort and her reason to go on when she wanted nothing more than to climb into the flag-draped coffin to be with her husband.

People could not understand why she had brought a baby to Lee's funeral. Sarah didn't care. Lee's parents wanted their son to be buried in the national cemetery to honor his ultimate sacrifice for his country. Sarah had honored their wishes even though she would rather have him close to her. With his grave at such a distance from home, the visits would be few and far between. Knowing she would probably only come once or twice a year, Sarah had chosen to bring Lila with her.

It was important that a daughter be present when her father was laid to rest. One day, when Lila was older, her mother would tell her about her daddy's funeral and they would return to his grave. Sarah was certain Lila would be grateful to know she had been a part of that final goodbye. Today, Sarah was grateful she had something to hold on to.

Many had come to pay their respects to Lee Waters, forming a sea of black against the rows of white slabs that stretched as far as the eye could see in each direction. He had been well-liked. Upon word of his death, people from his past made the trek to his ultimate resting place and the end of his future.

Sarah had seen familiar faces from high school and their hometown, family from both sides, and of course, brothers in arms. They were like statues, formal in dress uniforms, betraying no emotion except for the tears that fell unchecked and could not be stopped.

"Taps" began to play and Sarah rose to her feet, shivering, but not from the cold. It was the music that had always moved her and sent a chill through her body. Never had she expected it would be played for one of her own.

Four soldiers performed the task of folding the flag that blanketed Lee's coffin and one stepped in front of Sarah. He looked her in the eye, his face a grim mask, and handed her the neat, triangle of red, white, and blue with hands gloved in white. No longer able to fight it, Sarah's sobbing began in earnest. The rain fell harder, the sharp crack of gunfire filled the air with the twenty-one gun salute, and Lila wailed in her arms.

Sarah bolted upright in bed, the echoes of gunfire and her baby's crying still in her ears. She reached up to find that her cheeks were wet and wiped at them with her blanket. Heart hammering and body trembling, she burrowed back down under the covers and tried to go back to sleep. It had only been a dream, yet it was so real. For an instant, she had been in Arlington all over again.

Straining her ears, she listened for any sounds from below. No more coughing for the moment. It had been hideous in the night, a terrible croup with a rattle at the end that went on and on. How could a person live through that? Sarah had rushed downstairs to see what could be done only to find Kane with his sister, holding her, pressing a bloodied cloth to her mouth. She offered to help. He sent her away. Perhaps there was a need to do this deathwatch alone?

She returned to her bed and buried her head under her pillow, hands pressed to her ears as the horrendous sound continued below. At some point, exhaustion must have won out, giving way to the dreams. The house was silent now, eerily so. Sarah feared the worst when there were footsteps followed by the opening and closing of the door.

It must be over. The thought had her sitting up in bed. Holding herself. Rocking. Unsure of how she felt when the horrid coughing began anew.

Sarah fled down the steps to the tiny room and stopped in dismay. There was so much blood, a brilliant splash of scarlet across the covers, down Caroga's nightgown, coming from her mouth and her nose. A wretched gurgling now accompanied the rattle. Sarah hurried out, filled a basin with warm water, and found a towel before she returned. She gathered the ailing woman into her arms and simply held her. What else could be done?

After what seemed like hours, the attack let go, leaving Caroga wrung out and limp, light as a child resting against her shoulder. Sarah murmured words of comfort although there was none to be found and stroked her hair, like she did for Lila.

She washed Caroga's face and hands. Gently leaning her back against the pillows, the blanket was stripped away next and dropped on the floor. With hands that trembled, the nightgown was removed next, exposing a skeletal frame. Sarah couldn't help but wince. The illness was eating the poor woman alive.

Biting down on her lip to keep from crying, Sarah found another nightgown and pulled it over Caroga's head, found another blanket, and covered the woman. Her patient was shaking and her touch was like ice when Sarah pressed a cup of tea into Caroga's hands, fingertips and lips gone blue from a body starved of oxygen. Sarah continued to hold on, helping Kane's sister to take a few sips before she fell back against the pillows, utterly exhausted. Her eyes drifted closed and she appeared to sleep when her whisper broke the silence.

"I'm…sorry…sorry…for…what…Kane…has done….I…told….him….from…the …beginning…it ….was….wrong….that he had to…to….let…you…go." Caroga's eyes opened, catching Sarah in a blue ocean of sorrow, and her hand floated up. Sarah caught it and held on.

"You don't need to say sorry. This isn't your fault. Don't worry yourself. Rest, Caroga. That's all you need to do right now." Sarah's voice trembled and nearly broke. What this poor woman had endured.

The hold on her hand tightened for a moment as Caroga found the last of her strength. "Go….Go now….Your…job…is…done…I don't…have…much…longer…Go." One last squeeze and her hand dropped to the blanket.

Sarah hesitated for one moment then carefully gathered the husk of a woman in her arms. She pressed a kiss to the crown of her head and slipped out of the room without looking back. She scurried upstairs. What did she need? The camera, nothing more. Sarah slipped it in her pocket, streaked back down to the door, her hand on the handle when the next fit of coughing began.

She couldn't do it, couldn't leave Caroga alone, and now Sarah found herself sitting on a rock, shivering while Kane continued the heart-wrenching job of shoveling through ground hardened by frost. His breath rose in a cloud around him and his crying did not stop, tears occasionally accompanied by harsh sobs. Lost in his task, he did not seem aware of anything else around him.

Now, Sarah. Do this now! Glancing repeatedly over her shoulder, she slowly retreated, taking care not to snap a twig or rustle the carpet of leaves on the forest floor. The scrape of the shovel against dirt and rock covered any movement. Twenty feet and she put on a full, hell-bent burst of speed.

With no idea of which way to go, the need to take flight was the only thing that pushed her forward when a blow to her back rammed her down, face first. The ground rushed up to meet her as Kane's full weight bore into her. The breath was knocked out of her, her lip bleeding from where she bit it upon impact. There was no time to do anything. He hauled her up by the back of her sweater and flung her over his shoulder as if she was nothing more than a rag doll.

Sarah started to kick and beat her fists. His grip only tightened. She might as well have struck a wall made of stone. Back to the gravesite and he set her down none to gently, pushed her up against a tree, and yanked his coat off in jerky motions. He was shaking and his eyes were wild as he pulled his coat around her. He tied her down so tightly she cried out with the pain.

Kane's face was an inch from hers as he hissed. "You. Will. Show. Her. Respect." He returned to his task, completing the hole, and laying his sister's body down with the utmost tenderness. A flurry of shoveling began to cover her, revealing his rage. Sarah bowed her head and let the tears come for herself and for Caroga.

SARAH SAT ON HER BED, knees drawn to her chest, replaying the horror of the previous day and the worst—letting it slip about Graham. Her stomach twisted at her blunder. How could she have been so stupid? From the beginning, she had closely guarded the secret of the man in her life and his occupation, only to spill it now. Her family, Lila…they had been her focus.

Her reasons for keeping Graham to herself had been many. Foremost, he was hers and she would hold him safe in her heart, hidden away. Then there was the element of surprise. If Kane did not know about the environmental conservation officer, he would not expect him or be suspicious.

It was also a matter of faith. Sarah clung to the hope that Graham was coming for her. It was irrational, but saying his name out loud could jinx everything. The final reason for maintaining secrecy—self-preservation. Sarah was intimidated by the thought of Kane discovering she loved another man.

Kane's whole manner changed when she mentioned Graham, something dangerous lurking in his eyes. Frantic in his hurry to get home, he had practically dragged her through the woods, eyes wild as they darted from left to right. He kept watching his back and did not seem to breathe easy until they reached the cabin. He flung her in the loft and was restless for the remainder of the night, a wall of silence coming up as a shield. Who knew what was brewing in that mind or what the man would do next?

Sarah's choice was clear. She would have to get out and soon. She didn't trust Kane. He feared pursuit and had a daunting desperation with the loss of his sister. There was no telling what he was capable of if his way of life was threatened , especially now that he knew about Graham. A commitment made to herself, she finally drifted off for little catnaps and woke just before dawn.

The sky had lightened. The colors would be painted across nature's canvas within the hour. There was no movement down below. That was strange. Kane was always awake first to build up the fire and catch the sunrise. His departure was Sarah's cue to get up and prepare for breakfast. She contemplated slipping downstairs and out the door, but stopped herself.

He would hear her. The man always did. On the slim chance that Sarah made it outside, it would be too dark, making it too hard to find her way out. Waiting. She had spent seven months waiting for some sign of hope, for release. She could wait until daylight arrived and he left her alone.

Daybreak made its appearance. The birds chattered outside her window and flitted through the trees in a cheerful buzz of activity. Pink washed over her walls, followed by brightness. Sarah climbed out of bed and dropped to her knees by the tiny window. The woods had been transformed, wearing a white coat of wintry finery. So beautiful, like a prayer.

There was the sound of movement below. Something metal clattered on the stove. Kane was up. She took a deep breath, built up her nerve, and went down to face him.

He had fixed his own coffee and sat drinking it by the window. Sarah anxiously set the tea kettle on the stove, waiting for his first move. Dark shadows beneath his eyes and skin drained of color showed the marks of his anguish. Sarah brushed out her hair while waiting for the water to boil, and prepared her tea. She sipped at it quietly. Tried to escape notice. To disappear.

She should have known better. He was watching, always watching her. His voice was soft in the early morning hush and his words became a blur, something about Thanksgiving. Thanksgiving! Sarah could not tolerate being here on that day.

Kane rose and approached her, touching his mother's rosary that she still wore around her neck. Somehow, it gave her hope. His hand brushed her cheek next and it was all she could do to refrain from slapping him. He apologized for his actions the day before, his face nearly cracking with his grief. A few last minute preparations for hunting and he left her.

The heavy bar fell into place with a loud clunk and finality, followed by the shutters slamming shut over the windows. His footsteps receded into the distance. Sarah felt like she had been sealed in a cave. The only light came from a kerosene lamp that Kane had lit on the table and the small windows in the loft. She was trapped inside the tiny cabin until he would see fit to take her outdoors again.

There was a loud pounding, the beat of her heart, thundering in her ears and fluttering in her chest. It had to be now! She would not spend another day here with this man, Kane's wishes be damned! The tea cup trembled in her hands as Sarah sipped slowly and drank it down to the last drop. There had to be distance between Kane and the cabin. It was her only chance of escape.

She set the cup in the wash basin and went upstairs. Her fingers fumbled through the clothing in his mother's dresser and did not want to work. She made her hands into tight fists, breathed deeply, and tried again. There was a heavy, woolen sweater that was tan and might blend with the forest. Hopefully, it would be warm enough. Sarah pulled it on over the flannel shirt she had slept in, stepped into her own pair of jeans, and put on her hiking boots. The easy part was done. Now, to find a way out!

A charge at the front and back doors proved them to be of such sturdy construction that they would not budge. She might as well be a moth fluttering against the window, trying to get to the light. She lifted the windows on the lower floor but the shutters would not yield. Her feet carried her back and forth within the small interior of the cabin, her stomach knotting so tightly she almost doubled over. There had to be a way to get out!

The sight of the little bit of light in her loft brought her to a stop and then she was running up the steps. These windows would not open. Kane had nailed them shut shortly after Sarah's arrival. She studied one for a moment, grabbed a wash towel off of her dresser, and wrapped it around her hand. Sending up a fervent prayer that God would be with her, she pulled her arm back and sent it through the window with all of her strength.

The noise of its shattering seemed loud enough for the whole world to hear. Towel still wrapped on her hand, she knocked the shards of glass away and hoisted herself through the window. It was a tight squeeze. Sarah had to wriggle and stretch her body and her sleeve snagged on a piece of glass. She pulled hard and sliced a gash on the inside of her arm in the process. Biting her lip to keep from crying out, she crawled across the roof, grabbed the trunk of a tree, and shimmied down to the ground.

No time to think. Just do. It was a motto Lee had to live by in the service and Graham as a conservation officer. Sarah ran as fast as her feet would carry her, slipping in the freshly fallen snow and the wet leaves underneath, dodging trees, desperate to get away and find others. She had only made it a short distance when she pulled up short and tried to get her bearings.

That day they came from Pine Lake, she could swear it was to the west. Judging the position of the sun and the path it was traveling, she changed her direction and hoped it was the right way. Her legs pumped up and down, her lungs near to bursting, and her side ached with exertion. Nothing hindered her. One goal made Sarah keep moving. She had to get out of here. She had to get home to her baby. Her family and Graham needed her. It had to be today.

Her feet carried her further from the cabin. If she went fast enough and far enough she would find her way out of the woods to civilization. A small voice at the back of her mind reminded her of the immenseness of the Adirondacks. She refused to listen. Sarah glanced back over her shoulder and a root rose up out of the ground, sending her flying to the ground. She got back up and let out a scream. Kane stepped forward and grabbed her arms in a vice-like grip. It was over!

His eyes snapped and his fingers dug into her skin. For the first time, Sarah thought he might actually hurt her. "You dare to defy me, to break my trust! I told you that you are mine!"

His voice was loud and his chest heaved. His eyes fell on the rosary she still wore and he tore it off her neck. "You do not deserve my mother's cross. You do not deserve my compassion. It is obvious that I cannot leave you. I've told you. Now believe me. I *will not* be alone!" Kane yanked her by one arm, his fingers slick with her blood, and started the trek back to the cabin.

Sarah fought bitterly with everything she had. She might as well have tried to move the mountains. Kane was bigger, stronger with a body honed from living off the land, and he was stubborn. Nothing she did even fazed him. It felt like the journey into her nightmare all over again. All too quickly, they closed the gap and she found herself in her loft once more.

Thank God for small blessings, he left her alone. She wiped the cut on her arm with the wash towel she had used earlier and wrapped it around the wound. There was nothing else to do except curl up on the bed and get through another day. At one point, Kane came upstairs, surveyed her room, and went back down. He returned immediately, sealed both of her windows, and eventually brought food.

How could he expect her to eat? It became quiet downstairs while Kane dozed. Sarah drew herself more tightly into a ball and rocked, at a loss as to how she could possibly go on this way. Dying would be better. She began to contemplate a way to end this horror once and for all.

"*COME ON, GRAHAM! PICK UP!* Damn it, pick up!" Jim Pedersen sat in his cruiser with the engine idling and the heat blasting to fend off an unusually cold evening. Throughout the day, he had called Graham's cell. It went directly to voice mail every time, as if it was turned off.

A glance at the clock made his stomach clench. 5:15 PM. His shift was over, but the chief had agreed to allow Jim to take his cruiser when he explained the situation with Graham. There was one major problem. Exactly what was the situation?

Jim dialed his home phone number, tapping his fingers on the wheel, unable to sit still. His wife picked up on the second ring. "Hi Jeanie. Have you heard from him? No, I didn't think so. I don't like it, honey. I've got a bad feeling about this. I think he's still on Kane Mountain and something is wrong. I'm going to go up to the trailhead and see if I can find him. No, I won't do anything stupid. No, I won't go up the mountain in the dark. If he isn't there and doesn't make it out by morning, we'll have to begin searching in the daylight. I'll be careful, I promise. I love you. And Jeanie, say a little prayer… for everyone."

Jim hung up, eyes suddenly burning, and pulled out onto the road. It was sunset. It would be dark by the time he arrived. He hoped with all of his heart that Graham would be waiting for him when he got there.

JEANIE HUNG UP THE PHONE and sank down into a chair. She bowed her head to clasped hands, and began to pray. Graham was in trouble; he had been in trouble since the day Sarah disappeared. There had to be some light at the end of the tunnel, some good after all the pain, but it didn't sound promising right now. Their friend was out there, somewhere in the wilderness, and he was not answering their calls.

She had been unable to let well enough alone and had called several times herself. What if he was hurt? What if he had intentionally hurt himself? The latter possibility never would have crossed her mind in the past, but Jeanie couldn't be sure after the previous night. She sent up a litany of anxious prayers for Graham, for her husband, and for Sarah. *Please God, keep them safe. Bring them all home.*

AFTER WHAT SEEMED AN ETERNITY, darkness fell over the wilderness. There was the occasional hoot of an owl and the howl of a coyote. Otherwise, quiet reined. Graham stood slowly, his body shaking with the cold, and fought the stiffness in his joints. His jaw clenched tightly while he worked through the pain until he could move freely once again.

He reached inside his coat and pulled out his pistol. A quick rummage through his pack and he found his flares. Graham hoped like hell this plan would work because there was no plan B. He fired his pistol into the air, praying that he would not need to fire his weapon for any other reason. The crack reverberated loudly, shattering the peacefulness of the night. Graham counted to ten, lit a flare, and pitched it as far as he could throw. A soft glow rose up from the ground a good distance away. *Please keep burning,* he urged and waited.

KANE WAS OUT OF THE ROCKER LIKE A SHOT. Sarah ran down from the loft, a quilt wrapped around her shoulders, eyes huge with terror in a face gone white. He pulled on his coat, took down his rifle, and pushed her into the rocker. "Stay put and don't be afraid. I *will* keep you safe. I'll be back as soon as I can."

Kane stepped out into the night, secured the door, and headed in the direction of the gunfire. There was a dim light in the distance. He checked his gun and moved quickly with a stealth born of living in the wilderness all of his life. He vowed that no one would gain entry to his home and no harm would come to the woman inside because she had become his world. Everything else had been ripped away.

20

SARAH STAYED IN THE ROCKER because she didn't have the courage to move. She wrapped herself tightly in the quilt and set the chair in motion. She wanted to look out the window, but they were all covered from the outside. She didn't dare venture out with no idea of what awaited her. Her hands gripped the arms of the chair and her heart pounded, making her lightheaded.

The sound had been a gunshot, she was certain, and it was close. No one had ever come near before. Who could it be? If something happened to Kane, what would she do? The door opened and closed and she kept her eyes trained on the fireplace. She was afraid to turn around.

"Sarah," a voice said softly, hoarse with emotion. It was a voice she had heard nightly in her dreams, one she had imagined speaking to her every day of her captivity. Could it be real? She closed her eyes, her heart fluttering madly, and slowly turned around.

GRAHAM STAYED DOWN LOW, pressed to the rock, and watched as a shadowy figure moved past him into the night. Using every ounce of skill he possessed, he picked his way silently to the cabin door, checked quickly that the stranger was not headed back yet, and slipped inside. Across the tiny room, a rocking chair moved back and forth in front of the fire, a tumble of blond hair falling down a woman's back. For an instant, he couldn't move.

"Sarah," he croaked. She turned and his limbs unlocked. She was out of the chair, her blanket falling to the floor, and Graham had her in his arms. He crushed her up against him and could feel her heart hammering against his own, matching its wild beating. She was real, warm, flesh and blood. She smelled like wood smoke, some kind of home-made soap, sweat born out of fear, and that scent that belonged to no other. It was unique to one woman and her name was Sarah Waters.

"God, Sarah, I'm here. Hang on just a little bit longer and we'll leave this place." Graham buried his head in her shoulder and his body trembled with the effort to maintain self-control. They weren't in the clear yet.

Sarah was quivering, a flower tossed by a storm, and her hands came up to thread through the tangle of his disheveled hair. Graham stood firm, solid and strong when she needed him most. "How did you find me? He brought me in here and kept me from everyone. I don't even know where I am! How did you do it, Graham?"

He shook his head and looked into her eyes, still blue enough to make his heart hurt. The color of the sky, summer, and new beginnings. "It's a long story and we'll all sit down together to hear it another time. Right now I've got to keep you safe. I've only bought us a little time. He'll be back any moment and we have to be ready."

Graham glanced around the cabin, searching for the best place for himself and for Sarah. He set his hands on her shoulders and tried to project a calm that he did not feel. "Go back to the rocker and sit by the fire, the way you were when I walked in. I'm going to wait by the door. If there's a struggle, get down on the floor and find something to crawl behind. Go now!"

He urged her to go with a squeeze of her arm and took his place in a spot that would conceal him until the door opened and then...God be with him.

JIM THOUGHT ABOUT GOING TO PLEASANT LAKE FIRST. Graham might be there, sound asleep after the grueling schedule he had kept, aggravated by the recent turn of events. Maybe things had not gone as hoped on the mountain and he was getting drunk, ignoring the phone.

Flashes of that instant when Jim saw Graham disappear into the icy waters of the lake passed through his mind, making him start to shake all over again. Graham had promised he would never do such a thing again, but was he truly in his right mind? The only thing Jim could do was keep the faith and trust that his best friend would keep his word. Meanwhile, he still wasn't answering his phone.

Green Lake Road was dark with only a few breaks of light at the occasional year round residence. Jim took the side road down to the parking area for the hiking trails and his heart plunged. His headlights landed on a dark green truck from the Department of Environmental Conservation. There was no doubt that it was Graham's because of a unique bumper sticker.

His best friend was somewhere in the woods, not answering his phone. Swallowing hard and trying to rein in his heart, Jim hopped out of the car and tried the doors on the truck. They were locked. He scanned the interior with his flashlight. Nothing looked out of place. An inspection of the area revealed no evidence of others. Memory was cruel, making his stomach churn, comparing this night to that night seven months ago when Sarah had disappeared.

Jim had been wrapping up at work, ready to head home, when he got the call from Graham to meet him at the entrance to Rockwood State Forest, an order that would be issued shortly to all officers on duty, firemen, forest rangers, and local volunteers. Graham had not shared details except to say he thought Sarah was in trouble and he needed help. There had been an edge to his best friend's voice, threaded with panic. It was a tone Jim had never heard before from a man that remained calm and cool-headed in any situation. He hoped never to hear it again.

There had been no hesitation. When his friend needed him, he was there. That was what true friends did for one another, what Graham did in return time and again. Jim climbed into his cruiser instead of his own car. Something told him this was going to be official business. He called Jeanie and told her he didn't know how late he would be before driving up Route 29.

He would never forget pulling into the parking area and seeing Sarah's locked car, never forget the sight of his best friend's face, never forget watching someone barely able to keep a grip on his sanity. Graham kept going over his walk with Sarah, the timeline since he had pulled out, and the reason why he had left first. It was obvious that he blamed himself for whatever had befallen her.

Jim had joined Graham and walked the trails with him all night long. He followed him home and sat with him until Graham fell asleep still sitting up on the couch. Jim waited for his friend to awaken and he was there to help pick up the pieces when Graham fell apart. It was not a dream—Sarah was still gone.

Jim paced back and forth in the parking area below Kane Mountain, nerves strung tight. Every fiber of his being urged him to go up the mountain and search for his friend, but what good could he really do? Graham could be anywhere and Jim had no idea what he was up against.

The nagging voice of indecision poked at his mind. What if Graham was hurt or in danger? Until day light, Jim would be at a serious disadvantage. He was not a woodsman like his best friend. He'd probably manage to get himself lost. Jim felt helpless. He couldn't do anything but wait and pray.

KANE RETURNED WITHIN MINUTES, his footsteps heavy in his haste to get back to the security of the cabin and make sure Sarah was all right, that she hadn't gone anywhere. Someone was out there, most likely the ranger. Who else could it be? Kane paused when he caught sight of the door. The bar was no longer in place. Had he forgotten to drop it in his panic or had someone breached the cabin?

He hesitated long enough to steel his nerves, flung the door open, and stepped inside. His eyes rested on Sarah, rocking by the fire, and the peaceful scene within the small, living area. Everything looked in order. Kane lowered his gun only to catch a blur of movement out of the corner of his eye. He whirled around, the door slammed, and a conservation officer launched himself into the air, head on with a course of impact.

GRAHAM MOVED FASTER than he thought humanly possible, fueled by an adrenalin rush, and went for the gun before the woodsman had time to take aim. He grabbed hold of the barrel, raised it high, and swung the stock at the stranger's head. The man had incredible instincts as if he could anticipate Graham's moves. He ducked with a whoosh of air and rammed the ranger in the stomach with his head. Graham dropped the gun, kicked it away as far as he could, and prayed it wouldn't go off. His arms came up around Sarah's abductor and they wrestled.

It was like tussling with a bear, the man was that strong and all muscle. Graham considered himself to be made of a sturdy metal, but Kane was a serious rival. No matter. There was no way he was going to make it this far only to have it all go wrong.

Kane slammed the ranger up against the solid wood of the door and something inside cracked. It didn't stop Graham, only made him fight harder. He rammed an elbow into the woodsman's nose and hooked his foot around his legs, sending him to the floor in a tangle of limbs. The man lay still, gasping for breath.

Graham ignored the stabbing in his side—the bastard had broken his rib, he was sure of it—and dove onto the man lying on the floor. He grabbed hold of his head and slammed it against the unyielding wood once, twice, three times until his eyes rolled to the back of his head and the woodsman was out. Graham remained on top of him on his hands and knees, drawing in air with a catch in his breath, trembling uncontrollably now that it was over.

Sarah was beside Graham, her arm around him, making him wince when she hit the sore spot on his side. “Are you all right? You’re bleeding.” She reached up with a corner of the blanket to dab his mouth, nose, and the corner of one eye. “You look like a prize fighter, my hero.” Sarah’s smile wobbled and she started to cry.

Graham straightened until he was kneeling and pulled her close, breathing hard with his chin resting on top of her head. “It’s all right. It’s all over. You’re all right now.”

He stroked her hair, touched her cheek, and brushed her lips with his to reassure himself she truly was alive. For just a moment, the rest of the world could wait and they were in each other’s arms.

Sarah was the first to break away. She glanced down at the unmoving figure beside them. “What are we doing to do about Kane? I just want to go home. Take me home, Graham. Please take me home.” Her need was so strong that Graham could feel it slamming into him.

“We’re taking him with us. He has to pay for what he’s done and if we leave him, I know we’ll never find him again.” Graham pulled the pack off his back, moving gingerly, and took out his handcuffs. Unlike the teen burglar, this man could not be trusted. Graham slapped on the restraints, made sure they were secure, and stood up slowly, his rib protesting with every movement.

Sarah's blue eyes went dark with worry. "You're hurt! How can you bring him in? It will only get worse." She reached up and touched Graham's cheek with every bit of gentleness she had. "We can take the chance of leaving him behind. You can keep him cuffed and tie him up. Somebody can come back in for him. Let's just go, Graham!"

Graham shook his head and probed his side with care, his jaw tightening when he hit the worst spot. "No, it will be all right. Look, he's coming around. He can walk out on his own two feet. If there's anything you need, get it. I want to get you home. They've been waiting long enough." He nudged Kane with his foot and glared down at him. "*Get up.* It's time to go."

Kane stared up at him, unmoving for a moment, and then rose to his feet. He hung his head and his shoulders slumped in defeat. Sarah took the steps to the loft two at a time in a flurry, returning with her camera and the stick that she used to mark the days. "Nothing else belongs to or matters to me."

Graham took Sarah's hand and gave it a squeeze. "Ready?" At her nod, he opened the door and they were under way. "I've got to warn you. It's a long hike to the Kane Mountain trail. Just keep the end in sight."

He handed her a flashlight from his pack and turned on another. Its beam was weak in the inky blackness of the forest, but it would suffice.

The night had grown colder. Sarah was shaking, dressed only in the heavy sweater she had put on earlier. Graham shrugged out of his coat, grimacing as he aggravated his side, and handed it to her. She protested. He waved her off. "Are you kidding me? I haven't seen you in months and you won't borrow my coat. I'm offended!" Sarah smiled at him and took his arm, trying to pass on some of her body heat.

The journey out seemed to last forever. They tripped, wavered with exhaustion, and had to sit several times. Graham's stomach twisted with the fear that they were headed in the wrong direction when the fire tower loomed above them.

"It was right here all along? If I had only headed this way, I could have found my way out?" Sarah was dumbfounded.

Graham smiled at her as he caught her eyes glinting in the moonlight. "Kane Mountain was standing guard over you the whole time, calling to me. It's really strange, but somehow I knew all along that it was connected with you although I didn't know how. Ask me about my theories some other time."

Sarah leaned up against Graham for a moment and he held her close, still unable to believe she was really here and it was almost over. She looked up at the fire tower and tried to pick out the old, ranger station in the distance. "Lila!" She spoke her daughter's name out loud, a blessing and a prayer. "Take me to her, Graham, please!"

Exhausted beyond measure and hurting, his body would have to make it just a little further. "Let's go."

He took her hand and they worked their way down the mountain, Kane walking slowly in front of them. It was difficult going in handcuffs and several times he fell, but the woodsman never did stopped moving. If he wasn't about to quit, neither would Sarah and Graham. Time seemed to come to a halt as they stumbled and slipped their way down, finally staggering into the parking area where Graham's truck and a police cruiser waited.

"*THANK GOD, SCOTTIE! YOU MADE IT*!" Jim was out of his cop car and by his friend's side in an instant. He halted at the sight of the woman beside Graham. "Sarah…is that really you? Oh God, Sarah, you're alive! Graham was right all along. He never gave up on you! Thank God, Sarah!"

Jim grabbed hold of her in a bone-crushing hug, pressed a kiss on her cheek, and held on tight. He couldn't let go yet. Still in shock, he turned back to his friend. Graham was white, bruise like shadows under his eyes, and his face showed signs of a fight. He was breathing with a hitch, almost a hiccup with each breath, and favored his right side. "Scottie, you all right?"

Graham gave his best friend a tired grin and pulled him into a careful hug. "I am now, for the first time in a long time." He nodded his head toward the stranger standing next to them.

"This is Sarah's abductor, Kane Johnson. Would you please take him to the station? We'll come in when we can to file a report. Right now, I've got to get Sarah home."

Jim nodded, suddenly overcome with emotion and unable to speak for the moment. He hugged Sarah again and then grabbed hold of Graham in a bear hug. "You did it, buddy. I always knew if anyone could, it would be you. You kept the faith and you did it. Get out of here and I'll make sure Mr. Johnson is taken care of."

Jim wiped at his eyes and took the suspect's arm, leading him to his cruiser. He made sure the man was secure in the backseat and sat down in the driver's seat. Graham walked Sarah to his truck and opened the passenger door for her. The ranger paused to stroke her hair and touch her cheek as if making sure she was real. Reassured, he walked around to the driver's side and climbed in.

Jim waited until his best friend pulled out and followed him all the way to Pleasant Avenue. He didn't go to the station until the truck pulled into the Andersons' driveway. Letting go of a long sigh, as if he had been holding his breath forever, Jim moved on. Their world had been set right.

GRAHAM HELPED SARAH CLIMB INTO THE TRUCK and went around to the driver's side. He ignored the pain in his side and pulled himself in by holding on to the steering wheel. They sat in silence for a few minutes, their breathing the only sound, slowly calming down. It was over.

His body wilted with the let-down. He turned to look at Sarah. She was bent forward, face in her hands, shaking with silent sobs. What was going through her mind? What had she been through over the past months? He rested his hand on her head and began to stroke her hair. It shimmered in the light of the moon and was silkier than he remembered. The urge to touch her, to hold her close was too strong to deny.

"Sarah, come here, please." She looked up, the need equally great in her eyes, and fell into him. His arms came around her of their own accord and he began to rock. "I love you, Sarah, I love you with all my heart. You are my world and I am never going to let you go. I've waited seven months to be able to tell you that. You're everything, the only thing that has kept me alive."

SARAH SAT IN THE TRUCK and waited for Graham to get in. She saw him wince with the movement, watched the lines tighten around his eyes and mouth. He was so thin, like whipcord! What had her abduction cost *him*? She believed one thing with absolute certainty—he had never surrendered, a torch of hope held high until Graham found her.

Sheltered by his strength and love, she bowed her head and let go. It was over. She came undone. Whatever had held her together finally gave, turning her into a shaking tangle of emotions. She was going home. His hand rested on her hair and it was like sweet honey flowing through her, warming all of the cold places inside.

"Sarah, come here, please." His voice was strained. She focused on Graham, saw the love ready to overflow, and sank against him. He held her close, told her how much he loved her, said all the things Kane tried to say. This time, with this man, it was right.

Sarah reached up and took Graham's face in her hands. She hoped he could see the light in her eyes. It was there, strong and bright, because of him. "I love you more and I'll tell you one other thing. I'm here because of you and I'm not going anywhere."

IT WAS LATE. Lila was supposed to be sleeping, but her eyes didn't want to close. She kept thinking about all of the pictures she had made that morning . Lying in bed, hiding under the covers, she whispered over and over, "Mommy is coming home for Thanksgiving."

She could hear Nana and Pop Pop's TV in the bedroom. They were watching the Jimmy Fallon show. She had stayed up for it once when Mommy was on vacation and let her sleep in her big bed. Lila watched about five minutes and fell asleep. She had never managed to keep her eyes open that late again.

She sighed. She didn't think Nana and Pop Pop would let her watch it tonight.

Lila rolled over on her tummy and tried counting sheep. That didn't work either. She crawled out of bed and went to her window. She stared at the light, Mommy's light, and said again, "Mommy's coming home for Thanksgiving." There was the sound of a motor which was funny so late at night and then a truck pulled in the driveway. Crackers!

Lila stood up and pressed her hands and face to the glass, watching as Graham got out of the truck. He walked kind of crooked, his arm folded across his middle, and he wasn't wearing a coat. It was really cold. Lila could tell because she could see Graham's breath. He went around to the passenger side of his truck and opened the door. Somebody got out.

Lila squeezed her eyes shut really tight and looked again. It was somebody with blond hair. It was a girl. It was… "Mommy!" Lila shouted and ran out of the room.

"Lila, what's wrong?" Nana called after her from her bedroom door with Pop Pop right next to her. They started down the hallway, but they weren't fast enough for Lila.

"It's Mommy! Graham found her and brought her home! She's here! She's really here!" Lila scampered down the steps, unlocked the door, and flung it wide open. She ran out onto the porch in her nightie and her bare feet. Mommy was running up the walkway straight for her and scooped her up into her arms.

"Lila, my sweet Lila! Oh honey, how I've missed you! I love you so much!" Mommy was crying and she was hugging

Lila so hard she thought her stuffing would come pouring right out. Lila hugged Mommy back as hard as she could.

"I love you too, Mommy! I knew Graham would find you, I just knew it because he believed it so I believed it too. I really missed you too, Mommy! Don't you ever go away again!" Lila hugged her mommy again and then she kissed her cheek.

Suddenly, Nana and Pop Pop were there too and it was a great, big family hug. Everyone was laughing and crying. Lila finally had a happy bubble inside that was as big as she was. This one wasn't going to pop. Her mommy was home!

21

SARAH SAW HER BABY GIRL RUNNING toward her and it felt like she was breathing for the first time since the nightmare began. The empty place inside, that had been hurting so badly for so long, was full again and the crack in her heart began to seal. She swept Lila up into her arms and hugged her hard. Sarah didn't think she could ever put her down.

She buried her face in locks filled with sunshine and inhaled the scent of strawberry shampoo. Her girl was soft, warm, and real, not a dream or a memory. "Lila, my sweet Lila! How I've missed you! I love you so much!" Sarah began to cry, finally letting loose. She was back home on her parents' porch with all the people she loved standing by her. She was alive again.

GRAHAM HELD BACK, leaning up against the porch railing, and watched as Sarah was reunited with her family. A flood of emotions—relief, gratitude, overwhelming happiness—threatened to carry him away. It was finally over. The sorrow and frustration could let go of him. He reached out and held onto the post, in need of support as something inside of him crumbled.

Everything that had kept him going was gone now and there was no strength to hold himself up. He stumbled away to the back yard, away from the others. His legs gave out and Graham dropped to his knees. It was over. It really was over and he'd been given the fairytale ending, against all odds.

He fell forward and pressed his head to the cold ground. It was soothing to a soul worn ragged. "Thank you, God, for bringing her home safe and sound. I am forever grateful."

He remained that way, completely spent, with no reason or energy to move. Graham could stay there the rest of his days and be content. His Sarah was back where she belonged.

SARAH HUGGED HER PARENTS, kissed them, and touched them. She still held onto Lila and didn't let go, couldn't let go. She had to feel everyone, listen intently, ensure herself it was real. Everyone did the same to her and talked at once.

Her father couldn't take his eyes off her. It was as if he was drinking her in. Her mother held onto her waist and pressed her head to her daughter's shoulder. Sarah could feel her quivering. She glanced behind her and caught sight of Graham out of the corner of her eye. He was leaning on the post as if it was the only thing holding him up and then he staggered away.

Worried, she turned to her mother. “Mom, why don’t you and Lila start some hot cocoa for everyone and break out some cookies? I am starving! I just need to check on Graham and make sure he’s all right. It was a really rough night. Dad, why don’t you come with me in case he needs help?” Her mother hugged her again and took Lila while Sarah went around back with her father.

Graham was on his knees, head pressed to the ground. His body was shaking from the cold and silent sobs racked his body. It was very painful to watch. Sarah felt her heart fill and took off his coat.

She draped it over his shoulders and knelt down beside him. “Graham, sweetheart, it’s okay now. Won’t you please come inside with everyone? It’s a time to celebrate. I’m home and it’s because of you. Come be with us.”

He turned to her and Sarah gathered him into her arms like he was a child. “Dear God, Sarah. I still can’t believe it’s real. I don’t know what I would have done if I hadn’t found you. I had to keep going and believe I would bring you home. You’re here, but I’m not sure I believe it.” His voice broke and he was trembling in her arms.

Sarah stroked his hair and kissed his cheek. “Hush now. It’s over. I’m really here and you brought me home.” She held on until the weeping stopped and stood up. Graham tried but he couldn’t stand up to save his life.

"I'm sorry. I don't think I can move. I'm so tired. I don't care if I stay here all night." He kneeled on the ground, his hands pressed to his knees. He was swaying.

Sarah looked over her shoulder to her father and gave him a nod. He came forward and they managed to get Graham to his feet. He wavered, but made it inside with their help. The couch would be his bed for the night because he didn't have the stamina to walk the stairs to the spare bedroom. They all had cocoa and cookies. Sarah started to tell her story while Graham drifted off to his first solid sleep in months. Everyone basked in the miracle. Their girl was home.

GRAHAM COULDN'T BRING HIMSELF TO LEAVE the Andersons' home. He simply wasn't ready to let Sarah out of his sight. There was a slow unwinding of all the knots that had replaced his insides. For the first twenty four hours, he slept like the dead. He awoke, had a drink of water, and found his way upstairs.

Peeking in Lila's bedroom, he reassured himself that it hadn't all been a dream. Two golden heads were pressed together, wrapped in a tangle of limbs as if they couldn't get close enough to each other. Lila had begged her mother to stay with her and Sarah wasn't about to argue. Graham leaned against the door jamb and closed his eyes, sending up another prayer of gratitude. He couldn't say thank you enough. How fitting that Sarah was given back to him as Thanksgiving neared.

The touch of a hand on his shoulder gave him a start. Sally stood beside him, her eyes moist and glowing for the first time since the disappearance. Until yesterday, all of them had simply been going through the motions. "She's just fine and she's not going anywhere. Come lie down, Graham, before you fall down."

She took his arm and guided him to the spare room as if he were drunk or blind. A set of Steve's pajamas were resting on the bed. Sally helped Graham to remove his shirt, wincing at the angry bruising on his side, and slipped the pajama top on, taking care when he grimaced in pain. He fumbled, his hands made clumsy with fatigue, and was grateful for Sally's assistance in slipping off his belt, dropping his pants, and pulling up the pajama bottoms.

Graham gave her the sheepish smile of a child. "Thanks, Mom." She pulled back the covers and helped him to lie down in the blessed coolness of clean linens. His eyes closed, taking him to the brink of sleep when there was a weight beside him on the mattress.

Sally stroked his hair and brushed it out of his eyes. Giving comfort, as if he was a child again. It had a hypnotic effect, making it even harder to stay awake. She leaned forward and kissed his cheek. "Thank you, Graham, for bringing her back to us. We can never repay what you have done for this family and we love you with all of our hearts. Rest now." She waited until he was out. It didn't take long.

In the next twenty four hours, Graham awoke sporadically to find Sarah or Lila waiting by his bedside. They would give him a drink, a little something to eat, or just sit and watch. As long as they were near, he could sleep with a clear conscience. After two days of rest, it felt like he'd been hit with a Mack truck. No matter. The search was over and she was home.

Sarah wanted him to get his ribs checked, but there'd be no going to a doctor or anywhere for that matter. The only medicine he needed was Sarah and her family. John Christopher issued strict orders to take a vacation, as long as Graham needed. After putting in three years' worth of work in seven months, it was well deserved.

When he was up to getting out of bed, Graham took the girls to the Gingerbread Cottage. He didn't even try to hold back the tears as Sarah cried freely, a trembling hand to her lips, the instant she saw the door covered in letters. Graham couldn't even stay on his feet for the tour inside. The steps held him when he dropped down while Lila pulled her mother from room to room to see a little girl's faith in pictures.

Two days later, with a promise from Sarah that she would not go anywhere, Graham joined forces with a team of federal marshals, state troopers, and conservation officers. He led them up Kane Mountain to the fire tower and showed them where it all began, retracing his steps on the day he discovered Kane's lair.

They went on to trek through the forest to the cabin. More snow had fallen and the temperature had dropped, making the journey more difficult. The case had made it to the federal level. Kane had committed the crime of abduction on a nationally protected reserve. Moreover, he had broken building codes and evaded taxes for his entire lifetime on the property. He would be going away for a long time.

After several hours of trudging through the rough terrain, Graham came to a halt. He couldn't bring himself to enter at first, his feelings were that strong. The others were awe-stricken at the craftsmanship and resourcefulness of Kane's dwelling. Graham collected himself and led them inside, recreating the events of the night he brought the woodsman into custody. They investigated the premises, took photos, and made copious notes.

Graham walked through and noted the cardinal in the window, a picture of Kane's parents in his tiny bedroom, and steeled himself before going upstairs. This had been Sarah's cell. Tiny, delicate carvings of a consummate artist were scattered throughout the room. Sarah had explained they were gifts that she used to remind herself of home.

The cross from Kane's mother's rosary was on the dresser. There were a few items of clothing in an otherwise bare room. A flash of red caught his eye on the bed. Slowly, Graham approached and lifted the pillow. There was the sweater that Sarah had worn on their last hike with one sleeve torn off. She had kept it near her each night. She would hold on to it and think about her family and Graham. One more way to keep hope's fire burning.

Graham sank down onto the bed and with a hand that shook, he held it to his cheek. The tears came again, unchecked, and the others left him in privacy. He didn't know how he had been led to that sweater. It had to be a gift from above.

"FASTER, CRACKERS! FASTER!" Lila's voice rang out, her breath floating above her head. Graham put on a burst of speed, although it was awkward in snow shoes, and whipped the little, red sled over the trails of the Rockwood State Forest. Sarah tried to keep pace, but was not accustomed to her new footwear and fell behind. There were giggles and squeals from the passenger until her chauffeur ran out of steam.

"All right, enough already! The horse is tired! Let's walk a bit and enjoy the view. We're leaving poor Mommy in the dust." Graham gestured behind them and stopped on a small rise.

A fresh foot of snow had fallen, transforming the woods into a winter wonderland. Everything was coated, forming a lacy canopy overhead while the sunlight made a sparkling landscape. It was beautiful. None of it came close to the sight of Sarah, walking toward him, in a cheerful red cap and scarf that were a splash of color against her navy pea coat. Her hair was a shining curtain down her back that captured the sun, her eyes were brighter than the clear sky above, and her smile could have given Helen of Troy competition.

Sarah reached the twosome and swept Lila up out of the sled. A quick spin through the air had both laughing and breathless before she set her daughter back down to continue her ride. Graham held out a hand and Sarah's palm found its way home in his steady grasp. They walked on in silence, simply taking in the day and each other.

Graham couldn't take his eyes off of the woman at his side. He had pictured her in his mind countless times in the past seven months. Those images had been mere shadows compared to the living and breathing reality. Sarah was vibrant, glowing, his. Finally, he could truly breathe again.

They came to a stop quite a ways in where a tree had fallen to create a natural bench. Lila hopped out of the sled and began to jump with excitement. "This is the place! 'Member, Mommy? This is where you hurted your ankle and waited and Crackers came to the rescue like the prince in Sleeping Beauty!" She skipped around them, ran to the log, and climbed up on it.

"Yes, Lila, of course I remember. How could I forget the day my shining knight arrived?" Sarah sat down beside her daughter and gathered her in close. Mother and daughter were eye-catching, Lila's ladybug coat bright against her mother. Sarah tipped her head up toward Graham with a welcome smile and patted the spot next to her.

Graham stood still, holding on, drinking in the sight of the two girls that were his everything. His heart felt light with the happiness he had been given. He still pinched himself each morning, assuring himself he really was awake. He sat down and took Sarah's hand.

They were quiet for a little while until his words drifted between them, unbidden, but they had to be said. "I haven't liked the woods anymore, not for a long time, particularly this forest."

Sarah turned to study Graham and her steady gaze tugged at his heart. It was as if a cloud had passed, darkening her face and her eyes were shadowed with memories. Her hand tightened on his. "I know. It was the same for me. That's why I felt like we had to do this. We had to come back and reclaim it, fill it with joy. This is our place, Graham, and we can't let that be taken away from us."

He smiled down at her even though he still felt broken. Healing would be a long time coming for both of them.

Graham's lips brushed hers and his eyes closed. "How did you become so wise?" His reward was another kiss and her weight falling into him.

"Time and patience. There's one more thing you need to know. It wasn't your fault. It was his. I want you to forgive yourself and be whole again." She reached up to cup his cheek with a fuzzy, red glove. Graham's eyes were swimming and he couldn't talk at first.

He gave a little nod and copied her gesture with his hand on her face. "I am whole because of you. I love you, Sarah." He pulled her close. Lila climbed up between them, making them laugh as her little arms wrapped around their necks and she plastered them with kisses.

"Don't forget about me! I love you both even more!" Her voice was bright like a silver bell and she was a warm bundle of energy, barely contained. The three held on to each other for a long time, soaking up the sunshine together. A lifetime wouldn't be long enough to make up for those dreadful months of missing todays like these.

IT WAS THANKSGIVING and the Gingerbread Cottage was filled to bursting. Card tables had been brought in to supplement the kitchen table and were covered with colorful, autumn tablecloths. The whole family was together—the Andersons, Graham's mother, Sarah, Graham, and Lila. Jim and Jeanie were adopted family members. Everyone was animated with conversation, food and drink flowed, and Lila scurried through the house, showing everyone her "believing" pictures. Jeanie had officially shared her news and was positively glowing.

Graham sat by Jim on the couch, carrying on the yearly tradition of watching football after their meal. They drank beer and munched on chips with dip even though they'd been threatened to save room for dessert or else. Graham sank back against the cushions, comfortable in jeans and a button-up shirt, thankful Sarah didn't expect him to get really dressed up. A news update had him sitting up straight and holding his breath.

"I'm standing here on the steps of the Fulton County Courthouse, the oldest working courthouse in the state, established in the late 1700's. It seems this historical sight is being marked by a historical case as Kane Johnson is arraigned for the abduction of Sarah Waters. After seven months missing, the Johnstown teacher has been returned to her home. Questions remain on what happened while she was gone and what the consequences will be for Mr. Johnson in this one of a kind case. For NBC nightly news, I'm Gina Robinson. Happy Thanksgiving!"

Graham took another long swallow of his beer and set it down. The moment he saw Kane's face, he wanted to commit violence. He knew it wasn't right. Even Sarah had begged the courts to be lenient, saying Kane was overcome with grief, had never hurt her, and that he would die if imprisoned. She wanted them to find a mental facility close to his beloved mountains where he could see the outdoors and experience the fresh air.

Graham marveled that she could be so forgiving. Johnson had taken over half a year of their lives, a time they could never get back. A very small part of him felt bad when he saw the mountain man in regular clothes with haunted eyes, lost in the crowd of reporters, lawyers, and law enforcement. The feeling didn't last. If Kane hadn't taken Sarah, he could have gone on living in the woods without discovery for the remainder of his days. Graham could not have compassion for the man who had nearly destroyed the lives of so many.

Jim nudged him with his elbow. "What do you think will happen to him?"

He glanced behind him and was glad to see that the women folk were in the kitchen and had missed the report. A quick glance over at the recliner showed Steve rigid in his chair, eyes far away. He had seen it all. What an impact one man had on this family. Their lives had been changed forever.

Graham shrugged. "I don't know and I don't care. He'll probably die in captivity like a rare species of animal and it's probably just as well if he can't live by normal human standards."

He stood up and clapped Jim on the back. Lila ran by and Graham caught her in a bear hug. He worked his way toward the kitchen, giving his mom a kiss while she sat at the table sipping coffee with Sally, made sure he didn't leave

Sarah's mother out, and swung Jeanie in a little dance in the kitchen.

"Motherhood is sure looking good on you, Jeanie-girl. I can't wait until the little one gets here." He turned to find Sarah with her arms buried in suds. Graham put his arms around her waist and swung her around. "Oh Ma Ma! I can't wait to see that happen to you too!"

Sarah turned and dropped her arms around his neck. They started to sway to the soft music on the radio and everyone else left them to enjoy the moment. They moved in closer, foreheads pressed together, content in each other's company.

"You want to know what I kept thinking about all that time?" Sarah's voice was a whisper.

He was afraid to ask. It actually caused a physical pain to think of those days without her, to know what she had been through, but if Sarah could stand to tell him then he could stand to listen.

"What did you think about?" He held her close, felt the slightest trembling run through her body, and waited.

"I thought of my family, of Lila,…and always about you. I remembered what you said about your name meaning home, and that every time I saw you was like coming home. I prayed you'd make that happen and you did. Thank you for bringing me home." She looked up at him with her heart in her eyes and then she gave it to him in a kiss.

KANE SAT IN A TINY CELL, smaller than his bedroom in the cabin, staring at four gray walls. There was one tiny window with bars on it, letting in the moonlight. The sound of cars on the highway obscured anything of nature. It was Thanksgiving. He should be at home with Caroga, sitting in front of his fire, eating turkey that was a gift from the forest, giving thanks for his life.

The walls seemed to close in and Kane felt as if he would smother at any instant. He stood and ran his hands through his long hair. Without a leather band to tie it back, it flowed down to his shoulders and made him look like a wild man. He had seen it in the mirror. It suited his state of mind.

Kane couldn't stay here. He would die within these walls, he was sure of it. His daddy had been right to take them to the woods. It was the only place that a being could thrive and be one with the world around him. In the wilderness, he only took what he needed, giving back his utmost respect and appreciation.

He now understood his crucial error. He had taken something that did not belong to the wild and had paid for it. That did not mean he should pay with his life. He had not hurt Sarah. He had only needed someone to fill the emptiness. He was truly sorry for the pain he had caused her and would not repeat such a misjudgment. Kane did not deserve to die.

He had to get out of these walls, tonight or it would all be over for him. He dropped down on his bunk and began to scream and moan in pain. "Help! Help me, somebody, please! I feel like my insides are splitting apart! Please help me!" Kane bent over and began to rock, his face a true mirror of the mental torment within.

A guard came to the door, took one look at the man inside doubled over, obviously suffering, and his eyes sprang wide with alarm. "Hang in there. You're going to be all right." He opened the door and stepped inside.

In a flash, Kane was on his feet and had the officer in a head lock. He grabbed his gun, his keys, shoved the man back, and locked the door. Pain made the woodsman's eyes burn intensely. "I'm sorry but I can't live this way."

He headed for the door. It was a holiday in a quiet, small town jail. Only one other officer manned the desk. Kane leveled his gun at his head and backed out. As soon as he hit the door, he dropped the gun and ran straight for the woods across the street.

Once in the woods, Kane was at home. He knew what to do, could live anywhere as long as it was in the arms of the wilderness. When he had run until he was certain there was a safe distance between him and the outside world, he stopped and truly breathed for the first time since he had been taken.

Happy Thanksgiving, Mama and Daddy. You too, Little Sister.

I miss you.

22

JIM ROSE TO HIS FEET in one fluid motion as a news flash interrupted the game. He was glad to see Steve had dozed off and Graham was in the kitchen. They didn't need to have their night ruined with the unfolding tale.

"This just in. Kane Johnson, arrested for the abduction of Sarah Waters, has escaped. His picture is shown here. If anyone sees this man, be sure to notify the authorities. Consider him dangerous and unpredictable. Take the utmost caution and do not try to apprehend him on your own. Women should lock their doors and don't walk alone. We'll have more at eleven."

IT WAS BLACK FRIDAY. Fitting for the change in Graham's mood with word of Kane's escape. He took Jim with him and they returned to the woodsman's cabin. Graham would have his best friend by him, whatever happened. It gave him strength and courage.

Jim went with him to the top of the fire tower and zoomed in where Graham told him to look. The police officer actually had to try several times before he saw something. Even then, he doubted his senses. He looked at Graham and shook his head. "I don't know how you found it. It was a one in a million chance. Imagine if it had gone the other way."

Graham's hands clasped the railing with an involuntary spasm. "I already have and it isn't pretty. I'm especially having a hard time now that Kane is on the loose. What if he comes back, Pete? Am I going to have to spend the rest of my life looking over my shoulder? I'm tempted to move, take her far away. I don't think Johnson will go anywhere else. This is the only place he's known. He can't make it in the outside world. If I go across the country, we should be safe."

Jim squeezed his friend's arm and tried to give him a grip on reality. "Graham, you can't spend your life running away. There will always be some kind of threat or disaster. You have to have faith and keep going. I don't think Sarah would want to leave her family, not now when she came so close to losing them forever. You wouldn't be happy anywhere else either. If Kane comes back, and I doubt he will, we'll be ready."

Jim's shoulders were set, his jaw firm. He looked like he could take on the world and Graham knew he could count on him.

Graham gave his friend a quick hug. "Thanks for talking some sense into me. Let's get a move on."

They made their way down the tower steps and pushed on through the ice and snow. The journey took longer because of the conditions, making Graham thankful once again that the search for Sarah had ended before winter had the land in its grip for the duration. They reached the cabin. There was no sign of smoke or life and the shutters remained closed. He knew there would be no one inside, had known all along, but went in any way.

The cabin was empty and it had an unlived in feeling. Graham would have thought it had been untouched from his previous visit for the investigation if he did not look closely. Things were missing. The rifle was gone as were the hunting knives from the wooden block in the kitchen. The glass cardinal no longer sat in the window.

A quick scan in the bedroom revealed the photograph was gone and clothes from the closet as well. He took the steps two at a time to the loft and saw that all of the carvings had disappeared. The rosary cross and Sarah' hairbrush, both belonging to Kane's mother, were not on the dresser, along with the photo of his parents. One other thing had disappeared—the red sweater. Graham sat down on the bed because his legs would not hold him. Wherever Kane had gone, he took his keepsakes of Sarah with him.

IT WAS CHRISTMAS EVE. They were riding in a horse-drawn carriage, Graham, Sarah, and Lila. An amazing sundown, one that might beat all others had just touched down. Lila took lots of pictures for her book. Graham promised he would buy her a new one to fill with countless new photos, God-willing.

Now she was dozing off, snug under the heavy covers. The evening had been full, spent at Sir William Johnson's Colonial estate. A special dinner had been set up in the old home for the public, there had been caroling, topped off with hot apple cider and cider donuts. All three were stuffed to the brim, limbs pleasantly heavy, relaxed with the slow rocking of the carriage as it traveled around the parking loop and down the quiet lane.

Graham turned to stare at the woman and child by his side. His heart was full and he couldn't imagine life without them. He didn't plan on letting either one of them go. He reached into his pocket and pulled out a small velvet box. Taking Sarah's hand, he set the box in her palm and wrapped her fingers around it.

His hand closed over hers and held it steady. "We've known for a long time where we were headed. Now that you've come home, I want you to always be at home with me. Sarah, will you be my wife?" He waited and felt the answer as she fell into him and her lips pressed against his cheek.

"Yes, Graham Dylan Scott, I will marry you!" Tears glistened in her eyes and great, flakes of snow, like pieces of the clouds, started to drift down around them. She grabbed hold of Graham like he was a lifeline.

Lila woke up in the middle of a hug between the two and squirmed between them. "Can I be married too?" She called out. She grabbed hold of her mother's hand and Graham's fingers. He kissed the top of her head while her mother hugged her close.

"Of course, Lila! We'll all be married and we'll live together forever and ever!" Their laughter rang out as they finished their ride.

They took their time walking back to the truck, breathing in the night air. Lila caught snowflakes on her tongue and everyone laughed at her. Graham picked her up and set her on his shoulders so that she felt like she was on top of the world. It was the least he could do since he felt that way every day that they were in his life.

The little girl slept on the ride to Pleasant Lake. Thanksgiving had been at the Gingerbread Cottage. Christmas would be at Graham's. They had already agreed that his cabin on the lake would soon be their new home as a family. Santa had come early with a little help from Sarah. A black Labrador named Chip and a golden retriever named Dale were two new additions for Graham and Lila. The puppies scampered across their pen, happy to see their owners, when the trio opened the door.

Sarah took Lila off to the spare bedroom to tuck her in good night while Graham looked out at the lake, his candle in honor of Sarah still burning in the window, although it now burned in thanksgiving. Something drew him outside and he walked out onto the deck that was covered in a layer of fresh snow.

He glanced down and the hair rose on the back of his neck. There were footprints and they weren't his own. He surveyed the area and his eye was caught. Moving forward, he found a carving on the railing. It was small and intricate, depicting a buck, a doe, and a fawn. There was a small note underneath, written in an untidy scrawl. It said, *Leave me to the Adirondacks and I'll leave her to you.—Kane*

Graham's hands clenched on the railing and he peered into the night. Somehow he had known they hadn't heard the last of the woodsman. The authorities had returned again to his cabin, but it remained empty. Who knew where the fugitive was now or what he would do next?

Graham picked up the carving and closed his hand around it. "I'm going to trust you, Kane, wherever you are. Don't break my trust or you'll regret it."

He pocketed the carving, ran his hand over it, and went inside. He had a family to take care of now. Kane could take care of himself. The Adirondacks remained as guardians behind him. They had another secret to keep.

Afterward

Far to the north of upstate New York, stretching to the Canadian border, the Adirondack mountains remain immense guardians of the land. They stretch in a soft, rolling rise across the horizon, blanketed in forest. Only God knows the secrets they keep, the bones that sleep within the Blue Line, or the number of souls that take shelter in the wilderness. What other mysteries remain…lost in the Adirondacks?

Look for another Cordial Creek Romance in November 2015:

Against the Grain

Paulie Goodwin has pushed his limits in life. As a photojournalist, he goes wherever the wind blows, and has been around the world and back again, seeing its many faces and places through the lens of his camera.

When his most recent assignment as a photojournalist lands him in Afghanistan on an army base with the American soldier, his life is turned upside down. A young serviceman gives his life to save Paulie's, sending the photographer reeling. He'll come back home to his family to heal from a severe injury in the small town of Cordial Creek. He's gone against the grain all of his life, choosing the road less traveled, but this time the mountain of guilt may be too hard to climb.

Anna Peters has lived in Cordial Creek for all of her life. A teacher of fifteen years, she's always been content with her predictable routine, but lately has felt a need for something new in her life, some kind of spark. Change will literally run smack dab into her when she sweeps Paulie Goodwin off his feet at the airport. Once high school sweethearts, they've remained friends throughout the years, catching up whenever he's breezed into town. This time, he's here to stay and ready to fall to pieces. Anna may be the only one who can help put Humpty Dumpty together again.

COMING IN THE FUTURE:

The Edge of Forgiveness on Blue Mountain

Book Two: The Lost in the Adirondacks Series

You can follow me on Facebook at Heidi Sprouse Writer. I'm also on Twitter, Heidi Sprouse Author @heidi_sprouse. Find me on the web at heidisprouse.wix.com/heidi-sprouse.